DEATH IN POZZUOLI

James Allan Evans

Order this book online at www.trafford.com/08-1155
or email orders@trafford.com

Most Trafford titles are also available at major online book retailers.

Note for Librarians: A cataloguing record for this book is available from Library and Archives Canada at www.collectionscanada.ca/amicus/index-e.html

Printed in Victoria, BC, Canada.

ISBN: 978-1-4251-8656-2 (sc)

Our mission is to efficiently provide the world's finest, most comprehensive book publishing service, enabling every author to experience success. To find out how to publish your book, your way, and have it available worldwide, visit us online at www.trafford.com/10510

Trafford rev. 07/25/2009

www.trafford.com

North America & international
toll-free: 1 888 232 4444 (USA & Canada)
phone: 250 383 6864 ♦ fax: 250 383 6804

Needless to say, there is in no Palazzo Agrippina in Pozzuoli and any resemblance between the characters in this story and anyone, living or dead, is purely coincidental. As far as I know, there is no summer school in Pozzuoli and vicinity remotely resembling the Palazzo Agrippina. However, the impressive ruins of Cumae, where the ancient Greeks founded their first colony in mainland Italy in the mid-eighth century BCE, do exist, and so do the remains of Pompeii and Herculaneum, both of them buried by the eruption of Mt. Vesuvius in 79 CE. And there is the Gulf of Baia, where the emperor Nero tried to drown his mother, Agrippina, the last wife of the emperor Claudius, who had eased her son's succession to the throne by feeding Claudius poisonous mushrooms. Next to it is the Gulf of Naples, with the islands of Ischia and Capri, and on the shore of the Gulf, there is Sorrento, where Ulysses once heard the Sirens sing and lived to tell the tale. The action of this story takes place against a landscape that has endured many centuries of history.

DEATH IN POZZUOLI

I

THERE WAS this cool-looking guy on the airplane from London to Rome. Wavy, fluffed hair, sharp jacket, well built, Italian, I think, but spoke English pretty well. Wore a big ring on his left hand. We got talking. He wanted to know why I was going to Italy.

'Just for a trip?' he said. 'Lookin' around Italy?'

'Yeah,' said I, cool. Cautious, like. I wasn't about to give a complete stranger my life history.

'On your own?' he said. 'By yourself, I mean?'

'Like, well—why not?' said I.

'You look like an American student,' he said. 'They travel around in groups, don't they? With an older guy to look after them? Keep them away from the good-looking dames, huh?'

I didn't like that too much, but whatever. I wasn't going to tell him my mom and dad were on the plane, two rows back.

'Well, there you go,' I said.

'Where you heading for when you get to Italy?' he asked.

'Naples.' I said.

'Ah, Napoli!' he said. 'Beautiful place, Napoli. Watch your wallet, though. There are many thieves in Napoli. Cammora. Very bad people.'

'Yeah,' said I.

'I could tell you lots of stories about Napoli' He grinned as he said it.

'Actually the place I'm going to is outside Naples,' I said. 'It's a town called Pozzuoli. Do you know it? Outside Naples somewhere, but on the same waterfront?'

'Pozzuoli!' He perked up. He got interested. 'I know Pozzuoli! Nice place. My mama lives not far from there. I'm going to see her tomorrow and pick up some clean shirts.'

'Clean shirts?' I asked.

'Yes,' he said. 'I take my shirts to Moma to wash. She likes doing my laundry. That's what Italian mothers do. Did you know Sophia Loren came from Pozzuoli?'

'No,' I said.

'Well, she did. Pozzuoli is a real interesting town. Do you know there is a great big Roman amphitheatre there, just like the Colosseum in Rome, only just a little smaller? Lions used to kill and eat the Christians there while all the Italians watched.' He chuckled 'They had real fun years ago in Pozzuoli.'

'Awesome,' said I.

'I'm going into Pozzuoli soon, too,'' he said. 'I got a friend there who's making a video for me. It's all tourist business stuff. That's the business I'm in. Tourism. I make arrangements.'

'Like arranging tours for Americans or whatever?'

'Yeah, yeah, that too. I have a little travel bureau in Napoli, though my main business is films.Video—what you call it? TV commercials?'

That is interesting, I thought. I want to make films someday, myself. I brought my videocamera with me. Out loud, I said,

'I'm going to make videos and DVDs too. When I go to college, I'm going into Film Studies. I packed my camera and some tapes in my duffle bag, and I'm going to shoot some footage here in Italy.'

'You do? Hey!' He fumbled around in his pocket. 'Here. Here's my card. You want help? Come and see me. I know how to make arrangements for you. I have friends.'

The card was printed in gold letters. It said 'Giacomo Fini: Direttore. Fabiola Films', a telephone number and a URL. I put it in my shirt pocket. 'Grazie tanto,' I said. His face lit up.

'Ah, you know some Italian?'

'A bit,' said I. 'They tell me Italians aren't so anti-American if you try to speak to them in their own language.'

He screwed up his face. 'Italians aren't anti-American,' he said. 'It's all politics. Just some people like to make a big noise.'

'Actually,' I said, changing the subject, 'The place I'm staying at, like, *is on the edge of Pozzuoli.'*

'What's it called?' he asked. 'Bauli?'

'Arco Felice,' I said.

'That's a railway station,' he said. 'On the Cumana railway. There's an arch nearby, made by the Romans long time ago. I know where it is. It's in Pozzuoli, on the way from Pozzuoli to Baia. Nice beaches around there, and lots of girls. I got a lot of good friends there, too,' he said. This guy had a whole crowd of good friends. 'A couple friends of mine work in an hotel there'

'Oh, yeah?'

'So, where are you staying?'

'A place called the Palazzo Agrippina,' I said. He looked puzzled.

'Agrippina?' he said "I've heard of her, somewhere. Does she live in Napoli?"

'I think she was—like—the mother of the emperor Nero or something,' I said.

'Nerone?' he said. He looked puzzled.'Didn't he play the violin once while Rome was burning?'

'It's a summer school,.' I said. 'For students from America, like. Stateside.'

'A summer school' he repeated, slowly. 'You go to school? Here in Italia?'

'No, in America.I go to prep school, a place you'd never have heard of, called Gilead Academy. The Palazzo Agrippina is just a summer school, like. We live together in this palace—like—a big house, you know, and we learn about the Romans and things like that Like Latin, and the Roman Empire, and Western Civ, and why there's a western tradition and all that.'

'Western Civ?'

'You know, the western civilization, like, and the rise of the west and all that jazz,' I said. 'They teach it at school. It's supposed to make you understand yourself and give you culture.'

'Oh. You came here for culture? I'll bet you came to look at Italian girls' He made a fist and gave me a playful punch on the shoulder. 'Away from home for the first time, huh?"

I don't think he gave a shit about culture and all that stuff. Europe is supposed to be full of it and so I suppose it doesn't matter to them.

'Well, we're supposed to learn something, anyway.'

He became quite serious. 'Here in the south of Italy,' he said, 'we've got loads of culture. Five hundred years? In America that's a long time. Here it's nothing. We Italians here in the south of Italy, we're not the same as Italians up north. We're a cocktail. People'—he searched for the word—'different races all mixed together. The Greeks came here hundreds of years ago. They built their temples. The Romans came, they built amphitheatres, and huge baths where people came to take a bath. Then the Arabs came. Then Normans—like the same Normans in England. Why, did you know that even the ancient Trojans came here? So they told me in school. Part of us belongs to the west, another part to Greece, another part to Africa. We are all people mixed up together. Like a cocktail.'

'Cool,' I said.

'Italy is a very old country, you see, and Napoli is an old city of Italy. Italians have lived through everything—wars, disease, famine, revolutions—everything.'

'Awesome,' said I.

'I wish I could show you around Pozzuoli,' he said, ' but I got business in Palermo. In Sicilia.' He was playing around with his briefcase. It was a black leather case with a laptop inside. 'I wish I could introduce you to Luigi. He's got a nice business, like, in Pozzuoli. Makes lots of money. He's a good friend of mine.'

'Yeah,' said I. 'I'd like that.'

Actually, I'm not sure I would. My dad thinks the ancient Romans were great, but it's been downhill ever since. My dad thinks the Roman Empire declined and fell, and it's stayed declined and fallen ever since. Dad was probably watching me right then, from two rows back in the airplane, where my parental units got their seats. We couldn't get three seats abreast; otherwise I'd be back there with them. But the old man doesn't miss much. He's a teacher at Williamson Academy, the school I was supposed to go to, but my grades weren't good enough to get in, and, anyway, my old man wouldn't want a dumb son there embarrassing him. So I go to Gilead, which isn't all that bad. Dad pretended he was disappointed and said so, five times a day for two weeks, but actually I think he was glad not to have a dumb son at Williamson where I might embarrass him with my low grades. Mother was disappointed too, *but she didn't say anything. Her specialty is long silences.*

My name is Conradin. I am named after the last of the Hohenstaufens. Whoever they were. One of the big wheels in the history of this part of the world, I think. I used to hate my name, but now I think it has a kind of class. Conradin Thatcher. It could be worse. I'm taking a summer course in Italy in ancient Roman civilization. At least, I am going along with my dad and mom. I'm not exactly studying.. I'm going along, like. My dad isn't exactly signing up for the course, either. He's the big wheel behind the summer program at this place called the Palazzo Agrippina

He tells all the teachers at Williamson Academy that he is the head honcho of the Palazzo Agrippina summer school, and the head master is sort of impressed. Which is good, because the head master isn't impressed by dad, generally. He doesn't like dad very much, I think, and dad certainly doesn't like him. He's a chemistry teacher and dad teaches Latin, which is still a compulsory subject at Williamson, though the head master thinks it should be dropped to free up timetable space for statistics. Also he's the man who told dad there was no place at Williamson for a student with grades like mine. It's too bad, he said. I'm really sorry to have to tell you, he said, looking really delighted. He hates Dad. So since the head master says I'm not good enough for Williamson, I'm at Gilead.

One of my teachers at Gilead, Kowalski, is taking the course at the Palazzo Agrippina this summer. Kowalski's a cool guy. I should have a chance to get together with him here, I guess.

So, as we were claiming our luggage at the carousel at Fiumicino airport, I saw this guy Giacomo Fini again. He came up to me, holding a knapsack.

'Yo,' I said.

'Hello,' he said. 'Is this yours?' He was holding my knapsack in one hand.

'Yeah,' said I. Big blue knapsack with red trim and with my name tag and a Palazzo Agrippina label. Not easy to miss.

'I picked it up for you,' he said. 'I thought it was yours.'

'Thanks,' I said.

'Grazie, that's what you say here,' he said. He snagged another suitcase as the conveyor belt brought it around. 'Here's mine,' he said. His case was not large, but heavy. When he lifted it, you could see his coat

sleeve tighten as his biceps bulged. 'Have a good trip, Conradino,' he
said.

'You, too,' said I.

'Get some good Italian culture!' He slapped me on the shoulder,
friendly-like and winked and offered his hand. I shook it. Real, firm
grip. 'Maybe you'll meet Luigi at Arco Felice. Tell him Giacomo says hi!
Giacomo from Fabiola Films. He runs an albergo there—a hotel, called
the Albergo Felice, I think. I'll be in touch with him soon.'

'Yeah,' said I.

'Nobody pushes Luigi around,' said Giacomo, clenching a fist, and
his biceps bulged again. 'He's a good man to know.'

'Yeah,' said I. Fat chance, I thought.

' Ciao,' he said

'Arrivederci, signore.'

He grinned at my attempt at Italian.

'Who was that, Conradin?' asked my dad, appearing from behind my
left shoulder. He'd been watching me all the time. He really slays me.

II

SOL BERNSTEIN, New York tort lawyer whom malpractice suits had made comfortably rich, leaned back on his deck-chair which creaked ominously, and said to his two companions, Marcia Mellon and Paul Kowalski, 'I may be a burned-out lawyer—both my psychiatrist and my rabbi agree on that much—but if this chair collapses and I suffer injury to my hip that will require a replacement forty years on, I'm going to sue.'

'Surely, with a view like this, you feel at peace with the world.' Paul gestured to the prospect before them, olive orchards sloping down to the shore of the blue Mediterranean. They were sitting on the patio of the Palazzo Agrippina enjoying a drink before 'Happy Hour', when all the students who had just arrived at the palazzo for the summer course were to gather for *antepasti* in the library before supper, and get to know each other. Paul had retrieved a bottle of bourbon from his tote bag where it had travelled unobtrusively from a Duty Free shop at Kennedy Airport, found three glasses, and poured drinks for Sol, Marcia and himself. Marcia leaned back in chair, and regarded the broken strap on one of her sandals with profound discontent.

'Why are you burned out?' she asked.

'Too much work,' Sol replied. 'You have to be an attack dog in court, fighting off the attack dogs on the other side. There's big money in tort cases, but, by all that's holy, you have to work. You have to line up experts who will give the opinion you want them to give and you have to vet them to make sure they haven't given some other lawyer the complete opposite opinion a couple months before, all of it for a price. What experts are most expert at is how to send you an invoice for their services.'

'Experts have to eat,' said Marcia, 'particularly if they have to make up an opinion that they can reasonably back with their reputations. This might be the one time when their fancy university degrees pay off.'

'Oh, come off it!' Sol scoffed. 'Courts follow their own rules. Why, courts have recognized medical conditions that medical schools have never heard of, and awarded huge sums to the poor victims who suffer from them. It's a game and I was good at it. But you wanted to know why I am burned out.'

'Please'

'A really tough job. A marriage on the rocks. She accused me of having an affair and she was not quite accurate. I was having two affairs. But they were just sex. I wasn't really two-timing in the proper sense of the word. Then there were three kids, two in Ivy League universities and you know what they cost. The third was in an expensive prep school. Williamson Academy. Half the dads who have kids in Williamson have second mortgages on their houses. Then I lost a couple cases. You know what that means financially for a contingency lawyer. I reached the point where I just sat and looked into the distance. My rabbi said, "Go to the Palazzo Agrippina and take you mind off the law." My shrink said, "I'll analyze you at $500.00 an hour and here's a prescription for Paxil." My rabbi's advice seemed the most cost-effective and so here I am!'

'So,' said Paul, 'we have two people here who make a living from the law courts.' Marcia, Paul knew, was Marcia Mellon, writer of detective stories and TV scripts about court dramas with well-crafted plots. She seemed to be a lady of uncertain age, and certain experience. 'I feel like a humdrum fellow—a humble teacher.'

'Don't,' said Marcia. 'Don't ever be humble. But Sol,' she said, turning to him, 'you interest me. Court cases are grist for TV dramas which I write in an effort to make a living, but of course, you have to wind up the plot within an hour with room for commercials. It's not the real thing.'

'Damn right it's not', said Sol. 'But you know, when a client comes to me, what he knows about the law courts comes from TV dramas, and that's certainly true of juries. Juries have watched *Law and Order* on TV.'

'I'm old-fashioned,' said Paul. 'I like Agatha Christie.'

'So do I,' said Marcia. 'Dame Agatha lived in a world of logical crime. There was rhyme and reason to it.'

'I like Dame Agatha too,' said Sol, 'for relaxation. Hercule what-his-name? Her detective?'

'Hercule Poirot'.

'Hercule Poirot did not have to worry about DNA evidence which has thrown our courts into a tizzy. The courts which are never wrong have been shown up. DNA evidence is showing that they have been sentencing innocent people, some of them to death. Some of our lawyers find it hard to take. You build a beautiful case against a suspect, and DNA evidence destroys it all. Can DNA always be right?'

'It's science,' said Marcia. 'It's got to be right'.

'Yes", said Sol, 'but you're getting cases where a felon is legally guilty but scientifically innocent. I'm a legalist, myself.'

'I wish I could write detective stories,' said Paul. My English grammar is sound enough, for what that's worth. Teaching Latin has given me that much. But the latest methods of solving crime are beyond me. It's all science now, DNA and psychological pro-filing. But most of all, you need a really satisfying victim to mur-der. What we have is dope smugglers and mafia families and maybe some presidential candidates. I don't know much about crime. I'm just an innocent teacher of languages, living and half-alive, at Gilead Academy, and I've never committed a worse crime than conjugating Latin verbs.'

'Don't underestimate yourself,' said Sol.

'Perish the thought. But you know, Aristotle had it right. You can't write a successful tragedy if your readers look at the victim of the tragic fall and say "Who cares?' "

'I should think Gilead Academy would provide some decent victims,' said Marcia. 'Couldn't a department head mysteriously disappear, and be discovered two weeks dangling from the top of a maple tree only after the autumn leaves have fallen?'

'At Gilead, department heads never disappear. They continue to take meals at the head table even after they're supposed to be dead.'

'What about a steamy sex scandal that turns into a murder?'

'You want total realism, huh? No, that's not my gig.'

'I wonder what is,' Marcia thought. She found herself looking at him speculatively. He was handsome, and well-kept. Fit and muscular; youngish rather than young. Younger than herself by a few years, however. Marcia glanced down at her own overgenerous thighs with discontent. Paul looked as if he jogged regularly and lifted weights. Not a body builder, to be sure, but as teachers of Latin, French and Italian go, he had a trim physique. Marcia looked forward to seeing him in swimming trunks. The summer program at the Palazzo Agrippina included time at the beach at Paestum. *'Morning: archaeological site, temples and museum. Afternoon: beach'* read the printout of the summer course activities.

There were some nice beaches within walking distance of the Palazzo Agrippina itself, but students were warned sternly that they were polluted. The young Neapolitans whose bare flesh littered the seashore had grown immune to the local bacteria, but they lurked in hiding, lying in wait for new prey from across the Atlantic.

Paul would do nicely for a summer affair, Marcia thought. She brought her mind back to the subject of the conversation with some effort.

'Well, if you want to write a murder mystery, you must plan the murder carefully,' she said. 'But there has to be a clue that is overlooked by everyone except your detective. That's the chief secret. And it can't be a perfect murder. I remember that I constructed the perfect murder once, and then couldn't solve it. Ii could have been embarrassing.'

'What did you do?'

'Oh, I stole an idea from Jim Qwilleran and his Siamese cat Koko. My detective, Aristide Blanchard, has a pet too—a parrot, Willoughby, a smart old African Grey. Willoughby kept screaming "You're a bad boy" at the murderer so often that he broke down and confessed. He thought old Willoughby had his number'

'But', said Paul, 'what do you mean, you couldn't solve the mystery? You knew who the killer was all the time'.

'Of course I did, but Aristide didn't. My detective is limited by the exigencies of the plot. I don't pretend that he's any Hercule Poirot, either, talking on and on about his little grey cells. He depends heavily on the grey cells of his secretary, Leslie, who makes him coffee and keeps him on the right track.'

'A loyal secretary?' said Sol. 'Where do you find them? I must read some of your books. This Leslie must be having an affair with her boss.'

'Well, I have read some of them,' said Paul, 'and I think you treat poor Leslie disgracefully. She's far too loyal. Couldn't you turn her into a feminist, who tells old Aristide to brew his own coffee?'

'But she is a feminist, in her own way. I've made Leslie and Willoughby both smarter than Aristide. My feminism is always a sub-text. All the men in my books are big and stupid, and have a great deal to say, most of it not to the point. The women are smart.'

'You're a dangerous woman, Marcia. Are you going to throw poor stupid Aristide Blanchard out on to the scrap heap eventually?'

"No, I thought I might recycle him as a murder victim. I won't waste him. He was an imaginative creation of my youth, and I'm rather fond of him. I would have recycled him it long ago except that my literary agent thinks that I'll lose readers if I eliminate him.'

'So you would.'

'However, I think I can convince Joshua—that's my agent— that I can ease Leslie and Willoughby in the C.E.O.'s chair at Blanchard Private Eye, Inc. and my readers will accept it..'

'There you go,' said Paul. 'You're a ruthless woman, Marcia. Who will murder Aristide?'

'I'm working on that.'

'How about this for an idea?' suggested Paul. 'Leslie gets fed up with making coffee for her boss, and begins to add warfarin to the mix. It's easily available. Then she manages to get Aristide to cut himself accidentally with an Exacto knife, and he bleeds to death. Leslie pretends to try to save him, and administers multiple Band-Aids, and then she delivers a eulogy at Aristide's memorial service, where she lists all his virtues. It doesn't take long. His cadaver is cremated before there can be an autopsy. How about that?'

'To tell you the truth, I was planning to make Leslie the detective who solves the case. Not the murderer.'

'Well, then,' said Paul, 'forget about the warfarin in the coffee, and have Aristide run down by a speeding car, driven by a man who is madly in love with Leslie and wants to present her with her first murder case as a kind of birthday gift. Then Leslie solves the murder to everyone's satisfaction.'

'But what about the love-sick driver of the car that runs down Aristide? He could go to prison for life!'

'I said that Leslie should produce a satisfactory solution to the case. She doesn't have to find the right murderer, just one that satisfies a judge and jury. Leslie and the real killer can live happily ever after—that is, if they want to.'

'Paul,' said Marcia, 'you are a young man totally without principles.'

'Only on the level of literature. Otherwise I'm the soul of rectitude.'

'How very disappointing.' Marcia looked at Paul speculatively and tried to picture him as a cadaver. The bullet hole need not show; and his lips would be curved in an unnatural smile which might pass for angelic. He would seem to be in an untroubled sleep. Paul, meanwhile, took a sip of his bourbon on the rocks, and for a moment, his mind wandered, as he gazed down at the prospect from the Palazzo Agrippina's patio. Baia, Arco Felice, Pozzuoli, and Naples formed one continuous urban sprawl along the shore of the Gulf of Naples, stretching into a cloud of smog which veiled the volcano of Mt. Vesuvius, lurking and quiescent, but still menacing. Only that morning, Bathsheba Bennett, an assistant professor of Latin literature from Edwards College, who had just arrived at the Palazzo for the summer course, had recalled her first visit to Naples: she had slipped into the harbour on the old Italian Line ship, *Cristoforo Colombo*, and as she leaned over the rail, she saw the cone of Mt. Vesuvius looming on the horizon. There were fewer cars back then, and the air was pellucid, she said. Nowadays this corner of Italy was choking on pollution and traffic. Paul took a second, larger sip of his bourbon on the rocks.

That's progress for you, he reflected, and it's worrisome. This magnificent shoreline belonged rows of tanned, more-or-less naked bodies baking in the sun, absorbing ultra-violet rays without sunscreen, just as naked flesh had done here for two thousand years. Greek migrants, wealthy Roman senators, Norman freebooters, Bourbon kings, all had come here and taken their pleasures on these shores. Julius Caesar and long-winded old Cicero both once owned villas nearby. The mad emperor Caligula had built a floating bridge across this bay and Nero had tried to drown his mother in the once-pellucid waters of the gulf. The sailors from the Roman imperial fleet from its naval base at *Capo di Miseno* on the tip of the Gulf of Naples must have relaxed on these beaches, and only a brief voyage from Naples, on the island of Capri, the emperor Tiberius had secluded himself in a lonely villa overlooking the sea, and shunned the unfriendly world. He wanted to be alone, like Greta Garbo, but all Rome thought that what he wanted was a secret life of debauchery in a place where no one could spy on him.

Vergil studied here as a young man, and tourist guides point to a Roman tomb on the road from Naples to Pozzuoli, and claim it is his. His epic, the *Aeneid*, told how Aeneas, fleeing from an affair with the queen of Carthage, made his first landing in Italy near here, and the cave where the Sibyl of Cumae foretold Rome's future grandeur was only a short hike from the Palazzo. Tour guides still point to an artificial cave, cut into the limestone cliff at the foot of the citadel at Cumae, and call it the cave of the Sibyl, though modern archeologists are skeptical. Somewhere nearby grew the tree that bore a Golden Bough, which only Aeneas could tear from its trunk. From there it was only a short walk through the silvery dusk to the gateway where the Dark Lord, Hades, took in the souls of the dead. The Gates of Hell were a close neighbour..

In fact, the Underworld lurked close to the surface in Pozzuoli. Underground fires smoulder beneath it, and the surface of the earth rises and falls, as if a wild beast in the planet's core were thrusting upwards, and then subsiding back into its lair, exhausted for the moment by its effort. Near Pozzuoli at the Campi Flegrei, fumaroles vent smoke and steam from volcanic fires, and, lowering over the Gulf of Naples, Mt. Vesuvius slumbers, deceptively calm.

Yet the Palazzo Agrippina was an admirable base for a summer school. Paul had spotted an advertisement for it on the *American Latin Reporter* web page, which announced in boldface letters that 'The Palazzo Agrippina Group, Inc., president: Decimus Monroe Thatcher, A.M.' was running its tenth annual summer program at the Palazzo Agrippina at Arco Felice, which, the web page explained, was a station beyond Pozzuoli on the Cumana Railway that skirted the Gulf of Naples. It was the name 'Decimus Monroe Thatcher' that first caught his attention. Thatcher's son was a student at Gilead Academy. That might be a drawback. But the program seemed attractive. There would be trips to the major archaeological sites in the area, and lectures by experts. One name he recognized: Dr. DeWitt Fordham, the program director. Professor at Holyrood College. Holyrood was a top level school, the equal of Kenyon College and Mt. Holyoke. The program at the Palazzo Agrippina could not be all bad if a Holyrood professor headed it. Paul faxed an application. Was there a space for him?

Indeed yes, there was. The Palazzo Agrippina summer school professed to be impressed by his qualifications. As Paul discovered even before he reached Italy, the Agrippina summer school was not deluged with applications. It had no university affiliation and little standing in academic circles, for it had been founded a thirty years before by an Englishwoman whose eccentricity more than matched her surname, which was Twickenham. Sibyl was the name given her by her Twickenham parents, who thereby inadvertently shaped her sibylline personality. There was always something odd about her, and by middle age, her eccentricity blossomed into full flower. In a burst of self-discovery, she realized that her body had become the present residence of the Cumaean Sibyl. In her final years, the Sibyl had retired from the human dimension altogether, dismayed by the prevalence of unbelieving Christians. But she could not die, for she was immortal, and death will never give immortals release. Eventually she found another Sibyl's body to lend her hospitality, and a new entry into the world of the flesh.

This was the truth that dawned on Sibyl Twickenham in an epiphany she experienced one weekend which she spent alone with only a bottle of Famous Grouse Scotch as her companion. As the level of whisky in the bottle became lower, the logic of it all grew clearer. She became more convinced of it as the months passed.. The Sibyl of Cumae, driven from her cave by the chill of Christianity, had taken up residence in her body. Sibyl Twickenham's life had new meaning.

The Palazzo Agrippina had been a legacy from a grandfather who had passed his retirement in Italy, and since Sibyl's only means of support was a small pension from her deceased husband that dwindled with inflation, she and the Palazzo together might have faded into dismal penury, had not her namesake appeared to her one evening as she reflected on her overdraft, and instructed her to open a summer school. It was barely profitable at first, but she brought enthusiasm to her lectures on the great age of Italy in the first century of the Christian era, and eventually she supplemented her enthusiasm with some knowledge. During the winter months she made ends meet by giving lessons in English-as-a-second-language and the French horn. Death came to her suddenly one winter; a student found her lifeless body when he came for his lesson. Her grave could now be found shaded by a chestnut tree in the back garden, a close neighbour of the septic tank which her spiritual presence guarded in death with no less diligence that than she had in life.

Her heir was her nephew, a country vicar in England who was surprised to find himself the owner of an Italian palazzo, and quite astonished to discover that his aunt had run a summer school there for English-speaking students, mainly from North America. Yet, when a group of Agrippina alumni proposed to carry on the school, he heartily approved. 'Latin conjugations can only improve the level of civilization,' he affirmed in reply to their proposal, 'and Greek is the *lingua franca* in Heaven', claiming Gilbert Murray as an authority. He settled for a moderate rent. The summer school was incorporated in Delaware as 'The Julio-Claudian Group, Inc.', and fitted out with a board of directors, a president and C.E.O. The last two offices were both filled by one Decimus Monroe Thatcher, a Latin master at the Williamson Academy, which was an eastern prep school old enough to have several revolutionary heroes among its alumni. One of them was remembered for the great valedictory speech he gave on graduation day on 'Liberty and the Rights of Man,' after which he joined George Washington's army and died of dysentery. Heroes such as he had formed the proud past of Williamson, and the Williamson Academy lent Thatcher prestige in the local classical association.

Paul had met Monroe Thatcher once. He and his wife Millicent had visited the Gilead Academy on Parents' Day, to check on the progress of their son Conradin. Monnie, as his wife called him, was prepared to be critical of the Gilead Academy, which lacked the history and prestige of Williamson, and no doubt, as his body language implied, it failed to attract teachers of Williamson's caliber. He had just discovered a new Cambridge Beginning Latin course, and was surprised to learn that Paul already knew about it. But would students at a second-tier school, like the Gilead, master the Latin subjunctive if they used the Cambridge method? Monnie, his wife explained, thought the importance of the subjunctive should never be undervalued. By no means, Paul assured them both. He was a subjunctive man himself.

However, it appeared that Conradin was on Monnie's mind more than the Latin subjunctive. Conradin had failed to win acceptance at the Williamson Academy, and Monnie consid-

ered that a blot on the family record, for Thatchers had all been
Williamson men back to 1821. The problem now was Williamson's
avowal of 'Equal Opportunity' which meant that the scions of
Williamson alumni were sometimes shoved aside by Chinese or
East Indian applicants who wrote stellar entrance examinations.
Conradin, complained Thatcher, did not apply himself.

Conradin was a willowy, handsome lad with a ring in his
right ear. He wrote poetry. Paul had read some of it. It was full
of despair, idealism, the gloomy contemplation of death, and immense disgust with the contemporary world, and it did not scan.
Yet, for all that, it achieved a kind of dismal appeal. .

Monroe Thatcher, Millicent and Conradin were to arrive
at Arco Felice tomorrow, according to a notice on the Palazzo
Agrippina bulletin board. Monroe had decided to look in on a
Palazzo Agrippina summer session himself and perhaps take in
a few of the sights and sounds of Italy. He might set an example
for Conradin too, though this was a hope he kept to himself. He
also felt keenly the need to subject the director and the associate
director to periodic supervision. Last year they had purchased a
used Volkswagen van for the school, claiming it was necessary
for shopping and picking up stray students at the Naples train
terminal, and in the space of three months it had devoured two
new clutches. Pozzuoli had a mechanic who specialized in repair-
ing Volkswagens, and he claimed that Volkswagen clutches were
an endemic problem in an otherwise excellent model. Monroe
suspected that the endemic problem was a dishonest mechanic,
who tightened a bolt or two, dusted the headlights and charged
the school an atrocious bill. Twice. D. Monroe knew what foreign-
ers were like. They believed all Americans were millionaires and
tripled their bills whenever one of them came into view. DeWitt
Fordham, the director of the Palazzo Agrippina school, was far
too naïve. So, at least, Monroe thought, and his suspicions had
been intensified only a year ago when he caught Fordham mis-
translating the Latin motto of the Williamson school, mistaking
a jussive subjunctive for an indicative.

Marcia was talking again. She had finished her drink, and decided that a second one on an empty stomach would be pleasant

but imprudent.

'My plan is to have Aristide go on an assignment to London and I'll dispose of him there. His body will be found floating in the Thames. His career will end with a flourish in the land of Inspector Wexford and Commander Dalgliesh. Aristide has served me well, and he deserves to become a corpse within sight of Westminster Abbey.'

'What of Willoughby?'

'He'll go to London, too. Along with Leslie.'

A young male voice floated up from the garden below.

'Yo-yo, we've got time to walk to the beach and back before the fucking dinner. The view's fuckin' awesome'

'There's drinks in the library before dinner', replied another male voice, precise and slightly accented.

Marcia and Paul both looked at their watches.

'That's a reflex action of mine whenever someone mentions dinner,' said Paul. 'I look at my watch'.

'Mine, too,' said Marcia, getting to her feet. 'It's been pleasant—really awesome—our drink together. You know, I'm awful with names', she went on, 'I know your first name, but not your last, and if I don't ask you now, I'll be too embarrassed to ask you in a week's time, when we know each other better. I'll have to sneak up to someone and whisper, who is that Paul somebody-or-other from the Gilead School, if I don't come clean now and admit I don't know it.'

'Kowalski,' Paul smiled. 'A Polish name. Not your old Boston blue-blooded family.'

'Good to meet you. Your physique is too good for a blue-blood. I notice things like that.'

Paul looked embarrassed but not displeased. Before Marcia left, he interjected a final question,

'Incidentally, how does your Monsieur Aristide Blanchard manage to pay Leslie's salary? How much does he charge to solve a crime?'

'Aristide never discusses his bill. It's fiction, Paul. Pure fantasy.'

III

HAPPY HOUR before dinner arrived at the Palazzo Agrippina. The library was crowded and students spilled over into the lounge. A tray of *antepasti* had appeared on the table, and a bottle of cognac and another of white wine stood open beside it. *Lacrima Cristi*: 'the tears of Christ', a pleasant, dry white wine from grapes grown on the slopes of Mt. Vesuvius. A clump of students clustered about the open bottles. There was Paul's room mate, Percy Bass, an modern language and music teacher from the Williamson School who had brought his guitar and a copy of Bulwer-Lytton's *The Last Days of Pompeii* with him to the Palazzo. Percy had just done a two-mile jog and his thinning hair was still wet from his shower. A portly man in a seersucker suit, with a gut that ballooned over his belt was speaking to him and to the associate director, gesticulating with one hand and holding a wine glass in the other Beside him stood a tall, broad-shouldered black man who was listening intently and saying nothing. The associate director was a plump, ruddy-faced man in his early thirties with round glasses and a perdurable smile. Behind him, almost touching elbows, was a leathery woman wearing Tilley shorts who was speaking with emphasis, and listening to her was a big blonde with an affable expression and a lumbar region tightly encased in white slacks. In one corner of the room, standing alone, was a strikingly attractive young woman, whose wire-rimmed glasses proclaimed that she was a serious student.

Sol Bernstein was deep in conversation with a woman of a certain age, and an intense expression, wearing a stick-on label with "B. Bennett" scrawled on it with magic marker.. Paul maneuvered towards them, close enough to overhear.

'Asbestos has been good to me, and to a lot of tort lawyers,' Sol was saying. 'I made my first million out of asbestos cases.'

'But isn't asbestos more or less exhausted? Is anyone getting cancer from asbestos anymore?'

'Maybe yes, maybe no,' said Sol. 'But it's not about the cancer. It's about finding something or someone worth the trouble to sue. The poor people who've been exposed to asbestos—I feel for them. I really do. A man who'd been exposed to asbestos as a kid in school might live until eighty, always wondering if he was going to get cancer, and there should be compensation for that. That's his right. It's what the pursuit of happiness means. But there's no point wasting time on a lawsuit if the defendant doesn't have a big bank account or a fat insurance policy '

'You must feel really happy when you win a fair settlement for a client.'

'I do. I really do. By the way, what's your first name? You don't go around calling yourself "B. Bennett", do you?'

'Bathsheba.'

'Bathsheba Bennett. A pretty name. You can call me "Shlomo". I like it better than Sol. It expresses my personality better, I think. Well, well. Bathsheba.' Sol savoured the name. 'Can I call you Sheba?'

'If you wish. Some of my acquaintances call me "Batty Sheba" Don't ever call me that.'

Sol threw back his head and laughed.

There seemed to be no way of breaking into that conversation, Paul thought, and he made his way towards the sideboard holding the *antepasti*. Directly in front of him was a shapely rump, swathed in blue polyester and attached to a woman who was leaning over the tray of *antepasti*, with her back to him. Paul looked at the rump with a sense of recognition. It had to belong to Marcia Mellon, author, script writer, traveler and for the next four weeks, a student of ancient art and archaeology. Less than an hour ago, he had been speaking with her, and he had sensed friendly vibrations. She had asked his name when she might have consulted the list of students posted on the bulletin board, and that was a sign of interest. The rump was familiar even if the blue polyester was not. He gave it a small, experimental pat, and then repented immediately. What if it wasn't Marcia? What if the rump's owner exploded in a fit of feminist rage?

'Oh, Lord!' he thought remorsefully, remembering the zero tolerance policy at the Gilead Academy. 'What if the headmaster hears of this?'

The owner of the rump, having filled her plate, straightened up and turned around slowly. It was not Marcia. It was Sister Stella. Sister Stella was a liberated nun who had abandoned her habit for everyday street dress. She looked at Paul speculatively with a sense of wonder and something approaching a smile. Paul was abashed.

Good Lord, now what have I done? I used to be an altar-boy once upon a time—how many years ago? Surely the Good Lord still owes me some protection in return!

'Isn't this a wonderful place to be?' said Sister Stella, brightly. 'I'm sure it is going to be a great inspiration to me when I get back to my Latin class.'

The least I can do, thought Paul, is to carry on a civil conversation with her. Sister Stella was no longer young. There were little lines on her upper lip and crows-feet around her eyes.

'It's such a storied area,' Sister Stella went on. 'To think that Julius Caesar had a villa here! St. Paul, you know, landed at Pozzuoli when he was brought to Rome for his trial! Back when Pozzuoli was called Puteoli. St. Paul's boat must have touched shore not far from here.'

'I think Pozzuoli's port area's rather seedy nowadays.'

Sister Stella smiled. 'Time is a great destroyer. But isn't it just marvelous to be in Italy? I feel as if this were my real home. Here in Puteoli, surrounded by the past.'

'Did you come here directly from stateside or have you had some time to look around?' asked Paul.

'I flew to Rome and spent a couple days there before I took the train to Naples'.

'A couple days aren't enough for Rome.'

'Oh, but it was wonderful. Truly wonderful! I saw the Forum and the Colosseum. I thought of all the Christians being eaten there by lions! And I got to St. Peter's basilica in the Vatican. That was a wonderful thrill.' Sister Stella's eyes shone, but then clouded immediately. 'You know, I was kneeling and praying in St. Peter's before that magnificent high altar with the great twisted columns, and a man pinched my—er—my behind. A man! An Italian! I'm not a prude, you know, but it was in St. Peter's, you know, the Pope's church.....and I *was* praying.'

Paul felt a tinge of guilt. But he had not pinched her rump, he told himself. He had patted it gently, with immense respect, and she had not been kneeling at prayer. She was bending over a tray of *antepasti*.

'This is Italy,' said Paul. 'The man who pinched you was paying you a compliment.'

Oh Lord! Have I been politically incorrect? I shouldn't have said that. Please, God, may no one at the Gilead know I said that. .

'I mean,' added Paul, 'he meant no harm. It's not—like—violence against women. It's just what Italian men do. So I'm told, I mean.'

'I know,' said Sister Stella, with a voice brimming with Christian charity. 'But there is a proper place for everything. That sort of thing is all right—uh—in a place like here, for instance, but not in a sacred place like St. Peter's. You don't expect to be pinched on the—uh, you know, propositioned, I mean, in St. Peter's basilica.'

'Was this your first visit to St. Peter's?'

'Yes. I'm not a prude, you know. I move with the times. But in St. Peter's at prayer, you should not have to worry about your—uh—your bottom, you know. I'm not used to it.'

Probably not, thought Paul. He decided to change the direction of the conversation on to safer grounds.

'I wish I could hear the Latin mass again,' he said. 'I was brought up with it as a boy. It was a sad day for Latin teachers when the church switched to the vernacular.'

'He was not a young man, either,' Sister Stella went on, who had not yet exhausted the subject and would not be deflected from it. 'He was short—no taller than I am—and bald. Why would he want to pinch women? You'd think he would have grown out of that sort of thing.'

"I was wondering if we could hear a Latin mass here in Italy,' continued Paul, doggedly. 'I knew it as a boy. A mass back then was full of the smell of incense, and bells, and musical words I couldn't understand.'

'Still,' objected Sister Stella gently, 'it is good that worshipers can comprehend what they are saying. It adds to the interest.'

'But I wish that the new Catholic missal didn't sound so much like the Church of England *Book of Common Prayer* rewritten by a journalism student', said Paul.

The little lines on Sister Stella's upper lip tightened in disapproval. Now I've really said something wrong, thought Paul. This conversation was not going well. He looked about him for Marcia, but there was no assistance to be had there. She was talking earnestly to the director. However the big blonde in white slacks was pushing through the crowd and in a moment, she planted herself before them, balancing a couple *hors d'oeuvres* on a plate in one hand, and a wine glass in the other.

'Ellen Cross is my name,' she announced by way of introduction. 'Am I breaking up a conversation? Send me away if I am.'

'Not at all, ' said Sister Stella. 'I was just telling Paul here how a man pinched me while I was praying at St. Peter's in Rome.'

'How wonderful!' said Ellen. "Nothing like that happens to me. It's because I look like a great earth mother battling middle-age cellulite, but I can't help it. You know, I actually am a mother. I have a son at Yale. You know,' she went on, hardly pausing for breath, 'I was telling the director, or the assistant director—whatever—that blondes like me are the new victim group. There should be a society for blonde protection. Dumb blonde jokes should be outlawed.'

'But blondes are one of the few groups left we can laugh at,' said Paul. 'It's politically incorrect to make jokes about most groups now, except for dumb blondes and Poles'

'Poles!' said Ellen with a throaty laugh. 'I love Poles. I assume you mean Polish people, of course, not flagpoles and other poles like that?'

'Right on,' said Paul, 'But seriously. You can't laugh at blacks or Jews or Chinese any more. The acceptable victim pool is becoming very small. Take away dumb blondes and who have we got left to make jokes about? The common rooms of our colleges will fall silent.'

'No chance!' replied Ellen. 'And drop the serious stuff. Life's too short for us to go around being serious. I don't mind being classed with Poles as a fellow victim.'

'Good for you.'

'Your name's Kowalski, isn't it? Do I sense a Polish heritage?'

'Yes. My father.'

'Then we can be dumb together. Colleagues in ignorance.' Her deep laugh unsettled her bosoms.

'However,' broke in Sister Stella with compassion, 'the fact that you're here in the Palazzo Agrippina summer school proves that neither of you can be dumb.'

'My husband—he's in the hotel business and has done quite well—he laughed when I said I was taking a course in Italy to get culture. So did my son. He goes to Yale,' said Ellen with a toss of her blonde mane. 'But I'm not really a blonde, you know. It all came out of a bottle. My hair dresser made me what I am, but she can't change my brain cells, can she?'

'Sounds like a good research project,' said Paul. 'The effect of Clairol or whatever, on grey matter?'

'Research project? Does someone here have an interesting research project?' A substantial woman in a blue polyester Turkish dolman joined them. 'Madge Midgely's my name. Just an overweight journalist. A cat among the pigeons, and always on the trail of a good story.'

'Great!' said Paul, who thought he should say something in response. 'What do you write?'

'Well, I write a column called "Ask Midgely" for the Beaumont *Advertiser* and it's printed by five other local newspapers belonging to the same chain.'

'You write an advice column?' asked Ellen. 'How splendid! I know there's a lot of people needing advice in Seattle, where we live now. What sort of advice do you give?'

'Whatever I'm asked to give. It's mostly about sex and marriage. Just before I left for here I got a letter from a couple of men who had gone to Canada for a same-sex marriage and now they want to know how to get a same-sex divorce. But the most interesting letters are from survivors who have repressed memories of sex abuse. You wouldn't guess what the secret life of a place like Beaumont is.'

'Yes, I would,' said Paul, his thoughts going back to the Gilead Academy.

'The people who write me usually want their names suppressed, of course', Madge Midgely went on. 'But what they tell me has really opened my eyes.'

'Well,' said Ellen, with a laugh, 'a lot of families have secrets. I have an uncle who went to Yale. He said he used to drink with President George W. Bush.'

'I used to do obituaries before I was assigned to the lovelorn column,' Madge went on, 'and I can tell you it's a whole different world. While people are alive, they are regular unloved sinners but once they're dead, they become beloved husbands, and wives who will be sorely missed. You learn fast in journalism. I suspect that if you found ten people in one room, two of them at least have a secret event in their lives that the public has a right to know.'

'Even here?' said Sister Stella. 'In the Palazzo?'

'Well, I don't want to talk about here,' Madge replied. 'I've just come here, you know. For a few weeks I am just a student of Roman archaeology. But yes, I'm sure there are people with hidden pasts here. There has to be.' She looked across the room at Percy Bass' track shoes. He was talking to Bathsheba Bennett, who was listening intently and frowning.

'I'm sure you'll find something to write about,' said Paul. 'Even here.'

'Well, I might,' Madge conceded. 'Reporters always are looking for things to report. But I didn't come here for that. I came here for a change of pace. I want to learn something about the Greeks and the Romans.'

'My son—he's at Yale—he took a course in Classical Civilization,' said Ellen. 'He thought it was interesting.'

'At Yale?' said Madge. 'That's an expensive place to send your son.'

'Yes, well, but so is a good country club, and we belong to one of those. Our family has a Yale tradition, even though we're in Seattle now. There are some things you just do.'

There was a muffled gong from the dining room, and the library emptied slowly. The dining room was one end of the long hall stretching the length of the Palazzo's first floor. It had some pretensions to grandeur: a long sideboard in florid French provincial style, two chandeliers of Capodimonte ware, and a large, framed photograph on the end wall, showing a bullet-headed man contemplating a classical bust identifiable by its high cheekbones and boyish face as the young emperor Augustus. Attached to the bottom of the picture frame was a small plaque, with gilt letters reading 'Our beloved leader.' The beloved leader looked very serious and rather grim, as if he were digesting a profound thought, and finding it a disagreeable experience. Bathsheba Bennett remarked to no one in particular that he resembled her ex-husband, who had died fifteen years ago –'and not a moment too soon,' she added, with some vehemence. Below the picture was a reproduction of an Athenian black-figure wine jug, containing a solitary sprig of oleander.

In the centre of the dining hall was a long wooden table which a furniture salesman would call 'distressed'. DeWitt Fordham, the director, took his place at one end, with his wife at his right elbow and at his left elbow was the assistant director, Dr. Alex Baker. Marcia Mellon, who had changed Into a dress of scarlet and teal blue which made her look like a large tropical bird, found a seat at Dr. Alex's left elbow where she had an unobstructed view of the beloved leader's portrait. Paul trailed in behind Bathsheba Bennett and Percy Bass, padding along silently in his track shoes. He found a seat where a large bouquet of flowers effectively shielded Sister Stella from his line of vision. Madge Midgely squeezed into a chair beside Sister Stella.

'I wish they would make chairs a little wider,' she said. 'I know I'm carrying a little extra weight, but I can't help it. It's my FTO gene. Half of all people of European descent have it, and I belong to the unlucky half.'

'Can I move over a bit to make more room?' asked Sister Stella.

'No, that's fine. Thank you, thank you,' as Sister Stella nudged her chair to the left. 'I'm ready to eat. I hope there are no long speeches before the chow. Paul, why are you hiding behind that bouquet of flowers? Bathsheba, I haven't had a chance to talk to you, yet.'

'Well, we must make up for it,' said Bathsheba..

DeWitt Fordham rapped his glass with his fork, and when the conversation died, he rose to his feet.

'We'll say grace,' he said. 'Alex, you do the honours.'

Grace was said. A simple Latin grace. *Benedictus benedicat omnia*. Then the first course. Minestrone, followed by *frutta di mare*, served by Mario, a muscular young Italian who worked as gardener and luggage-handler during the day, and then, having changed into a starched white jacket and dark trousers, served dinner in the evening. There was *zuppa inglese* for dessert. 'English soup'. It was English trifle as interpreted by an Italian cook. Trifle had crossed a significant cultural divide to become *zuppa inglese*. It was very good. Madge Midgely finished her serving quickly.

'That was good,' she said. 'Mario, could I have some more?' Mario seemed not to hear. 'Mario, 'said Madge, again, 'That's his name, isn't it?' she asked everyone within ear shot.

'I think we finished the dessert,' said Sister Stella. 'It's all gone.'

'I hope they're not going to starve us on this tour,' said Madge, crossly.

DeWitt Fordham tinkled his glass again, and without rising to his feet, spoke in a voice made raspy by a lifetime of chain smoking.

'Let me take a few moments before we move into the lounge for coffee and liqueur. Some of you may have already learned that our beloved president, Decimus Monroe Thatcher, will be joining us tomorrow. Decimus Monroe Thatcher heads the Classics department at the Williamson Academy, one of the great prep schools of America which has educated the elite of our country for more than two centuries. In fact we are delighted that another faculty member from Williamson has joined us for this session, Mr. Bass.' He looked down the table at Percy Bass, who acknowledged the introduction with a perceptible nod. Fordham continued, 'Mr. Thatcher was elected president of the Julio-Claudian Group, which runs the Palazzo Agrippina summer program, some six years ago, but when his normal term was up, he realized that he could best serve Palazzo Agrippina by remaining in office and devoting all his spare time to it. He has given the Agrippina summer sessions a continuity and—uh—a consistency that it never had in the past, and he has also done a bang-up job fund-raising, though Heaven knows we can still use more funds. Without the efforts of our beloved president, we would not be where we are now.

'Mr. Thatcher is no longer young and some of you may imagine that he belongs to a bygone generation. Well, I assure you he does not. As Vergil said of the old ferryman Charon who rowed the souls of the dead across the River Styx, our beloved leader is sturdy and full of sap.' Fordham signaled with a short chortle that this was a joke, and his audience laughed obediently. 'Always keep in mind what we owe to our beloved president. He has been the heart and soul of this operation. Monroe Thatcher is a man who likes to be in charge. I hope we will all be patient and forebearing. And appreciative.' The director looked at the associate director. 'Do you have anything to add, Alex?'

'I think you've pretty well covered it, DeWitt,' said the associate director, without rising to his feet. 'We are enormously honored to have our beloved president join us for the first session of the program here at the Palazzo Agrippina, and I trust we shall all profit from his dynamic presence, and avail ourselves of it. He will be joined by his good wife and his son, who is an outstanding and—uh, dynamic—young Latin student at Andover...'

'Gilead,' corrected Fordham.

'Gilead,' said the associate director.' They will all three add spice and interest and—uh—great merriment to our group,' he continued. 'Our beloved president is a great lover of the Greek and Latin classics and his dynamic vigor and energy will amaze all of you. He is a tireless and dynamic promoter of the Agrippina program, and takes every opportunity to advocate it.' Alex Baker's jowls quivered. 'He's a man of dynamic drive. Last year he raised fifteen thousand much-needed dollars for the Palazzo.'

'Fifteen hundred, I think it was,' corrected the director.

'Fifteen hundred,' repeated Dr. Alex. 'Decimus will bring an energetic, dynamic presence to the program that will—uh—energize us all.'

'He must be sixty-one,' said the director.

'I've known people who can walk without a cane when they are well over ninety,' spoke up Bathesheba Bennett. 'Decimus what's-his-name is not a special case.'

'Last year we had a seventy-five year old who walked up to the crater of Mt. Vesuvius,' said the director. 'A really remarkable woman. She knew how to pace herself.'

'Was that a safe thing to do?' asked Ellen Cross. 'What if she met some lava on the way up?'

Marcia spoke up.

'What makes this Thatcher man so beloved? My old Latin teacher taught me how to conjugate the verb "to love"—*amo, amas, amat*—something like that—but there's a world of difference between conjugating and loving, I should think.'

The director wrestled with a sudden paroxysm of coughing. Percy Bass muttered something under his breath.

'He's a Latin lover, of course,' volunteered the man in the seersucker suit, with a mischievous gleam in his eye.

'Probably it's because he raises money for the Palazzo,' suggested Sister Stella from behind the bouquet of flowers..

'Ah, money. That would account for the love, I guess,' said Marcia. Percy Bass's lips had settled into a gently cynical smile, she noted. Percy, she thought, might be worth further study.

The director had by now he recovered his breath, but he declined comment. Instead, he smiled beatifically at the group sitting at the long table.

'I think coffee is ready in the lounge,' he said.

There was a great scraping of chairs as the group rose from the table and filed back into the lounge. The seersucker suit followed on Marcia's heels.

'Don't underestimate the power of conjugating, Marcia,' he said.

'By no means,' Marcia replied.

Outside in the garden Percy Bass began to play the guitar and sing softly in a light tenor voice to himself and anyone else who would listen.

IV

THE MORNING schedule for day one of the program called for a visit to the sculpture galleries of the Museo Nazionale in Naples. Lunch at a Naples restaurant famous for its pasta.

'Aren't all Italian restaurants famous for their pasta?' asked Marcia.

'The program says this one is famous,' said Paul, 'so it must be really famous.'

'Da Gennaro's pasta really is magnificent,' said Dr. Alex Baker, smacking his lips. His two chins quivered in anticipation, and he patted his paunch tenderly. 'Truly sumptuous.'

The full roster of students in the Agrippina summer course had appeared for breakfast. All except the Thatcher family, whose plane was scheduled to arrive at the Naples airport at two o'clock in the afternoon. Giovanni, the general handyman at the Palazzo would meet them with the Volkswagen van. The new clutch appeared to be working well. If the director and the associate director were apprehensive as they awaited the Thatcher arrival, they did not show it. But the director's wife was irritable. A mosquito had pursued her in her bedroom all night long, she said, and she was worn out. When she referred to the Thatchers, there was a light tincture of venom in her voice.

The bus which the Palazzo Agrippina directorate had chartered for the school group arrived in the courtyard. The driver extracted himself from the driver's seat and swung out the door.

'*Buon giorno*', he said. 'Me, I am Giuseppe.'

'*Buon giorno*, Giuseppe', chorused the student body, like a badly trained choir.

'What's he saying?' asked Ellen Cross. Giuseppe's gaze rested on Ellen's blonde hair for an eloquent moment.

The Agrippina group filed into the bus. Marcia settled in a seat too close neither to the front nor to the back. This seat was likely to be hers for the rest of the session, and experience had taught her that air-conditioned tour buses tended to be chilly in the front seats and too hot at the back. The associate director appeared, smiled benignly and proceeded to count the students.

They were a miscellaneous group. Sol Bernstein from New York, short, wiry and almost bald, wearing khaki shorts, a red jersey and a baseball hat. Sister Stella, sensibly dressed with stout walking shoes. Madge Midgely, wearing shorts revealing elephantine thighs and substantial buttocks. Sharing the seat with her, wearing sensible shoes, was her room mate, Sally Harvey, a leathery high school teacher of Spanish and Latin from California. Walter Druker, a philosophy and classics professor from a mid-west university called Spearfish State, squeezed into a seat behind them. He had exchanged the seersucker suit he wore last night for chinos and scarlet sweatshirt that proclaimed across his pectorals, 'For God, for country and for Spearfish State!'. Across the aisle from him was his room mate, a broad-shouldered, dignified black man who was wearing a light suit. His passport identified him as Edgar L. Smith, but he had applied to the school program under the name 'Kwame Assante', and that was the name that appeared on the Palazzo Agrippina's bulletin board. Behind him was Ellen Cross, magnificent with her great mane of light blonde hair, black at the roots. She was wearing shoes with open toes, revealing red toe nails.

Then there was Percy Bass, lean, fit and slightly odd. He had traveled to Italy with his guitar, which had almost caused an ugly incident on his flight from New York to Rome, for the security guards suspected that it concealed a bomb, and then, when they were satisfied that it did not, the air line insisted that he either buy a ticket for the guitar so that it would have a seat for itself, or check it with his luggage. Percy flew into an impressive rage. He knew his rights. His father was a lawyer, he said, and the airplane was only two-thirds full. The guitar got a free seat, and it arrived safely at the Palazzo Agrippina. It was he who was singing and playing the guitar in the garden last night while the rest of the students drank coffee in the lounge. He was a teacher at the Williamson Academy, where Decimus Monroe Thatcher was a colleague, and the director and associate director treated him with marked deference, for they knew that Thatcher would quiz him closely about his experience at the Palazzo Agrippina when he got back home.

Marcia's roommate, Miriam Kuntz, nodded pleasantly to Marcia, and claimed a double seat for herself. She was an assistant professor of classics and sexual diversity studies at McPhatter College in South Carolina, and was writing a book titled *The Anatomy of Roman Imperialism and the Penis*, which she hoped would bring her tenure and promotion. It would, if there was any justice in the world, she had assured Marcia, but perhaps not at McPhatter. Her knapsack contained a bottle of Evian water, a Dell laptop computer, and the *Lonely Planet Guide* to southern Italy. Apart from that, all Marcia knew of her as yet was that by day, in her spare moments, she read *Notes on the Ancient Monuments of the Naples Area* by the Palazzo Agrippina's associate director, which were mimeographed and available for $10.00 each, and that, by night, she snored like a badly-tuned violoncello.

Sitting together near the back of the bus were Dr. Gregory Donahue and his wife Mildred, who was never far from his side. He was professor of classics, department head and Dean of Men at the College of the Pacific Coast, and he had the demeanour and the walk of a man who was important and knew it.. Across the aisle from them sat Percy Bass's room mate, Paul Kowalski, whose measure Marcia had already taken. He had arisen early for a run and a shower, and his hair was still damp. He wore tight spandex shorts, which revealed a bulge at his groin. A well-hung young man, she noted with approval, and apparently single. Bathsheba Bennett, identified on the Palazzo roster as an assistant professor, was clearly a veteran of touring groups: she wore crepe-soled shoes with low heels, a Tilley hat and a jersey with a multitude of pockets. She alone of the group carried no camera. Piers Ellsworth was a large, barrel-chested undergraduate from the University of Massachusetts who was spending time at the Palazzo Agrippina while his mother took a honeymoon with her new husband, and beside him was his room mate, a Korean student registered as Kim Young Sam, but 'Yo-yo' to his friends. Then there was Shirley Perovich whose hair color was "Sunshine Bronze", the same shade as Marcia's, and probably originating in a bottle bearing the same label. With her was her room mate, Betty Laramie, strikingly attractive, but seemingly unaware of the effect that her beauty had on the male sex. Both were from St. Louis. The student list on the Palazzo Agrippina bulletin board identified Shirley as an 'Educationalist' with an upper case 'E', and Betty as a graduate student, working on her doctoral dissertation.. Marcia had not yet talked to them. They looked about them with bright eyes, interested but apprehensive. Marcia suspected that this was their first time beyond the borders of Missouri.

When the three Thatchers joined them, they would number twenty-one. A good number. Palazzo Agrippina study groups had run as high as twenty-four in the past, but that was pushing it, the associate director had remarked.

Then there was the directorate, which was listed as 'faculty'. The associate director was Dr. Alex Baker from Ancaster University, a small institution near Montreal in Canada. His résumé showed two Ivy league degrees, and he appeared to be well- known within the distinguished circle of Roman scholars. Marcia had mentioned his name to several of them she knew, and they had nodded sagely and said, 'Ah, Dr. Alex!' One remarked approvingly that he mixed an excellent Martini, and another said with a sage nod that he had read a couple letters of recommendation that Dr. Alex had written for students and colleagues. All agreed he tried to be dynamic. His *Notes on the Ancient Monuments of the Naples Area* was recommended reading for the summer session.

The director, DeWitt Fordham, came from a Holyrood College, a well-known upstate New York liberal arts school and brought some of the prestige of his institution with him to the Palazzo Agrippina. His wife and he shared half a bottle of vodka a day and three packages of cigarettes, and this, added to his teaching load of seven hours a week, had left him little time for publication. But he had a Princeton PhD and an M.A. Oxon., and he had been a Rhodes scholar in the past, more years and cocktails ago than he cared to remember,. Twenty-five years ago, he had been a classical scholar to watch. His dissertation, 'Imagery in the *Histories* of Herodotus, with an appendix on the Parthenon frieze' was still read, and a few years ago, he had caused a stir in learned circles with his paper, 'Violence against Women in Sophocles' *Antigone* and Shakespeare's *Othello.*' He was presently working on a history of the Palazzo Agrippina. He had already completed the first chapter, on Sybil Twickenham's uncle who had built the palazzo, and the enigma of its name was solved. Sybil's uncle admired women who made things happen, and his favourite example was Agrippina, the last wife of the emperor Claudius whom she had eliminated. Everyone who had read the chapter agreed it was marvellous. He and his wife Annie were old veterans at the Palazzo Agrippina.

Annie seemed on edge. Marcia had passed their room early this morning and heard their voices raised. The hall was empty, and she snatched a tumbler from a nearby table, pressed it to the door paneling and put her ear to it. DeWitt Fordham's voice said clearly,

'I thought you brought enough Prozac to last for the summer!'

A bedroom door opened. Someone was going to the WC. Marcia quickly replaced the tumbler and nodded pleasantly to Sol Bernstein who was headed in the direction of the toilet, clutching his crotch. He flushed when he saw Marcia, and looked embarrassed, but he did not loosen his grip.

V

THIS WAS going to be an incohesive group, thought Dr. Alex, as the Agrippina students straggled after him through the sculpture galleries of the *Museo Nazionale* in Naples. They seemed a torpid lot. Unresponsive. Two or three took notes. Most of the group looked solemnly at the sculpture with the expressions of people who are swallowing culture with the stoicism usually reserved for nasty medicine. However, once they reached the statue of *Venus of Capua*, standing naked to the groin, looking like the *Venus di Milo* before she lost her arms, Piers Ellsworth broke the silence with the first comment of the day, which was meant for his roommate, but overheard by everyone.

'Jeez, look at those boobs.'

Fordham laughed and Dr. Alex smiled. Miriam Kuntz left the group and wandered over towards *Farnese Heracles*, the great muscle-bound statue of Heracles that was found in the Baths of Caracalla in Rome. She stood in silence in front of it. Heracles looked tired, like a wrestler who has survived a titanic struggle, and he leaned heavily on his club. Age was beginning to take its toll on his vast physique.

'Who's been pumping iron?' It was Piers, who appeared at Miriam's elbow. 'What gym did this guy belong to?'

'It's Heracles,' said Miriam.

'Oh, the guy who had to do all those fuckin' labours? Twelve of them, or were there ten? We learned about him in my mythology course. The one we used to call "Storytime with Professor Parker".'

'The sculptor has shown him as he was after he finished the last of his labours,' said Miriam, in her instructor's voice. 'You see, he is holding the three golden apples from the Garden of the Hesperides behind his back. The effort has wearied him.'

'He's had a workout. He's in damn good shape, though.' Piers moved around behind the statue. 'But he's over the hill.'

'Why do you say that?' demanded Marcia, who had joined them.

'Well, he must be damn near thirty-five,' said Piers.

Marcia moved close to Paul.

'Wouldn't you rather have a drink of something?'

'Hold on a bit,' Paul replied. 'We're supposed to appreciate these masterpieces.'

'I'm on cultural overload,' said Marcia. 'My feet are sore.'

Percy Bass joined them. 'We all have sore feet,' he said. 'It's the marble floor. When the arches fall, the brain switches off. Da Vinci's *Last Supper* couldn't switch it on again.' He chuckled at his witticism, and since he seemed to expect it, Paul and Marcia laughed politely. "Miss Mellon,' he went on, "are you the Marcia Mellon, the detective story author, by any chance?"

'I own up,' said Marcia.

'The creator of the great detective Aristide Blanchard?'

'Great? Maybe. I'm getting a little sick of him, myself.'

'I admire him, tremendously. You were the last person I expected to see here. Of course, Agatha Christie used to go on archaeological expeditions with her husband, and so I always knew that archaeology and detective stories were compatible. I've been trying my hand at writing, myself.'

'Good for you,' said Marcia, waiting for what she thought he would say next. She was not wrong.

'I wonder if you would look at some of my stuff. I don't expect you to edit it, of course—I don't need that—but if you could point me to a publisher with vision, a sensitive puiblisher—you know what I mean....'

'Um,' said Marcia. 'Yes, sensitive publishers *do* exist, I'm told.'

'I love imagining the perfect murder. The murder that can't be solved. One that has a dozen solutions, none of them right.'

'What do you think of that mountain of muscle?' Ellen Cross appeared at Percy's left elbow and interrupted him. She gestured towards the Farnese Heracles, leaning wearily on his club. 'I think he's repulsive. Don't you?'

'If you're game for another gallery, we can see the best copy there is of Polyclitus' "Spear-bearer",' said Dr. Alex, who was trying to shepherd the group forward. 'It is the ideal Greek male nude.'

'My feet are destroying me,' said Ellen, 'but I guess an ideal man is worth a look see, now that I've come so far.'

'When do you think we can get together, Miss Mellon?' asked Percy.

'Never, I hope,' thought Marcia. Aloud, she said, 'Do call me Marcia. Miss Mellon makes me sound like a school teacher.'

'Marcia,' repeated Percy.

'Our beloved leader is arriving sometime this afternoon,' said Marcia. 'I expect that the rest of the day will be busy.'

'Our beloved leader.' Percy's tone was unpleasant. 'God preserve us. And he'll bring his consort, the delightful Millicent, and the mini-beloved, his son Conradin.'

'Conradin's not so bad,' broke in Paul.

'Not bad, perhaps, but old Thatcher leaves no personality undamaged. What sort of father calls his son after the last of the Hohenstaufen? Or was it the Hohenzollern?'

'The herd's leaving us behind,' said Marcia. The Agrippina group was moving on to the next gallery, with Bathsheba Bennett bringing up the rear. Mildred Donahue was saying something to her husband which made him smile indulgently. Marcia nodded at Percy Bass. 'I'll certainly keep you in mind, Percy,' she said.

'Please do, Marcia.'

'I like to help promising writers,' said Marcia. It was only a partial falsehood.

'I know. And don't overlook Paul, here, either, who, I'm sure,. has some fiction up his sleeve,' replied Percy in a voice that was not quite facetious.

'Dr. Fordham, can I ask a question?' said Ellen Cross. The tour of the sculpture galleries was done, and half of the group was now crowded into the gift shop to buy post cards while the remainder gathered in a coffee shop across the street for cappuccinos and lattes.

'Why, certainly, Ellen.'

'Why did the Romans make so many statues without heads?'

'Statues without heads?'

'Yes, out in the courtyard of the museum there were a lot of statues of togas, but they have no heads to go with them. There's a place between their shoulders to fit on a head if you want, but they don't have any. '

'Well, the heads were made separately so that you could have a new one when you wanted it.'

'Oh,' said Ellen. 'Why?'

'More efficient that way,' interjected Sol Bernstein. 'You go bald, you get wrinkles, you get a new head.'

'Oh,' said Ellen. 'I guess that's true.'

'Those are some pretty enormous heads of the emperor Vespasian in the museum, aren't there?' continued Sol. 'He looked like a big thug, didn't he? He reminded me of some of the gigantic statues of Lenin I once saw in Kiev before the Soviet Union collapsed.'

'Who was Vespasian?' asked Ellen.

'Roman emperor. Put down the Jewish revolt in Judaea at the end of Nero's reign. At least, he started to. His son finished the job.'

'Oh. Well, was he fighting the Palestinians then?' asked Ellen.

Sol took a sip of coffee. 'They're Arabs,' he said. 'They weren't there yet.'

'The pornographic art exhibit was cool, as my son would say,' Sol went on. 'So they kept it locked up for so long, to protect our morals. I guess the big cheeses who run this museum think we are mature enough now to see it.' The Naples Museum had marked the start of the third millennium by bringing out of storage its collection of erotic sculpture found in Pompeii and putting it on display. It was bringing a new clientele to the old museum. 'I hoped you would give us a lecture on it, DeWitt,' said Sol.

'Well, what's there to say?' said Fordham, his eyes twinkling behind his glasses. 'It's quite explicit. Explains itself. Most of it was collected by a Catholic cardinal back when the Kingdom of the Two Sicilies, as they called it, was a going concern and there were Bourbon kings ruling here.'

'The Two Sicilies?' queried Sol, looking puzzled.

'Yes, that was before Italy was united into a single country. Before 1870. Naples had its own kings and they were a branch of the Bourbon royals. You can still see their palace overlooking the harbour. Big red building.'

'Miriam was very interested in the cardinal's collection,' broke in Ellen. Miriam Kuntz had crossed swords with a museum guard who tried to prevent her from taking photographs. The encounter had been short and fierce and the guard retired in high dudgeon.

'I was interested, too,' said Sol. 'What about this cardinal under the Bourbons?'

'Well, it was a private collection.'

'So,' said Sol, with a mischievous glance at Sister Stella, who appeared unperturbed, except for a slight puckering around the lips. "So he enjoyed it all by himself. Selfish old goat.'

Mildred Donahue sat down heavily at a table.

'It's good to sit down,' she said. 'Museums are perfect hell on the feet.'

'Where is Professor Donahue?' asked Fordham.

'Greg's getting me a cold drink,' replied Mildred Donahue. 'My husband is finding this all very interesting. Of course, this Roman stuff can't hold a candle to Greek sculpture. My husband is an expert on the ancient Greeks, or Hellenes, as he calls them—more correctly.'

'Didn't your husband do some big project connected with Greece?' asked Walter Druker. 'I seem to remember his name in connection with something. Big conference or something?'

'Dr. Donahue, my husband,' said Mildred, 'is an epigrapher.'

'Ah, yes. One of those.' Druker's tone implied gentle disapproval.

'That must be a fascinating branch of medicine,' said Ellen, in an enthralled voice.

'My husband is not a medical doctor,' said Mildred, with dignity. 'He is a classical scholar. Epigraphers specialize in reading inscriptions engraved on stones. It is a very exacting science. My husband has only recently published a book.'

'Is there a big demand for that sort of thing?' asked Ellen.

Mildred ignored, or failed to hear the question.

'My husband has been working on the late imperial inscriptions from Teos, and when his work is published, it will be recognized as a very great work,'' she said. 'It is a superb piece of scholarship and it will completely change the history of Teos.'

'Oh,' said Ellen. 'Change history—that must be really awesome, as my son would say. He's at Yale, you know. Where is Tea-- what's its name?'

'Teos,' repeated Mildred. 'It's in Turkey. Along the Aegean coast.'

'Oh, does your husband speak Turkish? I had a neighbour who visited Turkey last year. It was fascinating, she said.'

'Teos was in the Roman Empire,' said Mildred. 'It's in Turkey nowadays, of course, because there is no Roman Empire any more. It declined and fell.'

'Oh, then the inscriptions would be in Latin. The Roman Empire spoke Latin. I know that much,' Ellen went on. 'My son who is at Yale...'

'My husband works on *Greek* inscriptions,' said Mildred. 'The Greeks founded cities all over the Mediterranean, you see, and that's why there are Greek inscriptions in Turkey. Ancient Greek is a more interesting and civilized language than Latin. It has a much more subtle grammar. You should ask my husband.'

Gregory Donahue joined them with an iced coffee for his wife.

'I hear you're writing a book,' said Ellen. 'Do you think it will sell well?'

Donahue smiled benignly.

'The people who matter will buy it,' he replied.

'Well,' said Ellen, consolingly, 'my husband, who knows something about the book trade, always says that you shouldn't worry if the hard-cover first edition doesn't sell too well. It's the paperback and the movie rights that matter.'

Donahue made a perceptible grimace.

'My husband,' said Mildred, 'doesn't write Harlequin romances.'

'I wish I could,' said Donahue. 'I hear they make money. Romances and murder mysteries.'

The bus appeared around the corner. Fordham rose to his feet.

'All right, let's go, group, and board the bus,' he announced. 'It can park in front of the museum for only a couple minutes before we get a parking ticket!'

'Yes, I know there's been a fine book written on the dominion of the phallus in ancient Greece,' said Miriam Kuntz as she and Alex Baker emerged from the museum and made their way to the bus which had just pulled to a stop at the curb. 'I always recommend it to my classes. It's an admirable book.'

'Absolutely,' said Dr. Alex.

'But I want to do something quite different. I want to examine the cosmic significance of the male genitalia for the warp and woof of Roman society.'

'The woof?' repeated Dr. Alex.

'You know, the fabric of the societal structure. I want to put it in terms that our multicultural, intergalactic world of today can comprehend. Something you can explain to *Women's Studies* 100, which is our first-year survey course for our major in sexual diversity.. I think I can also throw some new light on female repression through the eras, to say nothing of the *D and F.* debate.'

'Absolutely,' said Dr. Alex, blankly. 'Of course, the *D. and F.*'

'I think that Edward Gibbon's *D and F of the Roman Empire* has held the field far too long. There is no feminist perspective to it at all. It's time to move on and join the twenty-first century.'

'You're absolutely right,' said Dr. Alex. 'We need a dynamic new look at the–uh–D. and F. problem.

'Time to mount the bus,' said DeWitt Fordham, ushering them to the bus door. 'You two will have to solve the problems of the world somewhere else.'

'We're still dominated by the mindset of dead white males,'

Miriam continued, pausing in front of the door. 'Like Edward Gibbon and his concept of decline going on and on and on. And he's not the only one by any means.'

'We really must be on our way,' said Dr. Alex. 'The bus driver will get a ticket from the police if he parks here for more than a minute or two.'

'Oh, yes, well, in that case...' said Miriam, mounting the steps into the bus. 'We wouldn't want Giuseppe to have to pay a fine.'

'*Grazie, signora,*' said Giuseppe, with a melting smile. He started his engine and began to thread his way through a phalanx of Fiats.

Baker quickly counted the passengers on the bus and then, satisfied that none of the Agrippina group was left behind, took his seat and assumed the countenance of a man who did not want to be disturbed. Miriam leaned across the aisle to him and spoke.

'I think masculinity and femininity are such fascinating subjects, don't you think?' she said.

'Yes, very much so,' said Dr. Alex.

'But we mustn't get hung up on them,' continued Miriam. 'Sexual diversity in the classics will be the new thing in classical studies. Don't you think?'

'Yes, definitely,' said Dr. Alex, and leaned back in his seat, as if smitten by uncontrollable weariness.

This is going to be an interesting summer, thought Marcia, as she took her seat in the bus. Not much here for a detective, but the Palazzo Agrippina experience should broaden the mind. And perhaps provide a middle-aged body with amusement too, she reflected, looking speculatively in the direction of Paul Kowalski. Paul caught her eye and smiled.

VI

THE THATCHER family arrived at the Palazzo Agrippina in time for afternoon tea. The Volkswagen's engine died at the front door with an asthmatic wheeze, and the Thatchers descended to receive a rapturous greeting from the director, his wife, and the associate director, their teeth bared in broad, genial smiles. The welcome was loud and effusive.

'Monnie,' said DeWitt Fordham, clasping the Thatcher right hand and pumping it, 'it's wonderful to see you! We were so looking forward to your arrival!'

'Hello, there, DeWitt,' boomed Thatcher. 'You're looking well-tanned and rested. You've made good use of your time here, I see.'

'The beloved leader,' thought Marcia Mellon, who was looking on from the window of the library. 'The picture on the end wall of the Palazzo Agrippina's dining room in the very flesh.'

'DeWitt and I were thinking about you all day,' said Annie, throwing her arms effusively around Thatcher and receiving a brief peck on the cheek in return. 'Millicent, my dear,' she went on, turning from Thatcher to his wife, who was watching her with a fixed smile, 'it's so wonderful to see you!'

'And good to see you, too,' said Millicent, offering a cheek to be kissed. 'I hope you are feeling better.'

'Oh, much better. A great deal better. I hope you didn't find your plane trip too grueling.'

'Ugh,' said Millicent Thatcher. 'The American Airlines flight to Heathrow was O.K., but then we had Alitalia from London to Rome, and then on to Naples. I couldn't eat the lunch they served! Some sort of pasta that congealed in the pit of your stomach like a bunch of old wallpaper. No wonder Alitalia is broke. I'm going to have to take a Pepto-Bismol.'

'Isn't it awful the way you're treated on planes,' said Annie, who looked as if she were going to cry.

'Hello, there, Alex,' said Thatcher, turning to Dr. Alex. 'Great to see you. You're getting a tan, too, I see. Italy agrees with you.' He stretched out a limp hand and Dr. Alex grabbed it.

'It's wonderful to see you, too, Monnie,' he said, with enthusiasm. 'You're looking well.'

'DeWitt, have you met my son, Conradin?' asked Thatcher, with some distaste. Conradin was wearing a baseball cap backwards, a T-shirt with 'BALMY GILEAD' printed across its front, and braces enough on his teeth to pay off his orthodontist's mortgage.

'No, but I've heard so much about you, Conradin,' said Fordham. 'It's good to meet you at last.' He pumped Conradin's hand energetically.

'Hello,' said Conradin.

'We've got a dynamic group of students here, Conradin,' said Dr. Alex. 'They're waiting eagerly to meet you.'

'Do you hear that, Conradin?' boomed Thatcher. Without waiting for a reply, he turned back to DeWitt. 'Is everything going well here? Everything ticking along the way it should? I see that the Volkswagen van seems to be working. You must keep an eye on it and see it gets proper servicing.'

'Yes, of course,' said DeWitt.

'Don't let these Italians cheat you. Did you get it insured, DeWitt?'

'No problem.'

'How's the staff? Did you find a good cook for the summer?'

'We've found a wonderful cook. Her *fettucini alfredo* is out of this world!'

'Good, good,' Thatcher nodded. 'You know,' Thatcher's volume dropped several decibels to a confidential mode, 'I got a special letterhead printed up for our directorate to use when they are dealing with Italian bureaucrats. Got it designed by the art teacher at Williamson. He lived in Italy for five years and he says that when you want special permission for anything, you should always use a dago dazzler.'

'A what?' said DeWitt.

'A dago dazzler. I'll show it to you. It's official-looking stationery on good vellum paper with 'Palazzo Agrippina: The Julio-Claudian Group, Inc.' engraved on the letterhead. Then when you write your letter to some godfather who runs a museum and want to get into a gallery that's been closed forever, you always begin, "Dear Commendatore". *Caro Commendatore,* was what he said. Then you tell him how important a group of international scholars we are, and would he let us see whatever it is we want to see, and then you write something flowery at the end. Be sure to put the Palazzo Agrippina seal on it. We have one, don't we? He says that if you want permission to see anything in the museum that's not on public view, you should present a dago dazzler, and you'll get permission every time. Just as good as a tip to the museum guards, he said, and a lot cheaper.'

'Oh,' said DeWitt, nonplussed. 'Yes, we have a seal for the Palazzo somewhere, I think. What am I to do with it?'

'Well, use it, my good man,' instructed Thatcher. 'Make up a good dago dazzler with lots of sealing wax. Write a letter on this letterhead writing paper I've brought with me, saying that we want to see the things that everyday tourists can't see on these archaeological sites. And always call an Italian official *commendatore,* he said.. It makes a good impression. We want these wops to think we're their friends, so they won't steal us blind.'

'I'd like to get to my room sometime,' said Conradin.

'Oh, you have a single room for Conradin, don't you?' said Millicent. It was more a demand than a question. 'We promised Conradin a single room if he would come here with us.'

'Of course,' said DeWitt and Annie, almost in unison.

'And I applied for a single room,' thought Marcia, as she witnessed the scene, 'and I was told there weren't any available. That young man is going to be a real pain in the butt.'

VII

'I HAVEN'T used a typewriter in years, Joshua', wrote Marcia, 'but there isn't any printer available here for my IBM ThinkPad, and you wouldn't want to read my handwriting'. Marcia was writing her literary agent an overdue letter. 'This ancient Underwood typewriter was sitting forlorn under a dust cover in a corner of the Palazzo Agrippina library, and it still works! Back in the school I attended in the Jurassic period, we had to take either a course called 'Economic Theory' or typing. I chose typing, and we used Underwoods. That dates me. But it was a good thing. Typewriters may be obsolete, but all the economic theory that Miss Lugar taught is now antediluvian.

'However we're not entirely archaic here. The Palazzo Agrippina has a FAX-phone, and we're invited to use it at five euros a pop. Seems outrageous, but I am going to try it. The Palazzo does not have an internet terminal. However there is an Internet Cafe in the *Albergo Felice* which is a short walk from here, down a path fringed with prickly acanthus that runs from our back garden, and I am going to try to pick up my e-mails there. I need my daily quota of SPAM. Rumour has it that the *Felice* has a well-stocked bar run by two young men in starched white jackets. One of them is as handsome as a Renaissance youth in a Raphael painting, and the other is definitely not, but strong as a bull. Mario, the young man who is waits on the table, mops the marble floors, drives the Agrippina's Volkswagen bus, manhandles the luggage, and delivers bottles of Stock brandy to those of our colleagues who thirst for it, seems to intimate with his body language that we should be wary of the *Felice*. Nonetheless, I think the *Felice's* bar will be popular with our group.

'Life is fairly civilized at the Palazzo. A gong sounds for breakfast, lunch is usually laid on at some restaurant, then there is tea and cake at five, and then a gong sounds at seven-thirty for happy hour before dinner. Lots of local wine, and it's good. Ischia, the island next door to Capri, produces a fine white wine. You know, this area was once the Hamptons of the Roman Empire. All the characters you meet in Robert Graves' *I, Claudius*, had villas around here, and they lived lives of overdone luxury with nothing to occupy their time except sex and the occasional murder. There was no law against murdering slaves. I'm told that one immensely rich, wicked old man kept a pool full of piranhas wherein he tossed slaves if the service was lousy.

'We overlook the Bay of Baia where the emperor Nero tried to drown his mother, Agrippina. Nero invited her to dinner and when they'd stuffed themselves, he made his last farewell like a dutiful son, and sent her back to her villa across the bay on a collapsible yacht. The yacht sank on cue, but Nero's mother could swim like a fish. She made it home, and Nero had to send some thugs to finish her off. Nero was a very disappointing son, for Agrippina had always tried to be a good mother to him. She had wangled the throne for him by poisoning his stepfather, the emperor Claudius, and then pushing aside Claudius' own son. Like most overly ambitious mothers, she got little thanks for it.

'Apparently her ghost came back to haunt Nero. She was a tough old lady. The Palazzo Agrippina is named after her. She is an example of a controlling mother who wouldn't let her boy go, not even after she was dead, but still I think Nero handled the situation badly.

'This place is owned by a Church of England vicar who charges a reasonable rent and approves of us, it seems. I don't know if he has ever seen a Palazzo Agrippina summer session in full swing, and maybe he should not be encouraged to do so. He inherited this place from his aunt, who was told by the Sibyl of Cumae to start the summer school here. You remember the Sibyl of Cumae from Michelangelo's Sistine Chapel ceiling? A big, ugly woman with masculine muscles? Well, she lived in a cave near here, and since she was immortal and could not die, she simply shrivelled up as she grew older. She grew smaller and smaller until she was literally bottled up. Someone stuffed her into a bottle like a butterfly specimen. But presumably if she cannot die, she is still around somewhere, if we can only find the bottle. We'll go to visit her cave in a couple days.

'Anyway, the vicar's aunt who founded the Palazzo Agrippina summer school was sitting in the Sibyl's cave at Cumae, meditating and thinking the usual dismal thoughts about unpaid bills, and the Sibyl appeared to her. She asked the Sibyl for advice, and the ancient dame was overjoyed to offer it. No one had asked her advice for over two thousand years, and if you are in the advice-giving business, it can be soul-destroying to have no one to advise. The Sibyl suggested the summer school. I don't believe the story, but it makes a nice founding myth, doesn't it?

'Anyway, the vicar's aunt did found the school and the rest is history, as they say.

'We have a couple short evening lectures scheduled, which should be interesting if I can keep awake. Perhaps the wine at dinner should be rationed on those evenings. The first is by a visiting speaker who arrived in Pozzuoli and offered us a lecture for free. He is a psychologist practitioner, whatever that is, who has attended Princeton, NYU and Freiburg and has a graduate degree from Puget Sound University. He is going to talk on "Octopuses in the mentality of ancient Greece and Rome". Could you check the plural of "octopus" for me? I don't trust psychologist practitioners with English grammar. Isn't it "octopi"?

'The other lecture will be by the associate director here, Alex Baker. Subject: "Vergil, a Dynamic New Beginning in Augustan Poetry." Alex is wonderful. He lectures in the grand style of the Victorian era. Do you remember the style of Bulwer-Lytton's *Last Days of Pompeii*? We'll visit Pompeii as part of this program and I look forward to hearing Dr. Alex lecture in the House of Glaucus. We have a student here who is a Bulwer-Lytton fan. Percy Bass, who also writes detective stories. So he tells me. He wants me to read them.

'We are getting to know each other, for better or worse. My roommate is an assistant professor of classics and sexual diversity studies at McPhatter College in South Carolina. She's doing research on the phallus and what it did to, and for the Roman Empire. She has a theory that the phallus and Roman imperialism were two sides of the same coin, and she will explain it to you at great length if you give her the chance. She's writing a book about it, and I'm sure it will sell, if she can only persuade herself to write in English. Of course, plain English is a deadly enemy of academic theories, which do better with jargon, for once these theories have lost their special vocabulary, their nonsense stands stripped and naked to the world..

'Miriam was wildly elated today. We were at the Naples Archaeological Museum where there is an exhibit of erotic art on public display. The pieces come mostly from Pompeii, and have spent years imprisoned in the museum storerooms. They were liberated only a few years ago. Apparently a cardinal in the eighteenth century collected them. Priests in this corner of the world were never corrupted by Puritanism. Do you know that one of the really popular sculptures which decorated Roman gardens was of a naked woman crouching, and peering around behind her to see what is going on? The official explanation is that this much-copied piece depicts Venus who is just getting out of her bath and looking around behind her to admire her own rump! I don't believe it. Admittedly she has not much surplus fat on it, and I hate her. But then Venus wouldn't have surplus fat, would she? But my roommate, Miriam, claims she sees a worried look on the divine brow, and wants to know why, as any good scholar should. Is Zeus banging on the bathroom door? Is Pan hiding in the bushes? The question demands a learned paper.

'Miriam is very serious. She's working on getting tenure and at her college, tenure is handed out by a niggardly committee of academic dinosaurs. No book, no tenure. The dinosaurs are a junta of professors who got tenure themselves years ago, when standards were much lower, and tenure was just a reward for buttering up your department head. Miriam is bitter.

'Today, however, she was greatly excited. She found an ithyphallic bronze statue of a satyr in the museum. Don't bother looking up "ithyphallic" in the dictionary. It refers to a male who is sexually aroused, with a predictable effect on his organ. Miriam said that from the neck up, the satyr was a portrait of her dean, but she claimed ignorance of the dean's body from the neck down. She was determined to get a photograph of the satyr, and tried in her minimal Italian to explain to the museum guard that she needed it for research. The guard was not unpleasant but he was very firm. Miriam must have a *permesso.*

'Miriam said she was not surprised. She managed to sneak a picture anyway with her little digital camera. Expect to see it on the Internet soon, at www.KUNTZ.com.

'As for the men here, one looks interesting. Paul Kowalski, trim number who teaches Latin, Italian, and soccer at Gilead Academy. Not gay, I think, and not married at the moment, anyway. Incidentally, one of his pupils from Gilead arrived today, none other than Conradin Thatcher, only son of the beloved president and C.E.O. of the Julio-Claudian Society Inc., Decimus Monroe Thatcher. Conradin got a single room. I did not. Conradin and Paul nodded to each other, not unpleasantly. I thought I saw a wary look pass between them. But I keep looking for raw material for my books, and I must remember that the Palazzo Agrippina is real life.

'Yes, my writing has fallen into arrears and I'm sorry. I need to charge my batteries. I'm getting older and to be frank, I'm teetering nervously on the edge of menopause. You don't know what it is like. Don't complain to me that men have a menopause, too. Women in menopause get hot flashes; men in menopause get to elope with young female secretaries. Human biology is not fair. Hot flashes and the Italian summer do not mesh well. One source of heat at a time is quite enough, thank you. I am here to hold off the night, and I intend to do it.

'But, really, I'm thinking, and my thoughts will jell into a book. I have already written the first paragraph in my head. I've struggled with this typewriter long enough. I shall use a different technology for my next letter to you: a ball point pen. Have a good time, Joshua. Your irresponsible client and friend (I hope). Marcia.'

VIII

WELL, I got a single room. I told my mom I would go home on the next plane if I had to room with some dried-up professor at the Palazzo Agrippina. Dad nattered something about a dried-up professor being a better roommate that a professor who had not yet dried up. That was supposed to be a joke. Dad can sometimes surprise me. Anyway I have a single room. It's not the Ritz. Not even the Comfort Inn. Narrow bed, lumpy mattress, whitewashed walls with one picture hanging on them: an engraving of a round building with columns, standing in water. The caption says 'Tempio di Sarapide, Pozzuoli.' Temple of Sarapis? I checked the meaning in my Italian-English Dictionary. I guess it's important. Sarapis was an old Egyptian god, I think.

Talking about Italian, Kowalski is here. He's one screwed-up guy. But he's one teacher you can talk to, man to man. I'd like to get into his Italian class next year.

Dad is in managerial mode. He knows only five words of Italian: 'Quanto?', 'Troppo', 'Si' and of course 'Non', which is his favorite word, and 'Arrivederci.' That means 'I'm out of here'. But as our driver, a guy called Giovanni, drove us in from the airport, Dad kept acting as if he had lived here for a hundred years. He kept pointing out the sights to me as if he were a tour guide. Here's the Lucrine Lake, he said, pointing to a pond. The Romans had an oyster farm there, he said. There's Bauli, where the emperor Nero had his mom killed, he said. Why'd he do that? I asked. She'd lived long enough and was in the way, Dad said. But I couldn't see anything. Just cars and buildings and walls. The old man is

57

going to drive everyone around the bend.

We passed a little hotel about two blocks from the Palazzo Agrippina, with tables on an outdoor patio under an arbor and a sign reading 'Internet Café.' Cool. There was a vine with a purple flower covered with blooms, growing over the arbor. Really beautiful. I'll check it out. It doesn't look as if there will be a whole lot of life in the Palazzo Agrippina, and maybe the café can make up for some of the boredom of being Monroe Thatcher's son..

Still, the Palazzo's a decent enough place. What they call the student body is an odd group, but after all, a lot of them are teachers of one sort or another. Only one of the women has a build worth looking at and she wears glasses. We've got a big college student here, built like a quarterback, who spends a lot of time looking at her, and his roommate, who's Korean, looks, too, but says less. There's a nice walled garden at the back of this place with a big tree at the back of it, and a round stone with 'Sibyl' carved on it.. I can see myself sitting there under that tree, drinking the local wine, reading, or writing a novel while I just rotted away, watching the ivy grow around me. Or maybe I can interview some local character whose father or grandfather remembered Mussolini and make a videotape of it which I can use in the Studio 303 course, or even flog it to the TV History Channel. That would be cool, except that said local character probably could not speak English. I brought my camcorder and some spare tapes. Seven, but when I unpacked my knapsack and set them on top of the chest of drawers, there was an extra one. Not mine, I think. No label, but when I held it under the electric lamp beside my bed, I could make out FAFI scratched in one corner of the case.

I'll look up FAFI in my Italian dictionary.

IX

WHAT ATTRACTED Marcia first to the *Albergo Felice* was the sign, 'Internet Café', placed discreetly beside the main entrance. The second attraction was the sight of Walter Druker and Kwame Assante at the bar. Druker had a brandy in his hand, and he was a little drunk and thoroughly argumentative. There was a copy of *La Repubblica* beside him, which seemed to belong to him. Assante was nursing a beer and maintaining his dignity.

'I know --,' said Kwame, with emphasis, 'sure I know that the library at ancient Alexandria was not yet built until after Aristotle's death, but that doesn't mean that Aristotle couldn't have stolen his ideas from the libraries of other Egyptian temples. Egypt was full of temples. They all had libraries.'

'But I tell you,' Druker said, ' it is not possible that Aristotle stole his philosophy from Egyptian temple libraries. The Egyptian temples had nothing of value in their libraries and Aristotle never went there and anyway, the ancient Egyptians were not black.'

'How can you say that?' Kwame said. 'Herodotus says that Egyptians had woolly hair and black skins. Just like me. It is right there in his text. Herodotus was a great historian, and he visited Egypt, you'll have to admit. He lived smack in the middle of the classical period, and he should have known.'

'That passage has to be interpreted,' said Druker. 'You always have to correct Herodotus to bring him up to speed. Boy, *gar-*

çon, *cameriere*, whatever you're called. Luigi, that's your name, isn't it? Give me another drink, Luigi. Just give me the whole bottle.' The bartender put a half-empty bottle of Stock brandy in front of him, and Druker clasped it in his fist. 'Homer uses the same word that Herodotus does for wooly-haired. In Homer we translate it "curly-haired". This stuff hits the spot,' he said, as he filled his glass. 'Have some more, Kwame? Are you any relative of Molefi Assante who used to be at Temple U.? He's an interesting fellow.'

'Just half a glass', said Kwame. 'I want to be able to walk both of us back to our palace—the Palazzo. But the point I'm trying to make is that you white men have written black men out of ancient history, and it is not fair. It's not historical, either. Hannibal came from Africa. He whipped the pants off the Romans in spite of their white skins. Cleopatra was an African. So was Terence. A great Roman playwright. You'll have to admit it.'

'St. Augustine came from Africa, too, bless his bigoted soul,' said Druker. 'But they weren't black. Terence was a Berber.' He noticed Marcia for the first. 'Marcia! You've discovered this watering hole, too. Did Mario tell you about it? Here, have a drink.' He thrust the bottle of brandy towards her. 'This Stock stuff is not the greatest cognac in the world, but it has a nice kick.'

Marcia demurred. 'You're deep in a philosophic discussion.'

'Mired in it, you mean,' said Druker. 'Kwame won't be reasonable. However he has promised to get me back to the palace in time for happy hour. I can't turn down a free drink, even if it's only the Palazzo Agrippina's *Lacrima Cristi*.'

'Walter is the black man's burden,' said Kwame.

'Damn right. Kwame is my designated driver. He'll guide my faltering footsteps back to the Palazzo.'

'I'd try to guide his scholarship too, if he'd listen,' Kwame said to Marcia. 'Walter, it's too late to save your liver, but you can still save your mind. Read *Stolen Legacy* by G. R. James. Read *Black Athena* by Martin Bernal. There's a book for you. He's got enough footnotes to choke all the tight-assed historians in America!'

'Listen,' said Druker. 'That *Black Athena* stuff is crap but I'll say this for it. It got us classical historians noticed. It got front-page treatment in our local newspaper, the *Benwell Bee*. The *Killer Bee*, we call it, because it slays its readers with unadulterated boredom. I wrote an article on *Black Athena* for the Sunday *Bee*, and it was that, I bet, that got me my promotion to professor. The dunderheads who run Spearfish State U. would never have noticed I existed, if it weren't for that article. So I owe you Afro-Americans, Kwame. I owe you big. Why, that article got me an interview on a talk show on the local TV station with some dame with big hair who thought Latin was Mexican dance music, and Greek was a salad, but it was great. I loved it. We had a great conversation! I hadn't used my brain that much in ten years, and you know, it still works!'

'There you go,' said Kwame. 'Black man starts a new idea. White man exploits it.'

'Oh, come Kwame,' said Druker. 'You got too good a brain to fall for crap!'

'What I'm trying to get through your thick skull,' said Kwame, with some heat, 'is the concept of competitive plausibility in ancient history. It's plausible that Cleopatra was white, I agree. But it's also plausible that she was black. The two plausibilities have to fight it out for believers. Plausibilities have to compete. There's a great, big, free market for ideas and you buy the ones you want. You don't have to be nailed down by footnotes.'

'Sounds post-modernist to me, and I don't go for it. I think there are facts in history. Cleopatra was white because her daddy, the old Flute-Player Ptolemy, was white, and he was white because his daddy was white.'

'But what of her grandma? The old Flute Player was a bastard, wasn't he? I say Cleopatra can usefully be called black. Evidence isn't everything, you know.'

Druker topped up his glass with brandy and stared at the amber liquid ruminatively.

Marcia broke in. 'How did you discover this place?'

'The *Albergo Felice*?' asked Kwame. 'Walter here has a nose for bars.'

'A useful nose,' said Druker. 'Like a useful non-fact. Like this cognac here in my glass. A non-great drink, non-healthful, a mote in the eye of a prohibitionist, but damn useful. But the fact is, I asked Mario, and Mario said this was an O.K. place, but be a little careful, he said.'

'What caught my eye,' said Marcia, 'was the Internet Café. I spotted the sign outside the entrance.'

'Oh, yes. Conradin, our beloved C.E.O.'s offspring, told us about that.' said Druker. 'If you want to use it, you've got to ask one of the *camerieri*. Not the Luigi fellow that looks like a thug, and is built like a brick outhouse. The other one who looks as if he has just stepped out of a Renaissance painting. He's the computer man.'

Luigi loomed up behind them, large and expressionless. He set a drink down on the table in front of Marcia.

'Did you hear the news?' Druker went on, paying Luigi no heed. He gestured towards his copy of *La Repubblica*. 'The bodies of two men were washed up on the coastline quite close to where we are. An early-morning hiker found them. I was reading about them before Kwame arrived.'

'Corpses?' said Marcia with quickening interest. Luigi, standing beside her, tensed, and Marcia realized that he was reading over her shoulder.

'Real live—or rather dead corpses. But I don't think you can make a murder mystery out of them. They probably came from the boat that capsized north of Sicily a couple weeks ago, carrying illegal immigrants.'

'Africans,' said Kwame. 'Sailing from Libya.'

'That's a long distance from Naples,' said Marcia.

'Well, the Camorra is mixed up with the racket—selling passages to Italy on superannuated boats to desperate Africans,' said Druker. 'The Camorra mob is giving the police a run for its money in Naples right now—if you read the Italian newspapers. A young fellow was riding his motorcycle in the north end of Naples a couple days ago and took a bullet in the head.'

'Those Africans were dumped,' said Kwame. 'The poor devils couldn't pay the snakeheads, probably. That's my take on it.'

'Well, they were in bad shape,' said Druker. 'Hardly recognizable. The sharks had taken some bites out of them.'

'But there were two black men, all right,' said Kwame. 'They would be. No doubt of that.'

'I hope we don't encounter anything like that lying on the strand,' said Marcia. She looked across the road that separated the *Albergo Felice* from the beach skirting the Bay of Baia.

'Not likely,' said Druker.

'Poor devils,' said Marcia. 'I wonder how many illegals make it.'

'With the Roman Empire, the illegal immigrants were the Visigoths and the Vandals and the Ostrogoths,' said Druker, with befuddled wisdom. 'And the Lombards, and the Saracens and so on, right down to these tourists roasting their back sides on the beach out there.' He waved an arm in the general direction of the Gulf of Naples. 'It all started with old Vergil's Aeneas, you know, the primal illegal immigrant from Troy, which makes him a Turk, doesn't it?'

Kwame said nothing.

'You know,' Druker went on, 'things happen. When I came to America from England with my degree from Oxford which fitted me to be a gentleman, I had to find a job that fitted my qualifications, which was hard, for Oxford didn't give me any. So I got bit parts in movies which paid me enough to let me to subsist on hamburgers from McDonalds while I did a PhD at Stanford, and back then, if you had a good English accent you were in big demand for bad-guy roles in TV shows. Swindlers, international spies, con men: for all those roles, an English accent was an asset. Then the Arabs swept us Brits all out of the bad-guy business. Now if you want to be a good crook, you have to sound like an Arab with a two days' growth of black beard. I would never be able to pay my way through Stanford if I were a student now.'

'Give it time,' said Marcia. 'The theatre will recognize your talent as a crook once again in the future, I feel sure.'

'It will be too late for me,' grumbled Walter. "My future is to be the besotted sage of Spearfish State, with an unfinished biography of the emperor Tiberius gathering dust in my filing cabinet. I once thought Princeton or Yale would come begging for my services when it was published. Now doubt is coming in.'

'What goes around comes around,' said Kwame. 'Everything makes a comeback. Even the Ku Klux Klan may make one. Don't sell your white sheets yet, Walter. You may want to use them again.'

'Ah, Kwame, my dear fellow,' Walter replied in a conciliatory mode. 'Don't be angry at a harmless old drunk like me. If it will make you less bitter, I swear I'll believe that Queen Cleopatra was black. If she had visited Alabama fifty years ago, she'd have been sent to the back of the bus, and there she would have to sit, wearing her crown and her purple silk robe!'

Kwame laughed.

'Kwame, you must visit me at Spearfish State', said Walter, rising unsteadily to his feet and putting an arm around Kwame's shoulder. 'I'll arrange for you to give a public lecture. Then we'll go to a football game together, and we'll sing the Spearfish State song as a duet, you and I. It's quite easy. It goes,

"'We shall ever be true,
"Spearfish State, unto you.
"*Fortes et fideles*
"Let no doubts assail us,
"Or our courage fail us.
"Rah! Rah! Rah! Etc." Simple, isn't it?'

'Walter,' said Kwame, 'if your liver grants you a few more years to live, I'll come. I promise.'

'Kwame,' said Walter, having now progressed from the argumentative to the philosophic stage of intoxication, 'did you know that the old emperor Tiberius lived out his last, unhappy years out there in the Gulf of Naples, on Capri? There's a man who needed a psychiatrist. What a tangled bundle of—of—what's the word I want, Kwame?'

'Syndrome?'

'Sin, Kwame, not syndrome, or better still, sins. Forget about the "drome". Sin, Kwame. Our sins always catch up with us, including those we are too busy to commit. Poor old Tiberius!' He rose to his feet and stood, not quite perpendicular. 'Time to go, Kwame.'

'Walter, act your age.'

'Age, Kwame!' said Walter, waxing philosophical. 'Age, the sere and yellow leaf! Age, when the body redirects its hair growth efforts from the crown of your head to your nose and ears! Ah, age, which improves wine and destroys—what was I going to say?'

Kwame steered him out the door.

THE YOUTH out of the Raphael painting was standing outside the entrance of the *Albergo Felice* in a starched, white jacket, elegant and beautiful. Luigi, his heavy-set partner, was serving a couple, an elegant Italian young man and his female companion, with drinks. Yes, he might do as a thug, thought Marcia. Perhaps five feet nine inches tall, and three feet wide, with a great barrel chest. The sleeve of his jacket stretched tight over his biceps as he hoisted the serving tray loaded with drinks, and the seam on the underarm had given way under the strain. His hairline dipped low over his forehead. A brutish face. Perhaps he has a nice smile, Marcia thought. He did. He caught Marcia's stare, and smiled at her. A redeeming smile, that revealed a set of even, white teeth. But with the hint of a leer.

Marcia approached the Raphael youth. He was anxious to please. The Internet Café was little more than an alcove off the *Albergo Felice* bar with three terminals and green resin chairs set in front of the computer screens. The computers themselves were chained to the wall, but, thought Marcia, with muscular Luigi at the bar watching, it would be a foolhardy thief that tried to steal them. The Raphael youth showed Marcia how to sign on, and she downloaded a dozen E-mails. Most of them were SPAM, messages offering instant credit, low-interest mortgages, and a proposition from someone who identified herself as the wife of a deposed president of Nigeria who had sequestered a vast share of the Nigerian treasury in a Swiss bank and needed only access to Marcia's own bank account to liberate it. Marcia deleted them all, and was left with a query from a reader of the latest Aristide Blanchard novel, a message from an old friend reporting that her daughter was on the brink of matrimony, and another from Emma Sanchez, the young woman who was house-sitting for

Marcia while she was away, and caring for Marcia's elderly cat, Mikado. Better known as *the* Mikado.

Emma's message was troubling. The Mikado was missing. Emma had had a few friends in for a drink or two a couple days ago, and next morning, the Mikado did not appear for his regular meal of *Fancy Feast*. Emma did not sound too worried. The Mikado had not been gone for long, and Emma was sure he would reappear. Cats had nine lives. Marcia was not so sure. If the Mikado had any survival skills, he had forgotten them long ago. Emma had come to Marcia with the recommendation of the friend of a friend, and the Mikado had given her a lordly reception, but on the whole he seemed satisfied to have her wait on him while Marcia was away. Perhaps the few friends who had come to the house for a drink, and probably more than one, had disturbed the even tenor of his life. Marcia was suspicious.

The Raphael youth hovered close by.

'I speak English', he said.

'And you want to practice your English, right?'

'You from Palazzo Agrippina?'

'*Si*. And you must be Raphael.'

'Raffaello?' He was taken aback. 'Me? No, me Tony.'

'Well, Tony, I've got quite a few E-mails to read.' Marcia gestured towards her in-box displayed on the screen.

'Two men come here from Palazzo Agrippina today.'

'I know,' said Marcia, nodding towards Walter and Kwame who had bellied up to the bar. 'I think they'll be good customers. Treat 'em well.'

'No, not them. One young guy younger than me and one man who was older. His *professore*, he said.'

'Oh.' *Younger than Tony. That could only be Conradin..*

'You tell them at the Palazzo Agrippina, we rent rooms. Ten euros one hour in daytime. Fifteen American dollars.'

'An hour?'

'*Si*. Forty euros the whole night. Sixty dollars.'

'That's very useful to know, Tony.'

'You want?'

'A room?'

"*Si*. You want a room?'

'No, Tony.'

'That's OK.'

'Do you rent many rooms?'

'Oh, many, many. You want to see our rooms?'

'No, Tony. Did you tell the two guys from the Palazzo who came here today how much your rooms cost for an hour?'

'I told them, but they no want right now.'

'Well, that good to know, Tony.'

'That's OK.'

Well, you can never tell, Marcia thought, as she trudged back along the path to the Palazzo in time for Happy Hour. Conradin and his professor. That would be Paul. Of course, what must have attracted Conradin and Paul would be the Internet Café. Yet Marcia's mind wandered from Conradin to the Gilead School and from there to Decimus Monroe Thatcher. And Millicent. All ice on top, but what was there beneath the surface?

By the time Marcia reached the Palazzo she had sketched out the plot of a novel in her imagination, with Conradin as the young Nero, and Paul his guide and tutor. Another Seneca. Millicent Thatcher would be Agrippina. And old Thatcher? He could be shoehorned into the plot as the emperor Claudius. His manner was imperial and possibly he liked mushrooms.

X

PERCY BASS. *Funny guy. Odd, I mean. Not funny ha-ha. One of dad's colleagues, it turns out. Dad never mentioned him. I don't think he and dad ever have a lot of heart-to-heart conversations. He teaches English and he jogs six miles a day to clear his mind, Dad tells me. He also gives lessons in classical guitar but he can play anything. Drums, piano, what have you? He was standing off by himself during Happy Hour and I came up to him and said, 'Yo.'*

'You're Conradin Thatcher, from Williamson School's great rival, the Gilead Academy?' he said, with a little smile. It wasn't a jolly smile Only his lips curved. There was no fun in it.

'Yeah,' said I. 'I admit it.'

'Monroe Thatcher's son,' he said.

'I can't help that, either,' I said. 'But it's the only sin so far that I've had time to commit. Yet'

He grinned. 'You've got your whole life ahead of you.' He looked away. Broke eye contact. He wasn't exactly an easy guy to talk to. 'Lots of time yet.'

'What's this thing about Gilead being Williamson's great rival?' I asked. 'I thought the Gilead Academy belonged to a lower order.'

'You've been talking to your dad,' he said. 'We educate, so to speak, the whelps of America's elite, and you know what that means.'

I didn't; so I said 'Awesome.' This guy had a big chip on his shoulder. Making conversation with him was going to be a chore.

'What brought you here?' I asked. 'To the Palazzo Agrippina, I mean? Did dad talk you into it?'

'No,' said Percy. 'For that, at least, you can't blame your dad. I spotted a poster advertising the program in the common room at Williamson. Probably your father put it there. But when he learned I was coming, he enlisted me as an agent.'

'What do you mean?'

'A spy.'

'To spy on me?' I asked. My dad might just do that.

'No, no,' he said. 'Give me a break. I'm not your keeper, Conradin. I'm just a poor guitar player who tries to makes a living by teaching. Not much of a one at that. But Monnie wants a report on the quality of the lectures on site Fordham and Baker are giving to the students. He's checking them out.'

'Lectures on site?' said I.

'Well, when we visit archaeological sites, the directors guide us through them. Stone by bloody stone, if they are doing their job. That's what your dad thinks. He wants me to give him my impressions of how well they're doing.'

'Oh,' said I. 'That means the parental unit thinks they can do better.'

'Your father thinks everyone can do better,' Percy Bass said.

'Don't I know it,' said I. Bass grinned.

'What's your interest here?' he asked, 'or do you have any?'

'I'm scouting. I want to do film studies in college. I'd like to find the story line for a script here?'

'Here?' Percy raised one eyebrow.

'Not here in the Palazzo. Give me a break. Here everyone is respectability squared. But I'll bet that behind every doorway in Pozzuoli there's a drama. A little tragi-comedy. Someone mixed up in the Naples underworld.'

'Behind every doorway there's a mama doing her son's laundry, Conradin,' said Percy. 'Don't dig too hard. And what's more, I don't think everyone here is respectability squared. I hope you won't think that of me, by the time the tour is over.'

'Sounds interesting,' said I. Mother was heading towards me. She had spotted me with a drink in my hand from across the room.

'Mom,' I said. 'It's only orange juice.'

'I knew it, Conradin,' she said. 'I didn't doubt you.' I think she was *a little embarrassed because Percy Bass was there, grinning. Even mom was put off by his grin, and that's not easy. 'I think teenagers shouldn't drink when they're underage, do you?,' she said to Bass.*

'You can't be too careful,' said Bass. His lips curved in another smile. I think he was laughing at us, though he tried not to show it to mom.. He moved away to where he could watch Betty Laramie. She'd be really pretty if she ever took off her glasses. I wonder if Percy and Betty will be a couple by the time the tour is over, as Percy put it.

But, after careful thought and due deliberation, I have decided that Percy Bass is a prick. A cool prick, maybe, and he doesn't rate as a real A+ prick, but in the bell curve for pricks, he scores pretty high.

The day began with a trip to Cuma. The bus paused on the way to look at Lake Avernus from the highway above it. The traffic was heavy and unforgiving, but the group dodged across the highway and stared down at the lake, blue, smooth and sinister below.

'No birds fly over it,' said Thatcher.

'Why can't birds fly over it?' asked Ellen. 'Why, I see a bird now. It's flying over it.'

'Vergil says they can't. They die. Toxic fumes, you see. They kill birds.'

'Well,' said Ellen, 'then the birds need to read Vergil, because I see one flying over it.'

'It's a volcanic lake,' explained DeWitt. 'Probably at one time the fumes from it would have killed birds that flew too close to its surface.'

'The traffic's pretty bad here,' said Thatcher, looking down the highway. 'I don't trust those little Fiats.' One whizzed by, driven by a young man with a cell phone at his ear. 'And I don't trust their drivers, either.'

'This was Vergil's Lake Avernus,' said Alex Baker, assuming his public lecture mode. 'It was larger in Vergil's day than it is now. That hill I'm pointing to, over there, arose as a result of volcanic action in the seventeenth century, and reduced the size of the lake.'

'Where?' asked Ellen.

'Over where he's pointing,' said Walter Druker.

'*That* little hill?' said Ellen.

'If you look directly ahead,' continued the associate director, 'you can see Lake Lucrinus, famous for its oysters in the Augustan period of Rome. Beyond it, separating Lake Lucrinus from the Bay of Baia is the *Via Herculea*, built by Heracles, or Hercules as the Romans called him. You saw a statue of him in the Naples Museum. The Farnese Hercules. Remember?'

Bathsheba Bennett seemed perplexed. Miriam Kuntz looked thoughtful. Shirley Perovic from St. Louis breathed, 'Oh, yes. He was shown resting and thinking about something after he took the golden apples from the Garden of the Hesperides.'

'Marvellous,' said Sally Harvey.

'A splendid, dynamic figure,' said Dr. Alex.

'A mountain of muscle,' said Sally. 'A low IQ, though, I'd guess.'

'He was certainly a big bruiser,' said Sol Bernstein. 'Lots of cholesterol, I'd say.'

'Why was he here building roads?' wondered Miriam Kuntz. 'Didn't he live in Greece?'

Bathsheba Bennett frowned, as if she were incubating an appropriate comment.

'Well,' she said, "I once wrote a paper on Heracles. Heracles as an Italian hero was the subject. Do you know what I think about it?'

No one replied. 'Well,' said Bathsheba, 'I think---'

'And in the distance,' Dr. Alex interrupted, 'you can just see through the haze and promontory that looks like an inverted teacup. That's *Capo di Miseno*. Cape Misenus, named after Aeneas' helmsman who fell overboard here, and Vergil says that promontory was his tomb, erected by the Trojans to commemorate him. It's quite a hill to build in an afternoon with just shovels and no bulldozer.'

A wise nod from Gregory Donahue. 'Wasn't there a Roman naval base there, Dr. Baker?'

'That was where the Roman navy for the western Mediterranean was based,' the associate director continued, 'and you can still see the mooring rings for the Roman warships. Yes, you will get to see that on one of our trips. Back in 79 A.D., or C.E., if you wish, in mid- August, the commander of the Roman fleet spotted the eruption of Mt. Vesuvius from *Capo di Miseno* and set out with a squadron to see what was going on. He got too close and died of an asthma attack.'

'I remember,' said Sol Bernstein. 'I read something about that in a Latin class years ago. My school taught Latin back then.'

'Will we get to see it, Dr. Baker?' demanded Sally Harvey.

'See what?'

'The naval base.' Sally's ballpoint pen hovered over her clipboard. 'I have my new digital camera with me. I'd love to send a picture of the naval base back home to put on our web page.'

'Do you know what I think about Heracles?' Bathsheba Bennett demanded. 'Well, I think he was a culture hero –'

'DeWitt,' said Thatcher, 'do you think we should stop in this spot? The traffic here is too dangerous. Someone will get run down and we'll get sued.'

'We'll be on our way, Monnie,' said DeWitt. 'All right, group. Take your pictures and get back on the bus. Be careful crossing the highway.'

'And he was taken over by the Etruscans and the myth passed from them to the Romans –' continued Bathsheba.

'Be careful, Greg,' said Mildred Donahue. 'Watch out for the cars.'

'That eruption of Vesuvius was in 79 C.E., was it?' said Sol Bernstein as he followed the group into the bus. 'Was that in the emperor Nero's reign, or was it later?'

'What? Oh, later,' said Dr. Alex as he ushered the group on to the bus.

DeWitt was already counting heads. 'Everyone sit down so I can count,' he called out. 'Yes, we're all here. On to Cuma. *Andiamo.*'

'I think it was later, Sol,' said Sally Harvey.

'All right, then,' muttered Bathsheba, 'don't listen to what I have to say about Heracles. Nobody ever listens to me.'

'Sheba,' said Sol Bernstein, 'I'd love to hear what you have to say about Heracles. Let's make an appointment to talk about him sometime.'

'Thanks, Shlomo,' said Bathsheba. 'I'd like that.'

The bus veered out into a traffic lane, cutting off a Land Rover which braked sharply and sounded an indignant horn.

'So much for Lake Avernus,' said Miriam Kuntz to no one in particular, but Mildred, who was sitting across the aisle, replied,

'It was most interesting, I thought. It had a sinister look.'

'I remember where I've heard of the College of the Pacific Coast!' exclaimed Miriam. 'The name rang a bell when I heard you came from there. A friend of a good friend of mine used to teach there, in your department, I think, Gregory. You're the Classics department head there, aren't you?'

Gregory Donahue, who filled the seat beside his wife, nodded assent with some condescension..

'Jeremy Slutsky was the name,' said Miriam. 'I heard a lot about him.'

'Oh, Jeremy! We were all very fond of Jeremy, but he left us after three or four years for some school in Wisconsin. We were all very sorry to see him go.'

'What was the college he went to?'

'I don't remember, I'm afraid. Not the University of Wisconsin. I don't think he bettered himself when he left us, but he was determined to leave CPC. It was his own choice.'

'Jeremy didn't quite fit in,' said Mildred, with disapproval.

'Now, Mildred, said Donahue.

'How so?' asked Miriam.

'Well, for one thing,' said Mildred, 'when he came to CPC, I had picked out a very good house for him to buy, not far from our own, which would have been a good choice and a good investment, too, but Jeremy and his wife weren't interested in it. They wanted to choose a house for themselves.'

'Well,' interjected Gregory, 'he had a right to choose his own house, Mildred.'

'Of course,' said Mildred. 'I know that. I was only trying to help. But the house they bought was too large, and not at all suitable for them. Then when I made a call on Jeremy's wife, wearing my gloves and everything, I found her painting the living room and you know, she didn't even offer me tea.'

'I don't think Alice Slutsky is very fond of tea,' remarked Miriam.

'And then Jeremy was always publishing,' Mildred went on. 'The scholarly stuff was all right, I suppose, but he also wrote things for a popular audience, you know. Newspaper articles.'

'He even wrote a novel,' said Gregory, with deep disapproval.

'Yes, a novel,' said Mildred.'I read it. Greg wouldn't. It was a trashy detective story with a silly romance thrown in. One of these detective stories where the detective spends half his time examining his own navel, as Greg puts it. Not the sort of thing that brings prestige to a classics department at a first-rate college.'

'Didn't he publish other things, too?'

'Oh, yes, he was always giving Greg offprints of the articles he had written on something or other.'

'Yes, I was told he published a lot,' said Miriam.'

'Oh, one thing after another. He was always writing. Greg found his articles a real chore to read. Greg believes young faculty members should publish, of course, if they have something to write about. But it doesn't look good if one department member just publishes to attract attention.'

'I publish myself, of course,' interjected Gregory. 'It's important for a young man to have a publishing record nowadays, particularly when you don't have a reputation and you're trying to get one.'

'But,' said Mildred, 'a department head has limited time to write, what with all the committee work he has to do. Greg is terribly busy, what with his senate committees and work in the Dean of Men's office, and that sort of thing. Greg prefers to concentrate on teaching, when he has any spare time. This Slutsky, Greg tried to give him two or three new courses each term so he'd be kept busy preparing lectures rather than churning out articles.'

'In my school, we publish or perish,' said Miriam. 'The Sanhedrin that runs the place looks for any excuse to deny you tenure.'

'Well, publishing is important, of course, but other things are, too,' said Gregory. judiciously. 'You have to fit in, or you'll never be asked to serve on committees. You have to have the right background. The best man in my department never completed his PhD, but he's a most useful person. If I want advice, I ask him. He lets me know what the other department members are saying and thinking. He never publishes, but he is really a first-rate colleague and he's the person I always consult.'

'He could be a distinguished scholar if he wanted to be,' added Mildred.

'He works half-time in the office of the Dean of Arts, and the dean finds him invaluable, too. He told me he is his eyes and ears,' said Gregory.

'That's Dean Bonehead Bill,' said Mildred with a vicious giggle.

'Mildred!' reproved Gregory. 'You shouldn't repeat that nick-name!' He cleared his throat. 'The dean's a bit thick, but he's not a bonehead.'

'I think we're here at Cuma, now,' said Miriam as the bus passed under a Roman arch and the high citadel of Cuma came into view. '*Andiamo*, as our beloved director would say.'

The entrance to the archaeological site at Cuma was dra-matic. A stretch of Roman road, surfaced with paving stones of black basalt, led under a tall, narrow arch of Roman brick, the so-called *Arco Felice* which gave its name to the railway station closest to the Palazzo Agrippina. Beyond it the valley opened out, still covered with gardens and small farms though suburbia was rapidly intruding. Beyond the fields was the Mediterranean and an inviting beach, where the main sewer of Naples made its addition to the pellucid waters of the sea. Directly ahead, a steep hill rose out of the plain, like a great knoll on steroids: the acropolis of the ancient settlement. This was the site which the ancient Greeks chose for their first colony in Italy. More than two thousand, seven hundred years had passed since then, and the temples which the Greeks built on the acropolis had become Christian churches, which in turn fell into ruin. Beyond the acropolis was the edge of the Mediterranean Sea, where the first colonists beached their boats. They were far from their homes in Greece, and their ships were mere cockle shells, but at least they knew the terrain and they chose their site well. Already they had built a tiny settlement on the island of Ischia offshore, beneath a menacing volcano, for they had discovered that the mysterious Etruscans to the north were eager buyers of Greek wares. Still, thought Marcia, it was a pristine world they encountered, with forest untouched by the axe, and breathing the translucent air of primeval Italy. Once upon a time, when the atmosphere was clear, before the age of smog and the havoc of civilization. This is a land where the earth is scarred by a multitude of genera-tions, thought Marcia, and conceals ancient mysteries we have long forgotten.

Alex Baker, sitting at the front of the bus picked up the mi-crophone, tapped it gently to see if the amplifying system was working, and cleared his throat portentously.

'This is a storied region,' he said, 'marked by the vicissitudes of dynamic—uh—ethnic groups whose history conducted them to this area. In front of us is the acropolis, that is, the citadel, of ancient Cumae. Cumae is the Latin; in modern Italian it's just Cuma. The Greeks who founded a colony here called it *Kyme*, after a *Kyme* in their home island of Euboea in Greece. If you were a Roman about a century into the Christian era, making your approach as we are doing now, bumping over the black basalt paving stones of the Roman *Via Domitiana*, once you had passed under the archway called Arco Felice which we shall do in a minute, you would have seen the acropolis directly in front of you, and on it, two temples, one dedicated to Jupiter on top of the acropolis, and the other a monumental temple to Apollo built on a terrace lower down, where it would be first thing for the visitor to see on his approach. The word *acropolis*, you will remember, means the 'high city', the upper city, or the citadel, and an important place of refuge for any ancient city.

The Greek colonists found this steep hill that would serve as an acropolis, and no doubt that was one reason they chose the site. The natives of the area were the Opicians, a very—uh—dynamic people, though we don't know much about them. In the last half of the fifth century B.C., or B.C.E., if you prefer, native Italians called Samnites took over Cumae and built a forum at the foot of the acropolis. They spoke an Italic language known as Oscan and Cumae became an Oscan city until the Romans took over'.

'How did the Romans and the Samnites get along?' asked Sol Bernstein.

'The Romans beat the shit out of the Samnites,' said Walter Druker.

'Oh,' said Sol. 'Like they did with most people, didn't they?'

'There was a long struggle between the Romans and the Samnites,' said Dr. Alex. 'Three Samnite Wars. The second was the longest, and it was one that the Romans nearly lost. The Samnites were fearsome, dynamic warriors. You can see the ruins of the city that the Samnites built from the acropolis.'

The bus rolled to a stop before the entrance to the archaeological site, and Baker went to the kiosk where a sleepy *custodian* waited, and showed his *permesso.*

'Alex,' boomed the querulous voice of Monroe Thatcher, 'hasn't all that entrance ticket business been arranged in advance? Don't these Italians know who we are?'

'Just one minute, Monnie,' said Baker, as the *custodian* detached twenty-one tickets, one at a time, from his book of tickets.

'We still show our documents to the *custode* to demonstrate that we are genuine students, not just tourists, Monnie.' explained DeWitt.

'I should think that would be obvious,' said Thatcher. 'We're *bona fide* scholars. We come from the Palazzo Agrippina. They should know what that is.'

'I know, I know, but we still have to show our documents,' said DeWitt.

Thatcher turned away, disgusted. 'This is a place where we could have used our dago dazzler to save time,' he pronounced.

'The guards here should learn that we're not run-of-the-mill tourists.'

'And I thought Conradin would be a pain in the butt,' Marcia said *sotto voce* to Paul. 'He's a lamb compared to the *pater familias.*'

'Conradin is all right,' Paul replied. 'He has some things to work out. He's a teenager and he's scared, like all teenagers.'

'What's he scared of?'

'Life. What will be do with it? Will he muck things up? What sort of world will we leave for him and his age group? How can he deal with his raging hormones? Isn't that enough to make you scared?'

'It sounds gruesome. In my early youth, it was the war in Vietnam that frightened us. I think that was a worse bogey than hormones.'

'It depends,' said Paul.

'I got to the Internet Café yesterday, and learned you and Conradin had been there before me.'

'Ah, the *Albergo Felice,* a Camorra subsidiary, run by the gorilla Luigi. Yes, Conradin found it.'

'The Camorra? What's that?

'Naples' own version of Cosa Nostra. A detective story writer must surely know about the Camorra here in Naples. They control the garbage collection. If Naples smells, that's the Camorra at work—or rather, not at work.'

'I see you've been doing some detective work yourself. Tell me what you know about the Camorra.'

'Not much. It looks after organized crime in Naples and Campania just as the Mafia does in Sicily, the `Ndrangheta in Calabria and the United Sacred Crown in Apulia. But I'm no expert. I leave that to you.'

'How did you sniff out a connection between the *Albergo Felice* and the Camorra?'

'Oh, it's merely an educated guess. But I wouldn't be surprised. Keep your eyes open when you're in there. What did you think of Luigi?'

'Who?'

'The bouncer with big muscles who tends the bar? Don't you think he could be an efficient smasher of knee-caps? I think we had better leave no bills unpaid at the *Felice*.'

'They looked so nice, in their starched white jackets and their starched white shirts,' said Marcia. 'And Tony was very helpful and very attentive.'

'Well, we must talk more about it another time. *Il duce* is about to burst into a lecture.'

They had passed through the tunnel that runs under the acropolis of Cuma, and had gathered round the entrance of a cave cut into the side of the hill so that it formed a long gallery with windows looking out over the valley below. A sign identified it as the *Grotta di Sibylla*. Alex Baker assumed the demeanour of a lecturer about to utter winged words. The group fell silent in anticipation. Dr. Alex opened his mouth and spoke,

'This is the cave of the Sibyl ...'

'Is this the Sibyl's cave?' interrupted Thatcher. He peered suspiciously into the long gallery with its steeply-gabled ceiling, with the sunshine pouring through its apertures, making a pattern of light and shade on its walls. Dr. Alex appeared not to hear.

'This,' said he, 'is the cave of the Sibyl.' He opened his text of Vergil's *Aeneid*. ' Let me read the passage at the beginning of Book Six. You will remember that Aeneas has left Carthage where he had his tragic love affair with the Carthaginian queen, Dido, and, leaving Africa broken-hearted, he paused in Sicily for funeral games in honor of his father who had died there a year before. There he leaves behind the Trojan women who are weary with wandering over the sea, and with the remainder of his small but dynamic group of colonists, he sets sails for Italy. At last he reaches Cumae and encounters the Sibyl. Here is the site where these newcomers from the east first introduced their—uh—dynamic presence into Italy.'

'But Cumae was Greek, you said,' interjected Ellen Cross. 'I thought Aeneas was a Trojan. The Trojans weren't Greeks, were they?'

'Yes, that is, the Trojans weren't Greeks, but the Sibyl was really international. This cave was an oracle site.'

'Was it here he said "I'm afraid of the fucking Greeks even when they bear gifts."?' asked Piers Ellsworth.

'No, that was on a different occasion.' Dr. Alex cleared his throat meaningfully.

'I know the Greeks. I had a Greek girlfriend once,' Piers mused, aloud. 'Her dad had a restaurant.'

Betty Laramie glanced at him and smiled, and Piers, having attracted her notice, attempted a conversation.

'I want to go to Greece sometime. Have you been to Greece?'

'No,' said Betty, 'but I'll have to go there to do research on my dissertation.'

'What sort of research?'

'It's on the three-barred sigma. It's rather abstruse.'

'Sigma? That must have something to do with fraternities and sororities.'

'No. It's epigraphy.'

Piers looked blank. 'Do you do anything else besides this research?'

'Well, I like jazz, but the three-barred sigma takes up most of my spare time.'

'Does that mean you want to be—like, um—a fuck... I mean, a professor?' Piers asked, nonplussed.

Dr. Alex cleared his throat portentously again, and talking ceased. 'Here,' he went on, 'is Vergil describing this very spot where we stand now.' His two chins quivered and his voice deepened to bass-baritone.

'Excisum Euboicae latus ingens rupis in antrum
'quo lati ducunt aditus centum....

'The vast side of the cliff at Cumae had been hollowed out to form a cave', he translated, 'and leading into it are a hundred broad entrance ways and a hundred doorways, and from them emanate a hundred utterances, which are the Sibyl's responses. They had reached the threshold, when the virgin.....'

'This is quite a sizeable grotto,' boomed Thatcher, who had wandered into the entrance of the cave. 'Is this all man-made, Baker? That's remarkable, isn't it? They hacked all this out of the rock with hammer and chisel, did they?. What do you think of that, Conradin? Huh? It shows what you can do when you apply yourself.' His voice echoed back after him as he pushed further into the cave. A half-dozen students drifted after him. The rest still clustered around Alex Baker, notebooks open and ballpoint pens poised expectantly.

'Well,' said Dr. Alex, closing his book, 'we'll continue. It was here that Aeneas came to the Sibyl's grotto with its hundred entrance ways, and in the 1930s, this artificial cave was discovered by the great Italian archaeologist Amedeo Maiuri, who identified it, rightly I think, as the grotto which Vergil knew. Later archaeologists have had doubts, but I think that Vergil actually saw this cave. At the end of the cave there is a chamber with a trough for water, and that could have been where the Sibyl performed her ritual ablutions.'

'How many windows are there?'

'Vergil said a hundred, Miriam,' Alex replied.

'There aren't nearly one hundred. There aren't more than six or seven. And this virgin you were talking about—you mean the Sibyl?'

'Is that appalling woman your room mate?' Paul asked Marcia, whispering out of the corner of his mouth.

'Miriam? Yes. I don't see why you call her appalling. She's all right, except that she snores like a twenty-four rank pipe organ. I get a full toccata and fugue all night long.'

'We should be careful in here. These caves sometimes amplify sound. We wouldn't want everyone to hear what we say.'

'Well, we've said nothing compromising thus far, Paul,' murmured Marcia.

They heard a few musical notes issuing from deep in the cave. Percy and his guitar had gone to the end of the gallery and he was now perched on the edge of the rock-cut trough, strumming the guitar and singing.

'Should you sit on that thing?' demanded Thatcher, pointing to the trough. 'We must treat ancient monuments with respect. What would happen if everyone sat on them and sang songs? They'd soon be destroyed. That's what would happen.'

Percy stood up and stopped singing.

'You know, I am very interested in these feminine prophets,' said Miriam, who had reached the end of the gallery and joined Madge Midgely and Sol Bernstein who were looking at the Sibyl's bathing basin. 'Like Cassandra, and the Sibyl of Cumae and the Sibyl of Tibur and of Erythrae and so on. Why women? Why did they form a sisterhood? What did they have in common?'

'Well,' said Sol Bernstein, 'they could all say "I told you so" when the disaster they predicted took place. That's a favourite female occupation.'

Miriam cast him a baleful glance and he retreated. Madge Midgely was making notes. This could be raw material for her column, 'Ask Madge', a regular feature in the Beaumont *Advertiser*, where she admonished and warned the citizens of Beaumont, rather like a modern Sibyl.

'What's a ritual ablution?' asked Conradin, who had joined Percy Bass and was examining the water trough.

'I was wondering about that,' said Madge.

'That's when you wash your hands before going to chapel,' replied Percy.

'You slay me, Mr. Bass,' said Conradin. "They didn't go to chapel back then."

'Shall we go to the top, Yo-yo?' Piers Ellsworth asked Kim, his roommate, and the two led the way up the path to the top of the acropolis. Marcia followed behind, with Piers' solid rump a couple steps above her, his muscular legs heaving his hundred kilograms of solid flesh tirelessly upwards, one step after another. She soon began to lag. Paul caught up with her at the first landing, where she had subsided on to a stone bench beside the parapet.

'Overweight and smoker's lungs,' she gasped.

'I haven't seen you smoking,' said Paul.

'I was bullied out of it. There were "Absolutely No Smoking" signs in every building I was in. I had to stand outside in rain, sleet and snow whenever I wanted to have a cigarette. So I gave it up. So as a result, I put on weight. So I can't make it to the top of this—what-do-you-call-it? acropolis isn't it?—without taking a breather. But you go ahead. You look fit.'

'I'll wait with you. We can join the stragglers.'

Thatcher puffed past, but wasted no breath speaking to them. The back of his shirt was dark with sweat. Behind him was a group clustered about Dr. Alex, moving at deliberate speed. Walter Druker stopped and mopped his brow.

'It's damn hot,' he panted. 'What misery we endure for the sake of culture!'

'Dr. Druker!' Conradin loped up behind him. 'What's happened to the old "sound mind in a sound body" stuff? Aren't you going to set us an example?'

'Let me lose a hundred pounds and a twenty years, and I'll set you an example.'

'Dr. Druker, you should think what an example you're giving to an impressionable youth like me,' said Conradin, with a grin revealing a mouthful of metal braces, and he continued up the steep path like an antelope.

'I guess, Dr. Druker, that out in the Midwest where you teach, you don't have a lot of contact with the liberal arts,' remarked Millicent Thatcher who was trudging up the path in the wake of her son and paused to catch her breath.

'Madam,' said Druker, 'you do us an injustice. The president of Spearfish State defends the liberal arts in every public speech he gives! He has split more infinitives in defense of the liberal arts than Abe Lincoln split fence rails!'

Millicent looked at him as if he were an unusual and slightly repulsive zoological specimen.

'How interesting,' she said. 'Well, I must be on my way and see what is on top of this acropolis.'

'There are only mute stones on top of this acropolis,' said Druker. 'Mute, broken stones in disarray and daunting numbers.'

Millicent murmured something indistinguishable and continued up the path. Kwame Assante, looking lean and fit in a white T-shirt, came up behind Druker.

'Come on, Walter,' he said. 'We're a team, remember? Don't let me down.'

'Kwame, I have just been reminded by an easterner of the lowly intellectual status of the American Midwest where I eke out a living, and I doubt that a climb to the top of this acropolis can do anything to improve it.'

'Come along, Walter. The exercise will do you good. Remember the Spearfish State song: "*Fortes et fideles, let no doubts assail us*". Have I got it right?'

'Kwame, you'll kill me,' said Druker, but he trudged onward in Assante's wake.

Paul helped Marcia to her feet and they resumed the climb.

'I give you credit for cutting out cigarettes,' said Paul. 'My ex-wife failed in two attempts to give up smoking and she is a very resolute woman. Very determined.'

Ah-ha, thought Marcia. Wait long enough and the marital details will emerge.

'Ex-wife?' she said.

'Yes. She left me. We grew apart.'

'That usually means one of you wanted someone else,' said Marcia, thinking to herself, 'I must not pry. Still, I look on this as professional activity. I might be able to recycle this matrimonial saga in my book.'

'She said she wanted a horny husband with a six-figure income,' explained Paul.

'Well, I can see that a Latin teacher might not have the latter qualification,' said Marcia, cautiously.

Paul looked down at the plain below, extending to the seashore.

'See that stretch of completely level land down there, with bluffs on three sides of it? That looks like a bay which has completely silted up. Do you think there was a little harbour there when the Greeks first arrived?'

'Damn,' thought Marcia. 'He's on to harbours.'

'Did you notice, when Dr. Alex was talking to us about how Aeneas and his Trojans landed here, there weren't any women in his group of settlers?' asked Paul, reflectively. 'The Trojan women remained in Sicily. They never came to Italy. Do you think that's significant?'

'No,' said Marcia. 'They were just tired of doing the men's laundry.'

TIME HAS TREATED THE Roman amphitheatre at Pozzuoli more kindly than its coeval, the Colosseum in Rome. The Colosseum provided a good share of the stones which went to build St. Peter's in the Vatican, which was fair enough, for in its heyday it provided a venue for disposing of persistent Christians. The Flavian amphitheater at Pozzuoli has suffered from neglect and comparatively minor plundering. Replace the seats, add a throng of spectators, restore the trap doors in the arena which opened on to the chambers below where the wild animals were caged, cover the arena floor with sand, and the amphitheatre would be ready again for the games the Romans loved. This was the third largest amphitheatre in all Italy. DeWitt spoke briefly. It was already noon and before lunch the group was still scheduled to make a brief stop at the 'Temple of Serapis', which, as Dr. Alex's notes stated, was not a temple at all, but a Roman market building, complete with public toilets. It was DeWitt's turn to lecture, and DeWitt adhered to the principle that any lecture to a tour group that exceeded one minute was a waste of breath. Still, this was an opportunity to say something about the patron saint of Naples, San Gennaro, who might or might not have been martyred in this arena.

'Legend has it that he was brought to the arena, perhaps this one, and thrown to the lions, who wouldn't eat him. So he had to be taken out to Solfatara near here, where there's a convent now, and there his head was chopped off. There is a phial of his blood still kept in the Naples cathedral, and once a year on his festival day it liquefies, and that is a propitious sign.'

'Liquefies?' queried Ellen Cross.

'DeWitt,' said Thatcher, appearing suddenly in the rear of the group, 'could you tell us something more about this amphitheatre here?'

'Monnie,' said Millicent, 'where is Conradin?'

'Huh?'

'Where's Conradin?'

'I thought he was with you.'

'I thought he went with you.'

'Where is he, then? Who has seen Conradin?'

The group looked blankly about them.

'Oh, dear,' moaned Millicent. 'He could have fallen down any one of those holes in the arena and we wouldn't know. He's possibly hurt. Why doesn't someone keep an eye on things?' She directed a reproachful glance at Paul.

'Conradin!' bellowed Thatcher. 'Everybody spread out and look for Conradin!' He filled his lungs with air, and bellowed again, 'Conradin!'

Millicent progressed from a sniff to a snivel. She turned to Percy Basso.

'Percy, have you seen Conradin?'

'No, I haven't, Mrs. Thatcher,' replied Percy. 'He was carrying his camcorder. He is probably somewhere shooting film.'

'I do wish you'd keep an eye on him, Percy,' said Millicent. 'He's just a boy. Someone might mug him and steal his camcorder. This is Italy. Italians aren't the same as Americans.'

'Let's all look for Conradin,' said DeWitt. He looked glum.

'Yes, let's all look,' said Dr. Alex, as he sat down on a square stone block where an archway gave some protection from the sun. The group began to scatter.

'End of lecture for the day,' said Marcia *sotto voce* to Paul. 'What's your opinion of this little family drama?'

'Conradin has some issues to sort out,' said Paul.

'His father must be a cross to bear.'

'His father? Yes. But watch his mother's body language.'

'A nice average kid carrying an enormous weight of parental expectations?'

'That's part of it,' said Paul. 'He'd have got free tuition as a faculty brat if he'd made it into Williamson where his dad's a teacher. At the Gilead Academy, his dad has to pay tuition. Don't think that Conradin isn't reminded of that.'

Miriam Kuntz and Madge Midgely wandered off to examine one of the trap doors in the arena floor which had allowed the ravenous wild beasts stored below in their cages to be hoisted up from their dark underground quarters to the sunlight while the noisy mob in the stands howled for blood.

'You know,' said Miriam, 'I didn't come here on my own nickel to waste my time looking for a spoiled brat.'

'He's an over-protected teenager, all right,' agreed Madge. 'Wait till he breaks loose from mom and dad.'

'Well, I can fill my time with better things than waiting for him to break loose.'

'You know, I get a lot of troubled teenagers writing to my column in the *Advertiser*, and I'm often sure that their problem is forgotten sexual abuse in childhood that they've repressed deep in their subconscious, and it has to be brought to the surface.'

'Humpf,' said Miriam. 'Isn't that repressed sexual abuse-thing yesterday's science now? I thought psychology had moved on.'

Madge flushed. 'I shouldn't think so,' she said. 'Science doesn't age. You can't argue with science.' She fanned herself with her notebook. 'I had no idea there would be so much exercise when I signed up for this tour,' she went on. 'I'd take off weight if I could, but I can't. It's my glands, you know. Let's sit down and rest until Conradin turns up. He will, you know. The Conradins of this world always do.'

They found Conradin in the vaulted chambers underground, chatting in a mixture of broken Italian and English to a bronzed young workman who was stripped to the waist and stirring mortar with a spade.

'Conradin!' barked Thatcher. 'Don't wander off like that! You scared everybody.'

'Well, hello, parental units,' said Conradin, with a trace of resentment. 'I just went off to have a pee. Do you know that Ildo here spent a year in Toronto?'

'Bronx,' said Ildo, grinning. 'I know many people in Bronx.'

'Ildo had a great time in Toronto,' said Conradin. He put an arm over Ildo's bare shoulders. 'You should take our picture, Dad. I'll send a copy of it to Ildo.'

Ildo smiled expectantly.

'No,' said Thatcher. 'I haven't got film to waste.'

'Well, at least I've got you on my camcorder, Ildo,' said Conradin.

'You shouldn't wander off like that, Conradin,' said Millicent. 'We were all terribly worried about you.'

'Mother, you slay me,' replied Conradin. 'I just wanted to look around by myself. Are we leaving now?'

'We have to go to the Temple of Serapis next,' said Thatcher, testily, 'and it's late. You've held everybody up.'

'*Ciao*, Ildo,' said Conradin.

'*Arrivederci*. Good-bye,' Ildo replied, with a grin.

'Let's get on the bus,' rumbled Thatcher. 'Don't keep the driver waiting.'

'It's really neat when you get a chance to talk to the ordinary people here,' said Conradin to no one in particular.

'Yes, it sure is,' said Kwame, who was standing behind him.

'Get on the bus, Conradin,' said Thatcher.

Giuseppe watched Ellen Cross with a melting gaze as she mounted the steps into the bus, her hips undulating rhythmically. Millicent Thatcher watched Giuseppe.

XI

AWESOME AMPHITHEATRE. *I took my camcorder and got some good pics. Tony at the* Albergo Felice *had told me about it. He's—like—a kind of Pozzuoli booster. They kept cages with lions and tigers in the basement, and when wild beast fights were being held, they would hoist the cages up to the open arena and a slave would open the cage doors and then run away quickly. If he was not quick enough, he'd be eaten. Really awesome. Then the lions and tigers attacked the Christians whom the Romans condemned to death, and they sang hymns as the lions and tigers munched away at them. Tony told me that San Gennaro was thrown to the lions there, but they didn't like the way he tasted and wouldn't eat him, and so he was taken away somewhere to have his head was cut off. His blood is kept in the Naples Cathedral, all dried up. But on his festa each year his blood turns liquid again, and a stain on a rock kept at the church that was built where he was beheaded turns bright red whenever his blood liquefies. Tony believes this. He believes in miracles and the evil eye and all that. He thinks his San Gennaro keeps the earthquakes away. Yet I wouldn't call him religious. He laughs at priests. He says they're for women.*

I told Tony about the guy I met on the airplane. Giacomo from Fabiola Films who said he knew Arco Felice. Tony said there were lots of Italians named Giacomo. But maybe Luigi would know him, he said. Luigi knew a lot of people. Tony didn't seem to like me asking a lot of questions.

The fat newshound Midgley sat beside me on the bus on the way back from the Pozzuoli amphitheatre. She kept talking to me about sex-

ual abuse which kids suffer and then they forget about it, or else they don't want to remember. Said a lot of people were in denial. Just like me, she said. Suppressed Memory Syndrome, she called it. Had I heard of it? Jeez. I was glad to ditch her.

We improve our minds after supper. There's a man called Arthur DeSilva who's come to give us a free lecture. Dad says we should take advantage of lectures to improve our minds. Particularly mine. Dad really slays me.

I'd rather go to the Albergo Felice after supper. Luigi's an awesome guy when you get to know him. Strong as a horse. A lot stronger than Mario, and he's pretty powerful.

XII

ARTHUR DeSilva, the lecturer on 'Octopuses in the Mentality of Greece and Rome' turned out to be a rubicund man mired in portly middle-age and apparently enjoying it. He arrived with much luggage in time for drinks before dinner, and he proved a jolly table companion. He had met all the people in the world worth meeting, and was on first name terms with most of them. Yes, he had met Princess Diana before her untimely death, and had chatted with her, but what they had said he would, of course, never reveal. So sad! Charming girl! Monica Lewinsky? No, he never was introduced, but he knew a person who knew her well. He understood what made her tick, he said, and nodded wisely, like a judicious old owl, implying that he could say more if he wanted to. Yes, he took patients, but a small legacy made it possible for him to devote a lot of spare time to his chosen area of research, which was octopuses. No, he didn't use the plural 'octopi'. He didn't want people to think he was parading his learning.

After dinner, the group gathered in the lounge. DeSilva took a seat behind a small round table which had supported a potted spider plant until a few moments earlier. Madge Midgely had her notebook out and her ballpoint pen ready, waiting for the lecture to begin. Sol Bernstein wore the expression of a man prepared to endure any amount of nonsense. Piers Ellsworth and his Yo-yo, his Korean room mate, looked about them, saw that there were not enough chairs, and settled down comfortably on the

rug. Monroe Thatcher took a seat in the front row where his considerable bulk blocked Betty Laramie's view. Conradin and his
mother sat near the door. Dr. Alex manned the Kodak Carousel
slide projector.

DeWitt Fordham rose to introduce the speaker.

'As you are aware,' he said, 'the Palazzo Agrippina has attracted many distinguished visiting lecturers over the years,
and this evening we are especially honored to have with us Dr.
Arthur De Silva, an expert on octo*pi*. We have all encountered
calamari, of course, and so we know that immature octopi are
good to eat, but Arthur's research has gone far beyond deep-
frying them.' DeWitt paused to chuckle, and one or two others
joined in. 'Arthur's research has taken him from Minoan art in
prehistoric Crete to Jules Verne, and from artistic and fictional
representations of the octopus to the revelations of psychiatry.
Arthur DeSilva is not hemmed in by departmental boundaries
like most of us academics, but he has been free to pursue interdisciplinary research in the best meaning of the word. When
Arthur let me know he would be arriving in Naples, bringing a
collection of his slides with him, I felt we should not miss this
opportunity to hear him speak. So, of course, I took him up on
his generous offer, and we are all the more grateful because he
has waived his usual lecture fee as a favour for our group. And
so I present, Arthur DeSilva, who will talk to us on 'Octo*pi* in the
mentality of Greece and Rome.'

Fordham sat down, having emphasized his grammatical point
in a stentorian voice, and turned a beatific gaze at the speaker.
De Silva arose, and said,

'Thank you, Professor DeWitt, thank you. Ladies and gentle-
men, let me say first of all how delighted I am to be here, in this
splendid Palazzo Agrippina. When I heard of the summer school
here, I felt I could not turn down an invitation to speak to so
dedicated a group of students. I just learned over dinner that
the palazzo here is named after the mother, I think it was, of
the celebrated emperor Nero, and I think it is really fitting that
a great Roman statesman's—uh—emperor's mother should be
commemorated here, all the more so because I shall have some-

thing to say about mothers and sons this evening. Why, I might even add a footnote or two to Agrippina studies.' He interjected a high-pitched giggle. 'Now my interest in octopuses began early, but it has only been in the last five years that I have turned my attention to the fruitful field of octopuses in the Greek and Roman thought world. It has been a truly tremendous intellectual adventure. It has taken me into many nooks and crannies of ancient history. Now could I have the first slide, please?'

Lights went out, curtains were pulled, and the lounge was reduced to twilight. The first slide appeared on the screen. It showed a vase from prehistoric Crete with a stylized octopus spreading its tentacles over the side of the vessel, and it was upside down.

'Well, regrettably, the slide is upside down, but don't worry,' said De Silva, 'Pretend you're standing on your heads. If I were using Power Point, this wouldn't happen, but I'm old fashioned. This is a vase from the Minoan civilization on Crete prior to 1400 B.C. No doubt, since many of you are interested in the ancient Mediterranean world, you will know something about Minoan Crete. This was the mysterious civilization of a pre-Greek people on Crete, where there were a number of great sprawling palaces built, and where the people enjoyed watching bull-fighting. Some of you have possibly read Mary Renault's *The King Must Die.*' Ellen Cross nodded. Gregory Donahue assumed an expression of exquisite boredom. Thatcher coughed..

The second slide showed a more naturalistic octopus, sprawled over the belly of a Minoan vase.

'Here is another vase. You will notice the curious obsession with octopuses. Of course, the octopus is found in the Mediterranean and it is an edible fish—I guess it's classified as a fish and not a crustacean.'

The next slide showed a drawing done by a male patient in a psychiatric ward. It was a spider-like creature with long, prehensile legs.

'This,' said De Silva, 'is a spontaneous drawing. A doodle, you might almost call it. The man who drew it was a patient suffering from depressive moods followed by highs. Notice the subject

that he chose to depict. It is clearly an octopus. Those are magnificent tentacles.'

More slides followed. More octopods. The psychiatric patients
that DeSilva knew did seem to use the octopus as a symbol of
something.

'What does it all mean?' asked DeSilva rhetorically.

'They just liked octopuses, or octopi, or whatever it is,' spoke
up Sol Bernstein. 'Some people have favorite fish. I like salmon.
Lox.'

'Yes, but why not dolphins or flying fish?' demanded DeSilva.
'Why always octopuses?'

'They liked *calamari*', said Sol. 'So do I. Deep fried.'

DeSilva looked pained.

'But,' Paul interrupted, 'the Minoans, if I remember, did do
wall paintings of dolphins. I remember one from the palace
of Minos at Cnossos. Dolphins are a friendly fish. They like
humans.'

'But my patients did octopuses,' said DeSilva, flatly. 'These are
patients who came under my care as a practicing psychologist.
I've never had any patients who drew dolphins.' He sighed. 'So,
you see, I'm left with a dilemma. What does it mean?'

Conradin spoke up. 'Does it have something to do with despair? Desperation at living, I mean? Love of death?'

'Well, that is an idea,' said DeSilva. 'The octopus as a symbol
of despair. A very good idea. '

Thatcher snorted. 'The reason the Minoan vase painters drew
octopi was that they filled the available space on the vase. As for
your patients, they drew them because they were easy fish to
draw. This symbolism nonsense is just that: nonsense.'

'Oh, I can't agree,' retorted DeSilva. 'All pictures are conveyers
of meaning. We have to learn to read and understand them. They
are like words in an alien language.'

'Well,' said Miriam Kuntz, 'what do you think the meaning
is?'

'Let me show you,' said DeSilva. He showed another slide.
It looked somewhat like an octopus. It was badly drawn, but
with imagination it could certainly pass for an octopus. DeSilva

waited in silence for a moment, as if on the verge of uttering a momentous verity, and then, changing his mind, showed another slide instead. Then another, a childish spidery scrawl which with determination could be interpreted as an octopus.

'These are drawings of quite young children. They had been asked to draw something that represented mother. They drew a form that looked like an octopus. Not only did it look like an octopus, it *was* an octopus—even though these children had never seen a real octopus. Here, I suggest, we have the answer to our conundrum. The octopus symbol represents mother.' DeSilva beamed.

'Oh, no,' muttered Miriam, audibly. 'Not the mother thing again.'

'Now, what,' asked DeSilva, 'did that tell us about the Minoan civilization on prehistoric Crete?'

DeSilva did not wait for an answer. His next slide showed a woman's vagina, drawn freehand. The artist was inexpert, but the resemblance to an octopus was clear. Madge Midgely, who had stuffed her notebook back into her voluminous handbag, took it out again, and waited with ballpoint pen poised. Shirley Perovich said something *sotto voce*, and DeSilva paused, expecting a question. But none emerged, and he pressed on to classical Greece. Athens was a male dominant society without much evident interest in octopuses, 'which some of you classicists might want to call "octopi"', said DeSilva with the indulgent smile of a person who understood the stresses of interdisciplinary study. 'In the Athenian house, women had their own quarters. It would have been improper for them to wander about on the streets. Men, on the other hand, did go out and about, and there was a room inside the main entrance where men could banquet with their male friends.' De Silva coughed gently and called for the next picture. It was a picture of the Parthenon on the Acropolis of Athens which he identified as a symbol of masculine power. Imperial power. It was built with money collected as tribute from an empire.

Then DeSilva swept on to Rome, which appeared to have declined and fallen without any marked enthusiasm for octopuses.

Their absence from Roman art called for an explanation. When Aeneas fled from Dido, queen of Carthage, to Italy, was this a masculine Roman fleeing from the octopus that represented female power? Remember he had already fled from his first wife, Creusa, when he evacuated Troy, and though Dido was not his wife, she wanted to be, which was good enough. The fact that Carthage was a sea power should be kept in mind. That was a significant point. Octopuses lived in the sea and Dido ruled the sea. Aeneas sailed across the sea to get away from her. Classical scholars had all overlooked the role of the sea and the octopuses that swam in it. Dr. Alex's chins began to quiver. DeWitt Fordham had a distant look in his eyes as if his mind was elsewhere. Gregory Donahue cleared his throat.

'I find it significant,' asserted DeSilva, 'that we're here in a palazzo named after the mother of the emperor Nero. I can't claim to be a student of ancient history, but from what I've read, Nero's mother was a classic, pushy mother who shoved her son into the emperor job before he was ready. I think he tried to drown her somewhere near here, which should be a lesson to pushy mothers. Nero had an artistic temperament and I've no doubt that if he had turned his hand to painting, the octopus motif would have been his favorite.'

Conradin whispered something to his mother and slipped out the door. Millicent's sigh could be heard in all four corners of the room.

The room was stuffy, and the twilight and the gentle hum of the Kodak Carousel invited sleep. Sol Bernstein was already nodding off. Miriam Kuntz initiated a discreet snore which began at middle C and reached F sharp before she snapped awake. Piers Ellsworth looked about him to see if he could slip out the door without his bulk laying waste a couple chairs. Gregory and Mildred Donahue who sat side by side, swayed slightly in unison on their narrow folding chairs. Gregory wore an expression of utter skepticism. Dr. DeSilva continued , unperturbed, until his flow of words ceased, and the audience realized with a start that he had finished.

Fordham snapped to attention, and said that he was sure

that Dr. DeSilva would be glad to entertain questions. DeSilva beamed with anticipation. Professor Donahue rose heavily to his feet.

'One small point. Not many people realize that the final syllable of the word "octopus" comes from the Greek *"pous"*, in the genitive case, *"podos"*, and so the correct plural of the word "octopus" is 'octo*pods*", not "octopi" or "octopuses."' He sat down.

'Thank you for that point,' said DeSilva.

'I like "octopuses" myself,' said Walter Druker.

'However, "octopods" is correct,' replied Donahue, 'and we should stick to what is correct.' Mildred, seated beside him, nodded.

'We must, indeed,' said DeSilva. 'Are there other questions?'

There was a minute of heavy silence, and then Shirley Perovich cleared her throat.

'That was a fascinating lecture, Dr. DeSilva but I believe that for anyone engaged in the reflective process, the correlation between the octopus and classical society must remain a little vague. Muddy, almost. I wonder if you could enlarge on that a little, and explain precisely what your reference to the vagina means.'

DeSilva frowned. 'I thought that was clear. Octopus equals vagina equals mother. You can express it in an algebraic equation. If "octopus" is "x" and vagina "y", then x plus y equals "z" which is, of course, mother. Is that clear?'

'I think,' said Shirley, with some asperity, 'that it helps understand vaginas if you have one.'

DeSilva acknowledged her point with a very slight nod.

Miriam Kuntz rose to her feet. 'This was an interesting lecture, to be sure,' she said, 'though there was an odor of half-baked Freudianism to it. As we all know, the concept of revision has –um—led to potent transformations of images which have been denigrated for centuries. The tutelage of Dido, for instance, as a beautiful and—um—tragic victim—a Madama Butterfly figure—makes a challenge to the traditional subordination of the female body to the lust and male violence of Rome—um— as symbolized by the phallus, and it makes us rethink the hollow triumph of Aeneas whose sole achievement was to found the Roman Empire. If we think of the "phallus in opposition to the octopus equals vagina" equation, it—um—puts pressure on the psychoanalytic assumptions of gender relations which have become so dominant in discussions of this sort. I hope I've made myself clear. I wonder if you would care to comment, Dr. DeSilva?' Miriam sat down with slow dignity.

'Well,' said DeSilva, after a long pause, 'you may be right.'

'The problem with this line of research,' Miriam went on, rising to her feet again and speaking with grave emphasis, 'and with much of the research into the Roman Empire is that it completely ignores the social and cultural prominence of the penis. Why is the battle of Actium more important than the penis? Because the persons who fought it, and then wrote about it, were all men. The correct insight is that battles are mere extensions of the penis. That is how we should interpret them.'

'But,' broke in Piers Ellsworth, suddenly alert, 'wasn't Cleopatra at the Battle of Actium? Didn't she lead the Egyptian fleet?'

'I can't see what difference that makes,' said Miriam, rather crossly.

'But,' said Piers, 'wasn't Cleopatra a woman? So how would she have a—you know—what you're talking about?'

De Silva stirred uneasily. 'Perhaps,' he said, 'we have wandered rather far from the vagina to the penis. I fail to see that there's a good fit—uh—between the two topics. I was really talking about octopi, or octopods, which I have been reminded is correct.'

Madge Midgely rose ponderously to her feet, 'Dr. DeSilva, I think that the role of masculinity as it pertains to Octopus Studies is very important. What evidence did you find for sexual abuse in ancient Greece and Rome? How did the Greeks and Romans handle repressed memory syndrome, and how does it relate to the octopus?'

'Well, I'm sure that if we had all the literature and art of Greece and Rome, we would find—umm—evidence of the sort you want. You must remember that so much is lost. We are detectives with cold case files, so to speak.'

Dr. Alex's two chins quivered, but he rose to his feet with dignity. 'Well, we must not wander too far from the intentions of the Agrippina program. It's getting late and I must call a halt to this dynamic discussion. Thank you all for coming, and particularly Dr. DeSilva who has given us a dynamic lecture which will set us all thinking, and nourish our minds for a very long time.' He nodded to DeSilva who beamed back. 'Tomorrow we must leave early for Paestum, which the Greeks founded with the name of Poseidonia in the days of the dynamic Greek colonial endeavour here in southern Italy, and it's time to call a halt. We've had a taste of Arthur's dynamic personality and fascinating research and tomorrow you'll have a chance to discuss his ideas further with him, for he will stay the night at the *Albergo Felice*, which some of you know,' Dr. Alex coughed, 'and he will join the Agrippina group tomorrow day on our trip to Paestum. We are all looking forward tremendously to having you as our guest, Dr. DeSilva.'

'Thank you,' said De Silva.

'Class dismissed, I suppose,' said Sol Bernstein who had awakened from his nap.

'What a load of horseshit,' said Miriam Kuntz. 'I need a rye to clear my head.'

Marcia slipped outside, longing for fresh air. The night was cool, and lights twinkled along the shore of the Bay of Baia. Marcia wandered around to the rear garden, where a stele marked the spot where the ashes of the Palazzo Agrippina's founder were buried under a tree. She paused to look at the inscription on the grave marker, but it was too dark to make out the letters. She became aware of two other figures in the garden. They moved furtively into the shadows and out the back gate when Marcia appeared, but she recognized them nonetheless. One was Luigi, the beefy bartender from the *Albergo Felice*. The other was Conradin.

XIII

CONRADIN SAT at the bare, little table looking out from his bedroom window over the garden at the rear of the Palazzo Agrippina. The morning light seemed to give new life to the plants, as if they were roused from deep slumber. But Conradin was lost in thought. A poem was already composed in his mind when he awakened, and now he was trying to recapture it and write it down, before it escaped. He opened his notebook, picked up a ballpoint pen; and then abandoned it for a pencil.

> matt, you never meant to die,
> matthew, our life is sweet,
> i know it's not grown-up to cry
> yet there must be a reason why
> our hopes are trampled under feet...

Conradin chewed his pen. The words came reluctantly. Conradin's attention focused on a large acanthus plant under his window that had, overnight, sprouted a tall spike covered with blossoms.

> matt, we had long talks together,
> we mapped the future of our world,
> come stormy or auspicious weather,
> there was no hawser that could tether
> our little ship of destiny.

still, to the young, death comes unwanted.........

It hurt to think of Matthew. But it was a sort of hurt that Conradin accepted. He laid down his pen and gazed out the window to the garden below. The back gate that opened on to the narrow path to the *Albergo Felice* was ajar. No one had bothered to lock it. Luigi had been in the garden last night, waiting for De Silva, he said, who was staying at the *Albergo Felice* for the night, and wanted someone to carry his luggage to his room. When he appeared, Luigi heaved one heavy suitcase easily on to his shoulder, grabbed the other by its handle and loped down the path to the *Albergo*, with DeSilva following with measured dignity. The gate must have been left unlocked after he passed through it.

The Fabiola Films man had called at the *Albergo* night before, Luigi told Conradin, and had asked about him. Yes, Luigi knew Giacomo Fini. He shrugged. Luigi's English was minimal, not much better than Conradin's Italian.

Well, thought Conradin, he might mention it to Tony. Tony had looked at Giacomo Fini's card and told him a Fini was no good. No Fini was, he said.

Thatcher knocked loudly on Conradin's bedroom door.

'Time to get up, Conradin,' he boomed. 'We have an early start for Paestum today.' He tried the door, and finding it unlocked, entered the room. Conradin crawled back to bed and pulled the covers over his head.

'PAESTUM WAS FOUNDED AS a Greek colony named Poseidonia' read Arthur DeSilva in Alex Baker's mimeographed publication: *Notes on the Monuments of the Naples Area.* Dr. Alex had presented him with a copy when he voiced an interest in visiting Paestum with the Palazzo Agrippina group. 'The colonists came from Sybaris, itself a colony on the instep of Italy which was conquered and destroyed by its neighbor Croton at the end of the sixth century B.C. Poseidon became a site for the worship of Hera, venerated here as a mother goddess who helped women in childbirth. Two of the three Greek temples on the site are dedicated to Hera:

an early archaic temple popularly known as the "Basilica" and a temple contemporary with the famous Parthenon in Athens popularly known as the "Temple of Neptune." Both were, in fact, dedicated to Hera, though recently archaeologists have argued for Apollo as the god who owned the "Temple of Neptune". The third temple which dates to the early fifth century B.C. belonged to Athena. The temples owe their remarkable preservation to the fact that Paestum was lost in the middle ages for the whole low-lying area round about became infested with malaria and was deserted....' Arthur DeSilva stopped reading. Tony, wearing a starched white jacket, arrived with a *caffè latte* and set it on the table before him.

'And my fried egg. *Uovo fritto, per favore,*' said De Silva. Knowing that if he ate a breakfast consisting only of a *caffè latte* and a hard roll, his stomach would protest with loud rumblings before noon, he had ordered a fried egg.

'*A momenti arriverà,*' said Tony, who departed, and a minute or two later, emerged again from the kitchen with an egg sizzling in a hot stainless steel saucer. De Silva looked at it with some distaste.

'O.K.?' asked Tony.

'This place is a real dump,' said DeSilva.

'Something is wrong?' asked Tony.

DeSilva looked at his watch. 'O.K., O.K,' he replied, peevishly. 'I don't have time to send it back. I'll eat it.' He stuffed his copy of Dr. Alex's *Notes on the Monuments of the Naples Area* into his knapsack, and threw it on the floor. He broke a hard roll apart, showering his plate with bread crumbs. At least there was a tiny container of jam. What I wouldn't give for a Starbucks, he thought.

Doesn't someone here know how to fry an egg? But I'll eat it. I'm not going to be an Ugly American. The thug with his back to me behind the bar—the muscleman who carried my luggage here last night—looks like an enforcer straight out of 'The Sopranos' on TV. He didn't appreciate the Evil Eye that I gave him last night. Serve him right. Why should I have given him a big tip? I gave him enough. These wops always have their hands out when they see an American.

The schedule for the Agrippina group called for an early start to Paestum. Several of the students, making their way to the bathroom, later recalled hearing voices in Conradin's room. Monroe Thatcher's deep rumble. Then Conradin's tones, higher-pitched and angry. 'Dad, you kill me. I don't care. I won't do it. I won't.' Then Thatcher's voice, firm, its tone unyielding, but his words were indistinct. Then a wail from Conradin: 'I don't want to.'

Thatcher's voice. 'Grow up, Conradin! I can't make excuses for you forever.'

Whatever the problem was, it had blown over by breakfast time. Conradin appeared, a little bleary-eyed, but apparently in good spirits.

'Well, are we ready for a treat today?' asked Dr. Alex, with slightly forced cheerfulness as he joined the group for breakfast. DeWitt and Annie had not yet appeared. Dr. Alex was in charge.

'How is Annie this morning?' boomed Thatcher.

' Fine,' said Dr. Alex. 'She just didn't feel up to the long trip to Paestum today.'

'Is Mrs. Fordham sick?' asked Sister Stella, concerned.

'Just a little under the weather,' said Dr. Alex.

'If she needs some pills, I've got a small pharmacy in my room,' said Sally Harvey. 'I never travel without it.'

'We're pretty well equipped here,' replied Dr. Alex. 'Thanks anyway.' He raised his voice to public announcement level. 'It's a long trip to Paestum, group. So let's be on our way as fast as we can.'

'Yes,' roared Thatcher. 'Let's get on the bus as soon as we can. No delay!'

Fordham appeared, red-eyed, wearing clean Dockers. 'I'll be ready as soon as I grab a coffee and a *panino*,' he said.

'Is Annie O.K., DeWitt?' demanded Thatcher.

'Yes, how is poor Annie?' asked Millicent.

'She's fine,' said Fordham. 'She just wants to rest today.'

'Huh?' asked Thatcher.

'She's fine, Monnie.'

'Poor dear,' said Sister Stella. 'I thought her face was quite flushed last night.'

'She's had such a busy time of it,' said Millicent. 'She must be tired.'

The bus made a stop at the *Albergo Felice* to pick up Arthur DeSilva. He was waiting on the patio, sitting at a table and glumly picking his nose, when the Agrippina bus pulled up in front of the hotel. The bougainvillea was gorgeous, but DeSilva was impervious to its charm. He was in ill humour.

'Arturo,' Dr. Alex saluted him. 'Are you all ready for a great adventure?'

DeSilva managed a smile. He hustled on to the bus, acknowledging assorted greetings.

'I so enjoyed your lecture last night,' said Sister Stella.

'Thank you,' said DeSilva, managing a smile.

'Hypocrite,' thought Marcia. 'You slept through the last half of it.'

'How did you enjoy your night at the *Felice*?' asked Dr. Alex, as DeSilva settled himself into a seat.

'Not much, I must say,' said DeSilva.

'That's too bad.' said Dr. Alex , his voice resonant with simulated sympathy. 'What was the trouble?'

'I couldn't sleep. There was a helluva lot of noise in the hallway,' said DeSilva. 'I came down to complain to the fellow at the desk and he just shrugged. I was really pissed off. I gave him the Evil Eye. You know, two fingers.' De Silva chuckled as he remembered. 'You should have seen the look on his face. The service at breakfast was lousy, too. I asked for a fried egg and it came half-cooked.'

Luigi and Tony in starched white jackets appeared at the door of the *Albergo Felice*. Several of the students waved to them merrily. Luigi smiled gravely. Just a model waiter awaiting customers, Marcia thought. Tony followed DeSilva to the bus carrying

DeSilva's knapsack, which he had left in the hotel lobby, and gave it to the bus driver who passed it back to DeSilva. DeSilva muttered, 'Grazie'. Marcia shot a glance in the direction of Conradin. He was reading his *Lonely Planet* guide, and seemed to notice neither Luigi nor Tony.

'You know,' said DeSilva, 'that place has signs on its door saying it accepts Visa, MasterCard, American Express and Diner's Club, but in fact it won't accept any credit cards at all. What it wants is cash. Dollars or euros'

'There are too many bogus credit cards around,' said Dr. Alex.

'Yes, but then why have signs on your front doorway saying that you accept them?' demanded DeSilva, who was clearly aggrieved. 'And I absolutely couldn't eat that so-called fried egg they served me at breakfast. I should have sent it back to the kitchen.'

'That's too bad', said Dr. Alex. He picked up the microphone at the front of the bus and blew into it to test it.

'Group,' he said, in lecture mode, 'all ye disciples of Agrippina! This morning we head out through Pozzuoli, past the Phlegraean Fields, through Naples and then south past Sorrento and on to Salerno where we'll have a rest stop at a BP petrol station along the highway for those of you who want to visit a WC. Then on to Paestum for a late lunch. Those of you who have read my *Notes on the Monuments of the Naples Area* will recall something of the history of this area....'

'Et cetera, et cetera,' said Marcia to herself as she closed her eyes. 'It's time for a brief nap.'

'THEY'VE REPLANTED THE ROSES,' said Miriam, coming up to Marcia as they stood beside the rose garden in front of the so-called "Temple of Neptune", a smaller version of the Parthenon in Athens. Same date, possibly even earlier. Who knows? Dr. Alex had asked rhetorically. Perhaps this was the model for the celebrated Parthenon.

'Replanted them?' said Marcia.

'Yes. Paestum was famous for its roses in Roman times. Twice-blooming roses'

'Oh. I guess there is always an historical reason, isn't there? I thought the rose garden was intended simply to prettify the place.'

' "Prettify"', repeated Miriam. 'Interesting word. Do you use it in your novels?'

'Never,' said Marcia. 'In my novels I never prettify anything.'

'You know, I think Paul Kowalski likes you,' said Miriam, after a pause.

'He's an interesting person to talk to,' conceded Marcia.

'More than talking, I think.'

'Do you think so?'

'And Sister Stella, poor woman, likes Paul.'

'Sister Stella is a nun.'

'That's supposed to be a problem, isn't it? A complication which a novelist would appreciate, I should think.'

Marcia sought a change of subject. 'It's marvelous, isn't it, as Ellen Cross would say, to find so well-preserved a Greek temple here. Not just one temple. Three of them.'

Miriam was not to be diverted, however.

'There's something I'd like to talk to you about,' she said.

'Go ahead.'

'Not here,' said Miriam. 'I want some time to think about it. I'm not sure how to put it.'

'Something very private? The precinct of a temple is a good place to talk about it,' said Marcia, whose antennae were twitching with curiosity.

'Here comes Percy Bass,' said Miriam. 'It's nothing at all. Keep quiet about this, will you? I want to take a picture of this temple from the other side, if I can.' She moved off.

Damn the woman, thought Marcia, as Miriam parted from them. She had been avoiding Percy, and now he had cornered her, alone. Paul was nowhere to be seen.

'Have you had time to look at the chapter of my novel yet, Marcia?' asked Percy.

'Percy, I haven't had a moment of free time.'

'I gave it to you yesterday,' said Percy, reproachfully.

'We're kept so busy here, though.'

Percy was disappointed, and showed it.

'You have time for my roommate.'

'Paul? Where is he, incidentally? I want to see him before lunch.' And, as if by telepathy, Paul who was taking a picture of the Temple of Hera with his digital camera, looked across the rose garden at her, and caught her eye. He moved towards her.

'Percy,' said Marcia, 'I promise I'll read your chapter, but give me a little time. There's so many things to do. I have to write a letter to my house sitter who's looking after my house while I'm away. My cat is missing.'

'Your cat?' said Percy, dismissively.

'Yes, my cat,' repeated Marcia. 'My best friend. I'm revealing my private tragedy to you, Percy.'

'Oh?' said Percy. 'Your cat is more important than my manuscript?'

'I'll see you at lunch, Percy,' said Marcia, with steel in her voice. She walked off in Paul's direction, without bothering to notice the frown that passed over Percy's face. Nor did she notice Sister Stella watching her.

BUT SHE DID THINK of Percy again, as she sat on her bed that evening, balancing her IBM ThinkPad on her knees. Miriam had not reappeared. She had been distant at lunch, and when the group returned to the Palazzo Agrippina for a late dinner, she had taken a shower, dressed and gone down for a quick drink before the dinner bell sounded. After dinner she had joined a small group in the salon who were gathered around the piano, singing songs. Marcia had the bedroom to herself. Percy's manuscript lay beside her on the bed, but Marcia was in no mood to read it.

Instead she composed a careful e-mail to Emma Sanchez,

'Emma,

'Good to hear from you, but the news about Mikado is distressing. Please let me know as soon as he returns. I'm sure he will. Put out fresh food each morning and he will come eventually. Mikado does not like to go hungry.

"We went to Paestum today, a Greek site south of good old Napoli where there are three Greek temples. One dates from more than 600 B.C. Then we went to the beach—there's a splendid beach a short distance away—and there we had an accident with one of our group. Not serious, though. He's in the hospital now.

'I'll get back to you later. If the Mikado reappears, e-mail me. I'm worried. Otherwise, I hope everything is going well.'

I hope that's the right tone. Anxious but not accusatory. Emma was supposed to be a serious graduate student enrolled at the local university. But what about her friends who drop in for a drink? No doubt the Mikado had taken their measure and disapproved. Joshua would have some advice. He was used to her. Literary agents are a special type of person.

She began a second e-mail..

'Joshua, I am distressed.' Marcia wrote. 'The estimable Mikado, my cat, has decided to wander. There is not much that either you or I can do about it, and my house sitter is supposed to be competent. So I shall hope for the best and if you can advise, please do.

'Meanwhile, I am trying to imagine a plot for a story set in the Palazzo Agrippina, but must not let my imagination run on completely out of control. I can imagine someone being murdered in the Agrippina summer session, and Aristide Blanchard coming here to acquire a little culture and finding the murderer while he's here. Willoughby is a problem, however. Parrots don't travel well. Besides I need a motive for the murder. There must be evil lurking somewhere.

'But first, and most important, I've found an Internet Café where I can plug in my ThinkPad and send you an E-mail. I can receive e-mails too, by Hot Mail. So I'm dependent on snail mail no longer.

'The Internet Café belongs to a little hotel near the Palazzo Agrippina, called the *Albergo Felice*, which boasts a patio with tables and white tablecloths, and many strings of glass beads

screening its doorway. Some of our members have already discovered its bar. Two of our group, Walter Druker and Kwame
Assante visit it regularly, Walter to drink excessively and Kwame
to nurse a Campari Soda and then see Walter back safely to the
Palazzo. Kwame seems actually to enjoy Walter's company,
though he refers to him the "Black Man's Burden". Walter is certainly someone's burden, but in fact, he is an amusing soul. He
has been in the academic rat race a long time, and his career has
stalled a good many rungs from the top of the ladder, and he
doesn't care. He claims he never really understood the problem
of pure evil until he met the dean of the Arts faculty at Spearfish
State –I think that's the name of the place where he teaches.
Kwame is interested in Africanist interpretations of ancient history, but he has a mind of his own. He accepts no one else's opin-
ions without question. Interesting man.

'Paul Kowalski says that the Camorra is behind the *Albergo
Felice*. It's not my business, of course, but as a writer I should stick
my nose into everything, don't you think? The front men at the
Albergo are two waiters, or bell boys, or bartenders—whatever
you want—who wear starched white jackets. They are quite or-
namental. They no doubt have mommas who wash and starch
their jackets every day. The Italian male, says Madge Midgely,
enjoys an undeserved reputation as a great lover. The fact is that
he goes home to momma every day, and she cooks him gourmet
meals, makes his bed, washes his clothes and what's more, she
likes doing it. The other day, Percy Bass was groaning about it to
everyone in the Palazzo lounge, "Where did we American men
go wrong?" he wanted to know. Presumably he was trying to
be funny. Percy is our guitarist, and a would-be writer. I'm supposed to be reading a chapter of his novel at this very moment,
but I'm writing to you instead.

'Madge is on the editorial staff of a small daily newspaper,
and writes a syndicated column. She knows a lot about love, she
says, but I cannot believe that her obese body arouses much passion among the male sex Yet she has learned a lot, she says, because women write her to ask for advice. But I think her bag at
the moment is repressed memory. You know how it is. We've

been raped by our daddies or funny uncles at an early age but we can't remember a thing about it until our therapists reveal all. I think our group here at the Agrippina will be grist for her column.

'To return to the subject. The two waiters are Tony, who is slim and beautiful, and Luigi who is a burly specimen, with big muscles and a homely face. We endured a lecture last night by an itinerant guru named Arthur. DeSilva, and after it, I went into the back garden of the Palazzo for some fresh air and caught a glimpse of Luigi there. With him was Conradin, the son of the great muck-a-muck, our beloved president Monroe Thatcher. When they saw me, they slipped out the back gate. They may be no more than ten years between Luigi and Conradin, but they are separated, I think, by a whole world of experience.

'The lecture by the good Dr. DeSilva was a piece of wonderful nonsense. Some of our grammarians here took issue with his plural form of 'octopus', but he rose nobly above such trifling concerns. Or dived below them. Take your pick. He was utterly convinced of the importance of his findings, though I am not at all sure what they were. He tried to connect the octopus with a woman's vagina, but I found his knowledge both of females and of fish deficient. But he was a genial old fraud. Next day he joined us on our trip to Paestum, and that's where the accident happened.

'Paestum is a wonderful site. Among the Romans of old it was famous for its roses, and a rose garden has been replanted there. There are three ancient Greek temples, all well-preserved as Greek temples go. In the Middle Ages, when other classical buildings were being plundered, Paestum was protected by the malarial mosquito that bred in the swamps around here. The site was actually lost and had to be rediscovered in the modern period. The youngest of the temples dates to the same period as the Parthenon in Athens, and it is very similar, except that it is smaller, and the Italians would like to believe that it is earlier, and hence the model that the Parthenon copied. Not long ago, a Greek tomb dating to the early fifth century B.C. was found there, and it has the earliest classical Greek painting found anywhere. It shows a diver leaping into the sea, and so the tomb is called—you guessed it—the "Tomb of the Diver". The artist was no Caravaggio or Leonardo, but still he had wonderfully clean lines. The tomb has its own gallery in the Paestum museum, which is a jewel as museums go.

'The goddess Hera was much worshipped here. I always thought of Hera as the bitchy wife of Zeus, because that's how she comes across in Homer's *Iliad*. But here she was treated as a mother goddess. She was the great mother that women in the Mediterranean world worshipped, call her what name you will. You see little terracotta figurines which show her cradling a child on her knee and holding an apple in her hand. They were buried in the ground as offerings of some sort. Women praying for healthy children. Women carrying out their only purpose in life, to reproduce the species. That was before the pill. Thank Heaven for it!

'I was quite unprepared for the Greek art I saw here. Paestum was a Greek city before the Samnites took it over and outlawed the use of Greek except for on one day each year, the story goes. When the temples were built here, Paestum must have been a little island of Greek culture surrounded by barbarism. The barbarians weren't long in coming.

'Having explored the site and had lunch, we moved on to the beach, which is relatively clean. We found it more or less deserted, which is unusual in this part of the world. The Mediterranean Sea is not exactly pristine pure anywhere, and the determination of the northern Europeans to get skin cancer has littered whole shorelines with bare human flesh. But not at Paestum yet. It is a nice beach. We got into our bathing suits. Walter Druker' waistline overflows his bathing suit but he is not quite as unfit as I thought. Betty Laramie was a lissome sight. DeWitt Fordham wore a suit with "DEWITT'S END" printed in upper case letters across his butt. It was a present from last year's class.

'It was just as we were setting off for home that the accident happened.

'We had already boarded the bus when Dr. DeSilva put his hand in his knapsack to take out his water bottle and a scorpion bit him. It must have been lurking in there. It could have crawled inside at Paestum, if he took his knapsack down to the beach with him, though he says he left it behind, on the bus. Imagine the general consternation! Fordham and Baker may have doctorates, but they're clueless about medical emergencies. DeSilva himself took it well, after some initial howls and curses. Sister Stella was all full of concern. The bus had a first aid kit, but nothing for scorpions. But Sally Harvey dove into her knapsack, having checked it first for any unwelcome guests, and brought out some antihistamines and a needle with adrenalin. She administered them to DeSilva with much advice. The bus driver killed the scorpion before it could do more damage, and we set off for home.

'However by the time we reached Naples, DeSilva's arm was badly swollen and he was having some difficulty breathing. Sally thought we should get him to a doctor as soon as we could. So we dropped him off at the International Hospital. It seemed the best place where he could get medical care. He has an emergency health insurance policy, and DeSilva was anxious to have us call the insurance company to notify it of what had happened. The conditions of his policy insist that he must do this in any case where medical assistance is needed abroad. For that matter, so does mine. It warns me that I must give my insurance company twenty-four hours notice if I have an accident. But the hospital was more interested in his Visa credit card than his medical insurance.

'Anyway, things seem under control. Just a little excitement. Incidentally I did see Paul Kowalski in a bathing suit. Quite acceptable. He's lean and fit. Did I tell you he has a crooked nose? We ate lunch together at Paestum. At least I sat on one side of him, and on the other sat Bathsheba Bennett, and she never stopped talking.

'Not much else new. The afternoon sun can be quite brutal. Bathsheba, our old-timer, says it was not so hot once; so maybe Global Warming is catching up with the Mediterranean. A notice on the Palazzo Agrippina's bulletin board warns us to use sun block. There's also a post card from a last year's alumnus saying how much he had enjoyed his Palazzo Agrippina session, and a handwritten notice that a fine leather belt with a silver buckle had gone missing and would finder please notify Decimus Monroe Thatcher. That's a funny thing to lose. Walter Druker supplied us with a number of scenarios which would account for Decimus' loss, all of them slightly obscene.

Well, that's my life story up to the present, Joshua. E-mail if you have any news. MarciaMellon@hotmail.com.

'Yours most faithfully. Marcia.'

Marcia closed her ThinkPad and yawned. Time to read a few pages of Percy Bass's novel. She could not keep putting him off forever. What sort of novel would an admirer of Bulwer Lytton write? Marcia pulled the manuscript of the first chapter out of its folder and read:

'It was a dark and stormy night when Algernon Bulwer shoved open the front door of the mansion on Sussex Street and encountered Sidney, hanging by his belt from the chandelier in the front hallway. Sidney's face was black. He had not died easily.

'Sidney was never a considerate man, thought Algernon.'

Marcia put the manuscript back into its folder. It could wait until tomorrow.

XIV

MARCIA DECLINED an invitation next evening from Miriam to join a cluster of her fellow students who were setting off to the *Albergo Felice* for a drink before going to bed. She had seen Paul return from a jog, and now, unless her timing was out of kilter, he would have taken a shower and be on his way back to his room in his dressing gown and slippers. She intercepted him in the upper hall.

'Miriam's gone to the *Felice* for a drink. I have a room to myself for three-quarters of an hour.'

'Oh,' said Paul.

'Come on in.'

'Into your room?'

'Where else?'

Marcia closed the door behind him.

'Paul,' she said, 'I'm a lady who is approaching menopause, and I'm eager, but I won't beg. Are you man enough for me?'

Paul sat down on the bed. He looked stunned.

'Lie back,' said Marcia. 'You know, you're a nice specimen. You've got a great body as Latin teachers go. I haven't seen any other male Latin teachers with their clothes off, but I'm sure you stack up with the best.'

'But Marcia --'

'We haven't got a lot of time. I don't know when Miriam will be back.'

'Marcia---'

'Come along, Paolo.'

'Marcia,' said Paul. 'There's a problem.'

'What's the matter?'

'It's hard to explain.'

'Don't tell me you're gay?'

'No, not that,' exploded Paul, blushing furiously.

'You're HIV positive?'

'No.'

'You can't be a virgin. You've been married. Is there a mother with high moral standards in your background?'

'Have you ever heard of erectile difficulties?' said Paul, in barely more than a whisper.

'Oh, that,' said Marcia. 'Yes, that's a downer.'

'I'm taking gingko biloba pills,' said Paul, 'but they take quite a while to work. I have to be patient.'

'Patient!' exclaimed Marcia. 'You want to be patient? In half an hour Miriam Kuntz will be back and if she sees a man with a limp prick in our bedroom, she'll have to rewrite her whole book! She'll never get tenure!'

'I can't help it.'

'Yes, you can. Have some mercy on the poor slob. Look, Miriam's whole book is based on the premise that billions of women are raped every year, and if she sees a husky young male with a limp prick, what will she think? Here.' Marcia dived into her purse and produced a small package of Viagra. 'Take a couple.'

'Don't you have to take them an hour in advance?'

'What do you mean?'

'Well, before they work. It's not always like it is in TV commercials.'

'We do what we have to, Paul. It's a tough world out there.' She picked up a bottle of Evian water from the table beside Miriam's bed. 'Here. Wash the pills down with this. We'll combine French mineral water with American know-how and we'll beat your problem.'

'Will I get headache?'

'What? At a time like this? Who cares? Lean back and think

sex. Let me pull off your underpants. There. You know, your shorts are far too tight. Your gonads have to be able to breath if you want them to operate properly. Let me massage the poor things a bit. They were terribly crowded there in your underpants.'

Paul relaxed.

'You know,' said Marcia, 'you're a well-hung young man. Did your ex-wife ever tell you that?'

'No.'

'Well, there you are. Ah, good. Now relax. I'll massage your balls a little. Ah, very nice! Very nice, indeed!'

'But we teach zero tolerance at our school,' said Paul, tense again as he remembered suddenly. 'I am to ask you if you consent before I penetrate. I've got to remember that no means no.'

'Damn right' said Marcia, 'and yes means yes. Now hold that little bugger of yours steady, will you?'

With a sigh, she mounted him.

XV

'I**T STRIKES** me as very odd that a scorpion should be in Dr. DeSilva's knapsack,' Marcia said to Paul as they entered the gate to the *Scavi* at Herculaneum. Pompeii, Herculaneum, Oplontis and Stabiae had all been buried by the same eruption of Mt. Vesuvius of 79 C.E., and Pompeii was the most celebrated of them, but Herculaneum was the earliest to be excavated. Digging began there while the Bourbon kings were still ruling from their rose-coloured palace overlooking the Bay of Naples. The digging was difficult. Herculaneum had been buried in forty to sixty feet of lava and mud, and it had to be removed with pickaxes and pneumatic drills. But what the archaeologists found was a well-to-do Roman community where life had stopped one summer day in the year 79, and where the shoreline used to be before a stream of hot mud pushed it forward into the Bay of Naples, they found a cache of human skeletons: residents of Herculaneum who had lined the beach waiting for rescue boats that never came.

'I suppose a scorpion could have crawled into the knapsack if he left it open on the beach,' Paul replied.

'But the knapsack was on the bus. So DeSilva says.'

'Well, it was one of those things,' said Paul. 'Things happen.'

On the way to Herculaneum, the bus had made an unscheduled stop at the International Hospital to check on DeSilva. He had spent an uncomfortable night, but there was no cause for concern. What troubled the hospital more was a fax from

DeSilva's medical insurance company, instructing it to undertake no medical procedure without first telephoning a one-eight hundred number in the United States. The hospital front office had tried telephoning without success. Could the Agrippina staff try to make contact? There seemed to be no danger in a little delay. The doctor in charge shrugged.

'Remember what Aristide Blanchard always says in the much-acclaimed detective novels of Marcia Mellon' added Paul. *'Stick to the significant evidence. The rest doesn't matter.* You must take your creation's advice.'

'Aristide has a limited imagination,' said Marcia.

'You've got too much imagination,' Paul replied, 'but I guess that's what a writer needs. Yet in Dr. DeSilva's case, we have a motive of sorts for an attempt on his life. Someone in our group took offense at DeSilva's lecture. He struck back. Or she. Remember that all the great poisoners were women.'

'But a scorpion is a defective murder weapon,' said Marcia. 'Death isn't at all certain. A viper would be better. I dispatched a man with a viper once—in a novel, I mean.'

'I remember that one. The murderer was the snake fancier's teenage daughter who wanted revenge on a man who raped her and then claimed mutual consent. Aristide was quite brilliant, I thought. The girl took a viper belonging to her herpetologist papa's collection, and put it in the rapist's mattress. It bit his left buttock as he lay in his bed, probably contemplating another rape. The court decided that girl was justified in doing what she did'

'You've oversimplified the plot. That was my first mystery where DNA analysis played a role. But in DeSilva's case, there's the question of availability, too. How available are scorpions in Pozzuoli, would you say?' said Marcia.

'Well, one was available, and only one was needed.'

'Except that one hasn't killed him. He's still quite alive.'

'Shall we return to reality?' asked Paul. 'Let's listen to what *il duce,* our Dr. DeWitt Fordham, has to say, and improve our minds.'

The group had descended the path into the excavation area,

and entered the great *Casa dei Cervi,* the 'House of the Deer', so-called from a group of stag figurines found on its front patio. It must once have been a splendid summer house for a Roman noble. Or perhaps its owner was a *nouveau riche,* a freedman who had made his money in trade, and had more wealth than taste. In one of the rooms there was a fountain showing a pudgy Hercules urinating, the sort of *objet d'art* that might appeal to an owner who had struck it rich. Fordham paused in the front patio, and assumed the pose of a cicerone about to burst into informative discourse.

'Now, DeWitt,' said Thatcher, as Fordham opened his mouth to speak, 'would this terrace have overlooked the bay before the eruption took place?'

'Probably. Originally the ground must have dropped off sharply just beyond this house. Herculaneum was buried over a hundred feet deep.' DeWitt took a breath and started once more to speak in public lecture mode. 'The houses found at Herculaneum are generally more opulent and deluxe that what we find at Pompeii....'

'What a great view this place must have had before the eruption,' boomed Thatcher. 'And look at the view it has now! We haven't improved things much in the modern world, have we? The view is blocked by ugly modern buildings!'

'You will notice one thing about the streets in this place,' Fordham continued. 'No wheel ruts in the paving stones. In Pompeii you will see deep ruts cut into the paving. That means, I think that there was never a lot of wheeled traffic on the streets of Herculaneum and consequently, not a lot of commercial activity. The residents must have been upper class Romans, though we will find here an apartment building built cheaply of wood and rubble and typical of the tenements that burned so well in Rome in the Great Fire which destroyed much of the city in the emperor Nero's reign.'

'Was that when Nero fiddled while Rome burned?' asked Sol Bernstein.'

'Well, he might have fiddled if the fiddle had been invented then,' said Fordham. 'But it wasn't. Now, if you will just stick together a while longer,' he went on, as he noticed a small group led by Miriam Kuntz gravitating towards the statue of the urinating Hercules, 'I'll take you through the highlights of this site, and then you can have some free time to look about by yourselves.'

'DeWitt,' said Thatcher, looking down from the terrace where the "House of the Deer" stood, 'if the sea came up this far before the eruption, was it around here where they found a lot of bones?'

'Yes, the remains of some residents trying to get away by boat, who never –'

'Conradin!' Thatcher summoned. Conradin had joined Yo-yo Kim and Piers at the edge of the terrace, Yo-yo with his camera aimed at the view below, and Piers talking to Betty Laramie. Millicent was looking distressed. 'Don't wander off, Conradin. Listen to what DeWitt has to say.'

'Dr. Fordham,' asked Ellen Cross, 'how did they heat these houses? Isn't it ever cold here in the winter?'

DeWitt nodded. 'Quite cold and wet, sometimes.'

'So where is the furnace? Of course, I guess they didn't have natural gas back then. How did people keep warm?'

'Charcoal heaters. In the Pompeii museum, you will see a little charcoal stove. But warm temperatures indoors in winter time is a modern expectation.'

'You know,' said Ellen, adjusting her wide-brimmed hat over her blonde mane, 'these houses have lots of room for guests to stand around at cocktail parties, but where did they go when they had to pee? And where is the kitchen?'

'Ellen cannot be a suspect,' Marcia said *sotto voce* to Paul.

'Suspect?'

'A suspect as DeSilva's assailant, the malefactor who planted the scorpion.'

'Why not? She would be as likely as Sally Harvey, or Shirley Perovich, or Shirley's roommate, the lovely Betty Laramie.'

'She cannot have a motive. She could never be a crusader against academic nonsense, for she could never recognize it. Once you eliminate the academic nonsense motive, what do we have left?'

'I don't know. I thought her point about no place to pee was a good one,' said Paul. 'Check out any book on Roman domestic architecture and you'll find it says almost nothing about toilets. Public latrines, yes, lots of them. But what is there on your humble WC? Ellen is on to something. What's more, if you eliminate academic nonsense, you will empty our library shelves.'

'Don't be bitter,' said Marcia.

'You're quite a dame,' said Paul. "Are you sure you are menopausal?'

'Too sure, I regret to say. Menopausal and overweight, complete with hot flashes. I can't look at Betty Laramie without feeling jealous. It's a real bitch.'

'Betty *is* looking fetching this morning,' said Paul, reflectively.

'Hush, our leader speaketh,' quoth Marcia. 'We're here to improve our minds.'

The group had arrived at a *thermopolium*, an open bar which sold stews and soups. It was a Roman fast-food outlet. But there was nowhere for customers to sit down and eat. Ellen Cross noted it immediately.

'Was it only for take-out?' she demanded.

It seems, Fordham explained, that the government was suspicious of taverns where people could gather to eat and drink and chat with one another. Talk could lead to sedition, and taverns were potential nests of revolution. *Thermopolia* were safer, and a hungry Roman could fill his belly at one of them just as well as at a tavern.

'The emperors must have been nervous,' remarked Bathsheba. 'Uneasy is the head that wears the crown. Isn't that a saying from somewhere?'

'They had reason to be nervous,' said Sol Bernstein. 'Of course, our leaders can get assassinated, too. Look at Yitzak Rabin in Israel.'

'Or JFK in Dallas,' added Sally Harvey.

'One moment, they're there, in charge,' said Sol. 'Next moment, some punk fires a gun and they're gone and can't be replaced. Of course, that didn't stop people from wanting to be emperors, did it?'

'Dr. Alex,' said Piers.

Alex Baker, who had been progressing with a measured pace in the rear of the group, had caught up with Ellsworth and Kim.

'Yes, Piers?'

'We were just talking, Yo-yo and me. We were wondering why you decided to become a professor. After all, you're a pretty cool guy, aren't you? You could have made a living doing something else.'

'Well,' replied Dr. Alex, with obvious patience, 'when I was your age, I thought I'd be a doctor. But I didn't like sticking needles into people and I did like classical studies. So one thing led to another.'

'But professor aren't paid all that much, are they? In my college, I know there are some instructors and assistant professors who get less pay than the cleaning staff.'

'We're underpaid, all right,' replied Dr. Alex, sagely. 'Overworked and underpaid.'

'But then, my dad says that professors are all liberals; so what can you expect? My dad hates liberals,' Piers went on. 'Me, I'm going to be a lawyer, like my dad.'

'Good for you.'

'I want to make a change for good with my life,' said Piers. 'I'm going to get into class action lawsuits. That's where the big bucks are, my dad says.'

'Oh?'

'It would really give me satisfaction to help some guy who's been screwed by his priest or his teacher when he was a boy, and now he can't get closure because no one will pay him any money. An altar boy should be fucking safe with a priest, I say. If he's not, the priest should –uh—damn well pay, or his church or whatever has the money to pay. So he can get closure.'

'Closure? What do you mean by that?'

'Well, that's when you make someone pay up for the mental damage he has done you,' said Piers. 'Then you feel better and you close the case. That's closure. If you don't make someone pay, then you never get it, and you can't get on with your life, like. Your inner self or whatever stays damaged. It's like—uh, a psychological thing.'

'Like wergild?'

'Like what?'

'Wergild. It was a price the family of a manslayer paid the family of his victim as atonement. In Anglo-Saxon law.'

'But that would be a sort of private thing, wouldn't it? How would lawyers come in?'

'Ah,' said Dr. Alex. 'Good point. A contingency lawyer needs a big payout or the case isn't worthwhile.'

'That's what my dad says. My dad isn't my father,—I'm the sole product of my mom's starter marriage, as she calls it, but my dad is her second husband and he always treated me like a dad. Mom's on her third husband now, though. I'm stashed here with you until they get through their honeymoon'

'Dr. Alex,' said Kim, interrupting. 'What are those?' They had reached a house with a colonnaded courtyard and in the interstices, between columns that had once been painted red, hung round discs with relief sculptures on them. They spun slowly in the light breeze.

'What?' asked Dr. Alex, looking blank.

'Those round things, like plates,' said Kim, pointing.

'Those frisbees—like—those fuckin' discs dangling down between the columns of that courtyard,' said Piers, pointing to the house with red columns. 'In that peristyle. Isn't that what you call it, a peristyle?'

'A peristyle. You're right.'

'Hey, I remembered!'

'Those are dangling discs, Piers,' said Dr. Alex, with patience.

'I know they're diskettes. But don't they have a name?'

'They're called oscilla, Piers.'

'Oscilla,' Piers repeated. 'Why are they called oscilla?'

'Because they oscillate.'

'I know that,' said Piers. 'But what do they oscillate for? Like, do they scare off the fuckin' mosquitoes that carry malaria?'

'No.'

'Are they magic? What about the Evil Eye? Do they scare it away?'

Dr. Alex snorted. 'They're just decoration, Piers. They have relief sculptures of satyrs on them.'

'The Evil Eye is a serious business here, isn't it?' said Piers.

'Isn't it everywhere, if you put stock in that sort of thing?'

'Yeah, everywhere, like, but particularly here, isn't it?'

'Why do you say that?'

'I learned it from Luigi. Luigi doesn't talk much but he knows a little English. You know Luigi? The bouncer at the *Albergo Felice*.'

'Luigi? The bartender, you mean? Why do you call him the bouncer?'

'Because he does whatever bouncing is necessary with some help from Tony. Me and Yo-yo were talking to them. Luigi is one awesome guy. He can hoist me above his head and hold me there with one arm.'

'You seem to be settling in to the local social life.'

Piers laughed. 'Don't worry about me and Yo-yo,' he said. 'We make out.'

The group moved on, past the entrance to the gymnasium and then along the edge of the Herculaneum forum, most of it unexcavated. Fordham stopped to point out an inscription honouring the *Augustales*, a club of ex-slaves who had climbed the social ladder. 'They were the Rotarians of Herculaneum,' said Fordham.

'A service club, you mean?' said Ellen Cross.

'Sort of, organized under the emperor's patronage,' said Fordham.

'My husband's a Rotarian,' said Ellen. 'I must get a picture of this,' and she pointed her camera at the inscription while the rest of the group moved on. They turned a corner, and continued down a street which Fordham identified as the *decumanus maximus*. He stopped in front of a doorway.

'This is the House of the Bicentenary,' he said, 'so called because it was excavated in 1938, exactly two hundred years after archaeologists began digging here at Herculaneum, before Italy was united. It was a rich house, and there was a nice mosaic in the dining room. The family that lived here had a decent income.

But what was most interesting is what was found in a room on the second storey.'

The students climbed the staircase, two or three at a time, into a small upper room, where something had been wrenched from the wall, leaving a cross-shaped hole in the plaster, and beneath it was a battered *prie-dieu.*

'Now what do we make of that?' demanded Monnie Thatcher. 'It looks like a cross once hung her on the wall.'

'This is our only evidence of Christianity in Herculaneum,' said Fordham. 'Whatever it was that was on this wall, it left a cross-shaped hole when it was wrenched off. So it might have been a cross or a crucifix. Possibly as disaster hovered over Herculaneum, a Christian tore his crucifix from this wall to take with him as he tried to escape.'

'But did Christians use the crucifix as early as 79 C.E.?' asked Sol Bernstein.

'That's a problem,' Fordham admitted. 'I don't know. We can't be sure they did. This is the earliest evidence we have for the use of the crucifix, and all it is, is a cross-shaped hole in the plaster of the wall.'

'So it could have been something else.'

'It could have been,' agreed Fordham. 'Still, the cross-shaped mark is suggestive.'

Sol nodded. Sister Stella crossed herself.

'The date of this cross would probably be later than the first persecution of the Christians by the emperor Nero,' observed Thatcher, wisely. 'So there could have been a little cell of Christians here. Maybe a few slaves.'

DeWitt Fordham raised an arm to attract attention.

'All right,' he said, ' take three-quarters of an hour free time to look around on your own, and take pictures if you wish.'

'Not a moment too soon,' muttered Madge Midgeley. 'I've got to get off my feet.'

'Here's a chair,' said Conradin, turning up with a dusty resin chair that had seen better days. 'Sit on it carefully to make sure it doesn't collapse. It's not made for XXL persons.'

'Thank you, Conradin,' said Madge, subsiding gingerly on to

the chair which did not collapse. 'I can't help my extra weight. It's genetic—my FTO gene.'

'Well, if God had meant you to walk, He'd have made you half a ton lighter,' said Conradin.

'Humpf,' said Madge.

'The Villa of the Papyri which was the model for the Getty Museum. Whereabouts is it?' demanded Thatcher. 'Isn't it here at Herculaneum?'

'You can't see it, Monnie,' DeWitt replied. 'It was excavated by tunneling and the tunnels filled with noxious gases. We are standing under a volcano, remember.'

' Well, I hope it doesn't blow up again soon and fill in all these excavations,' said Thatcher.

A stray cat sitting on a crumbling rubble wall surveyed Thatcher with grave suspicion. Marcia thought of Mikado, still lost.

XVI

D R. ALEX's public lecture was very different from DeSilva's. It was solid in substance and Victorian in style. The group gathered in the lounge and DeWitt Fordham manned the Kodak Carousel at the back of the room. A battered lectern emerged from a storage closet. Monroe Thatcher and Millicent arranged themselves somewhat uncomfortably on a settee at the front of the room where Thatcher's considerable bulk blocked the joint view of Shirley Perovich and Betty Laramie. Madge Midgely, who had abandoned her notebook for a pocket tape recorder, positioned herself where she had a clear sight line. Conradin entered just as Fordham was clearing his throat, prior to making the introduction, and joined Monroe and Millicent.

'Yo, parental units,' he said. 'This is like church. You get the best seats at the front if you come in late'

'Sit down, Conradin,' replied Thatcher. 'De Witt wants to speak.'

Fordham cleared his throat a second time, and began,

'As you know, this area is famed for many things,' he began, 'but not least for its associations with Vergil, who wrote the great national epic of the Roman Empire, the *Aeneid*. We are fortunate to have a world authority on Vergil here at the Palazzo Agrippina, Alex Baker. Alex comes from Canada, from a place up there called Ancaster University. But we won't hold that against him. He has a good Harvard PhD, and he is a veteran of our

Palazzo Agrippina program. He needs no introduction. You all know him already. Alex, the floor is yours.'

Dr. Alex approached the lectern with ponderous dignity and there was an expectant hush. He cleared his throat and began to speak. This area is full of associations with Vergil, he asserted. Epicureanism was a dynamic presence at Naples two thousand years ago. Vergil himself had studied the philosophy of Epicurus here. Dr. Alex reminded the group that in the Villa of the Papyri at Herculaneum there was found a badly charred library that must have belonged to an Epicurean devotee. Two or three students nodded wisely. Vergil has been a rather feminine youth and had the nickname 'Parthenius', which could be connected with the Greek word for virgin, *parthenos*. Dr. Alex cleared his throat again, gently.

'Vergil was gay, don't you think?' whispered Marcia to Paul, whose leg was pressing hard against hers.

'So?' Paul whispered back. 'It's an occupational hazard with poets.'

Dr. Alex went on to remind the students that the name of the street in Naples which ran along the waterfront was the 'Via Parthenope', named after one of the Sirens that had tried to lure Odysseus' ship on to the rocks. Odysseus' little ship had rowed past the Sirens on the Sorrento peninsula, paying them no attention, for Odysseus had plugged the ears of his sailors with wax. The Sirens, unable to bear the insult of being ignored, had hurled themselves into the sea and drowned. Parthenope's body was washed up where the Via Parthenope is now. Gregory Donahue cleared his throat loudly, and looked around the room. Dr. Alex then described the turmoil in Italy after Julius Caesar's assassins were defeated on the plains of Philippi. Mark Antony took over the eastern half of the empire and went off to squander his future prospects in the arms of Cleopatra of Egypt. Another throat clearing, this time from Kwame Assante. Octavian, whom Julius Caesar had made his adoptive son in his will, had the tough job of settling demobilized soldiers in Italy and suppressing a revolt in southern Italy and Sicily, led by Sextus Pompey, Pompey's surviving son. The students remembered Pompey, didn't they

Julius Caesar's dynamic rival whom he defeated on the plain of Pharsalia in central Greece?

Octavian's dynamic general, Agrippa, had made the region around Cumae his military base, and the great tunnel under Monte Grillo that connected Cumae with Lake Avernus was the work of his military engineer, the dynamic Cocceius. The tunnel was mined in World War II, Dr. Alex explained, and the danger from unexploded land mines was still too great for the Palazzo Agrippina's students explore it. So don't try.

Octavian, with the help of his dynamic general, Marcus Agrippa, made himself master of the Roman Empire. The senate gave him the surname 'Augustus' and Augustus founded the Julio-Claudian house to which 'our namesake', the unfortunate Agrippina the Younger, belonged. 'And so,' said Dr. Alex, 'through Agrippina, who tried so hard and so unsuccessfully to be a good mother to the emperor Nero, we have a direct connection with the majesty of Rome.'

He continued. Augustus wanted an epic poem written on himself which would celebrate his victory over Cleopatra of Egypt, and Mark Antony, and some poets did oblige with much forgettable verse. Vergil chose instead to write on Aeneas, the Trojan warrior—and thus an oriental—who escaped the fall the Troy and whom the family of Julius Caesar claimed as its ancestor. The result was the *Aeneid*, still unfinished when Vergil died, and Vergil wanted it destroyed, but Augustus refused.

The *Aeneid* made Vergil's reputation for all time. Dr. Alex said the words slowly, with weight, and paused for a sip of water to give them time to sink in. Madge Midgely flipped the tape in her tape recorder. Thatcher stirred restlessly. The lecture continued. Vergil in the Middle Ages was considered a wizard. Did the students remember seeing the *Castel dell'Ovo*--'Egg Castle'— on the Naples waterfront? A twelfth-century castle now transformed into a convention center? Where Conradin, the last of the Hohenstaufen royal house, was imprisoned and beheaded? A few students vocalized assent. Legend had it that as the castle was being built, the walls kept collapsing, and the master masons were at a loss what to do. But Vergil in the Middle Ages had a great reputation as a magician, and he was called in and built castle with an egg as its foundation. The castle walls remain solid to this day. 'But the legend goes on to say', said Dr. Alex, 'that if the egg ever breaks, the castle will fall and if the castle falls, the world will fall.'

'Humpf,' sniffed Gregory Donahue, audibly.

'An egg?' said Madge Midgely. 'How could he build a castle on an egg?'

'Ours is not to reason why,' replied Dr. Alex. 'Wizards can perform feats that we can't,' and he continued his lecture.

Aeneas became the paradigm of the dynamic Roman hero who puts personal feelings behind him in the pursuit of duty. He was the stalwart, dynamic soldier-type that builds empires. Duty to the state is everything. A decade and a half after the World War II, Dr. Alex continued, Robert Graves, author of *I, Claudius*, wrote an article for the *Virginia Quarterly Review* where he spelled out how much he despised Vergil's *Aeneid* and his pious hero, Aeneas, who had been thrust down his throat at school. Tsarist Russia and the Germany of Kaiser Wilhelm had encouraged the reading of the *Aeneid* in schools, and a generation of dynamic youths, their schooldays only a few years behind them, had marched into battle and died, following Vergil's precepts, or so they thought. But with the Vietnam war, scholars began to look again at the *Aeneid* and discovered an undertone of sympathy for the defeated. War for Vergil entailed tragedy, both for the winners who sacrifice too much and for the losers, who perish. The defeated characters in the *Aeneid*, such as Dido, the oriental Carthaginian queen, and the Italian native, Turnus who led the brave resistance of the aboriginal folk against the Trojan invaders, all trigger the reader's reserves of pity and fear.

'Poor Dido, whom Aeneas deserted, was the model for Madama Butterfly in Puccini's great opera,' pronounced Dr. Alex, caught up in the full flood of his eloquence. 'He admired Henry Purcell's *Dido and Aeneas* and he modelled poor, deserted Butterfly on Dido, who also was left bereft, and probably pregnant, by Aeneas, and killed herself. Aeneas represented the thrusting, dynamic force of imperial Rome, whereas Dido was the girl he left behind. His victim.' He paused a moment to allow his sagacity to penetrate the intellects of his listeners. 'Now,' he said, 'a few slides of Vergil's Italy.'

De Witt Fordham turned on the Kodak Carousel.

'Now we'll look at our first slide,' said Dr. Alex.

The first slide showed a view of the Sibyl's cave.

'Well, you can recognize that as the Sibyl's cave at Cumae,' said Dr. Alex. 'Where Aeneas made his first landfall in Italy. But let's move on to the second slide, which is more important for my lecture.'

Mario came to the door of the lounge and gestured to Fordham, who excused himself and slipped out. He returned a minute later. Mario had brought news. Arthur DeSilva was dead. Out of respect for the dead, it seemed best to suspend the lecture. Fordham seemed not displeased. Alex Baker looked annoyed. Marcia turned to Paul.

'So we've got a corpse,' she said. 'This must be murder.'

Conradin leaned over to his mother. 'That's two downers too many tonight,' he said. 'I'm going to bed.'

'I died in Egg Castle, it seems,' he said to Paul, as he squeezed past him and out of the lounge.

LUIGI AND TONY WERE *surprised when I told them that Arthur DeSilva was dead. Not particularly sorry, but surprised. They didn't like Arturo. He gave them the Evil Eye. You shouldn't do that, said Tony. He didn't like his breakfast, either. The police will come to check out the Albergo, said Luigi. But we had nothing to do with Dr. DeSilva's death.*

Then I asked Tony what FAFI meant, the word I found scratched neatly on the extra tape I found in my knapsack. He shook his head, and talked very quickly to Luigi in Italian. I couldn't follow it at all. Then Luigi said in reasonably good English,

'This tape, where is it?'

'In my room,'

'You've used it? In your photo machine.'

'Camcorder,' corrected Tony.

'No. I haven't tried It's not mine.'

'Good.' Luigi smiled and put his arm over my shoulder. 'Where is it now?'

'Where do you keep your tapes?' Tony explained.

'It's in my bedroom at the Palazzo.'

Luigi and Tony broke into Italian again. Then Tony said to me,

'Connie, I like you. I don't want you to get into trouble. The police will be suspicious about Arturo DeSilva's death. We can look after that tape for you.'

'Why?' Perchè, I said. Tony and Luigi usually laugh when I try to speak Italian, but this time, they didn't.

'We do lots of things here, Connie. We help poor people who want to get into Italy. It doesn't pay much, but we want to help. If guys want pretty pictures, we can help. We know photographers. If someone wants something done, Luigi's got big muscles. We do a lot of things.'

'You know FAFI?'

Tony hesitated. Luigi still had a heavy arm over my shoulder and I could feel the muscles tighten. He laughed.

'I go with you,' he said.

We took the path that led from the Albergo Felice to the gate into the Palazzo Agrippina back garden. On the way, Luigi took me by the elbow and shoved me to one side of the path.

'Scorpione' he said, and there was one: a big scorpion on the path. I almost stepped on it.

We slipped in the back door of the Palazzo. No one saw us, I think. I let Luigi into my bedroom while I went off to the WC to piss, for my bladder which wasn't going to wait any longer. When I came back, there was Luigi, nearly naked. He had taken off everything but his underpants. He crooked one arm behind his head so that the biceps bulged, and when he saw me staring at it, a glint came into his eyes.

'You like?' he said, gesturing towards his balls which bulged beneath his underpants.

'No, Luigi.' Luigi was a gorilla, and there is nothing beautiful about a gorilla..

'You no like?'

'Not here, Luigi. Not now.' I didn't know what to say.

'You like Tony.'

'Not tonight.' I was frightened. Luigi was a powerful man.

Luigi grinned. But I don't think he was pleased. Then, slowly, he put on his pants first, and then his shirt, and let it hang out over his belt..

'Some other time,' he said. 'Where's the tape?'

I found it and gave it to him, as Luigi slipped into his clothes. Then I opened the bedroom door and looked up and down the hallway. It looked clear. Luigi slipped out behind me and I saw him out the back door. He gave me a pat on my bum and disappeared into the night.

XVII

WO ELEGANT Italian *agenti di pubblica sicurezza* arrived in a Fiat at the Palazzo Agrippina the next morning at breakfast time. The older of the two had an ample waistline and wore white gloves, and the lean young man who was his assistant was armed with a notebook. They retired into the library with DeWitt Fordham and Monroe Thatcher, and closed the door. The rest of the group ate breakfast with no great appetite. Annie Fordham seemed close to tears, but she carried on a conversation gamely with Mildred Donahue at the far end of the table. Mildred's mind was not on Arthur DeSilva's death. Something had put her in a good mood. She seemed elated.

'I'm Decimus Monroe Thatcher,' said Thatcher loudly, offering his hand to be shaken by the older of the policeman as soon as the door was closed. 'I am the president of the Julio-Claudian Society which runs the programme here in the Palazzo Agrippina.'

'*Buon giorno,*' said the policeman, taking the proffered hand in his own white-gloved one, and dropping it almost immediately.

'This man DeSilva really had nothing to do with us,' said Thatcher. 'He just arrived here, and offered us a lecture. He wasn't part of our group at all.'

But the policemen had only minimal English and Thatcher knew only five or six words of Italian, including '*si*' and '*non*'. Thatcher tried again, speaking slowly and very distinctly,

'Not one of ours,' he said. 'Not a member of the Palazzo

Agrippina group! He came from outside.' He waved a hand towards the window. 'From outside!' he repeated.

The older policeman smiled with dawning comprehension.

'From Oosa?' he asked.

'What?' demanded Thatcher. The younger policeman stood
with his ballpoint pen poised over his notebook. DeWitt broke
in.

'He means the U.S.A., Monnie,' he said and then turned to the
policemen and broke into fluent Italian. They looked relieved.

'Tell them, DeWitt,' said Thatcher, 'that this man DeSilva did
not belong to our group. I can't make them understand me.'

'I will, Monnie. I think they already know it.'

DeSilva's scorpion sting had been painful but he appeared to
be in no danger. Then the nurse had come to check his tempera-
ture and pulse at seven o'clock in the evening, and found him
dead. It was a case of heart failure, the doctor thought, triggered
by an allergic reaction to his medication. The policemen were
fatalistic. Death was a universal evil. When a sick man. enters a
hospital, he will either get better, or he won't. That's what happens in hospitals. But there were forms that had to be filled out.
A report had to be filed—no one could be allowed to die without
one—and there were a few questions the police wanted to ask.
Would the *dottore* mind?

What information did Fordham have about the *dottore*
DeSilva? Very little, it turned out.

'He was not registered with us as a student,' Fordham explained in Italian. 'So I don't have any record of his next of kin.
He mentioned a son, so I suppose there must be a wife, present
or previous.'

The older policeman nodded, gesturing with elegant white-
gloved hands to indicate that he understood. He was world-
weary and overweight. Fordham asked him if he would like an
espresso.

'*Grazie tanto,*' he replied. Yes, his partner would have one too.
Fordham put his head out the door to transmit the order to his
wife.

'Why was he here in Palazzo Agrippina?'

'He gave us a lecture.'

'Ah! A professor.'

'Well, no,' said DeWitt. 'He was a private researcher. He was pursuing his interest in octopods and what they meant in history.'

The officer was incredulous. '*Piovre*?' he asked.

'*Si, commendatore.*'

'Fish?'

'Well, ' DeWitt explained, '*Dottore* De Silva was working on the symbolism of octopods and its meaning for the mindset of ancient Rome. Something like that. He wasn't staying here at the Palazzo, of course, but he offered us a lecture on the subject of his research, and we took him up on his offer. That's his connection with the Palazzo.'

'Ah. I understand. You study fish here.'

'No, we are interested in the history and archaeology of ancient Greece and Rome. But many Greeks and Romans took an interest in fish, and what octopods meant for the culture of the ancient world. So obviously we wanted to hear what DeSilva had to say. He had interesting things to say about the symbolism of fish in everyday life. Like octopods and how they symbolized mothers.'

'Ah,' said the officer as if he understood, which clearly he did not. 'So Dr. DeSilva was explaining how the ancient Romans ate fish and how the fish was a mother.'

'The octopus. It was a mother symbol, you see.'

'*Si*,' said the older officer. The younger officer solemnly wrote something in his notebook. The older officer continued, 'And so this researcher DeSilva joined you on a trip to Paestum to look at fish?'

'No, he wanted to look at the Greek temples. He had never seen them.'

'So he was also interested in temples. So while he was looking at the temples, a scorpion stung him?'

'No. After we had looked at the site and the museum, we went to the nearest beach.'

'Where the scorpion stung him?'

'When we were leaving the beach and got on the bus to come back to the Palazzo Agrippina, the scorpion bit him.'

'On the bus?'

'Yes. It seems to have got into his knapsack.'

'He carried a scorpion in his knapsack?'

'Well, that's where the scorpion was, anyway,' said DeWitt. 'It must have got there somehow. He put his hand into his knapsack and the scorpion stung him.'

'Ah,' nodded the officer. 'This DeSilva had a room at the *Albergo Felice*, yes?'

'Yes. We had no spare room for him here at the Palazzo.'

'Ah,' said the officer. 'The *Albergo Felice*. It's a nice place. Very nice.' A glance passed between him and his young colleague.

'So I'm told,' said DeWitt.

'I know the owner. He's a friend of mine.'

'You questioned him?'

'Question?'

'Did you ask the owner of the *Albergo Felice* any questions?'

'Ah, the owner. The owner is a very busy man. I talked to Antonio at the bar. He doesn't know anything.'

'What about Luigi?'

'Ah, Luigi. The big guy.' He glanced again at his younger colleague. 'We will talk to Luigi,' he said. 'He won't know anything either.'

Annie Fordham opened the door and brought in a tray with four espresso coffees. Her hands were trembling as she set the tray on a little table.

'I brought teaspoons and sugar,' she said.

'Thanks, Annie,' said DeWitt.

'*Grazie,* said the officer, picking up his coffee cup in his gloved hand. 'So you brought the *dottore* back to the International Hospital in Naples.'

'Yes. He didn't seem to be critically ill until he reached the outskirts of Naples. Then his breathing started to be difficult.'

'Scorpion stings are always serious.' The officer sipped his espresso. 'So. You can tell us nothing more about this DeSilva? He was from a university in America?'

'No, I believe he was an independent scholar. He had a private income.'

'Ah,' said the officer. 'He was rich.'

'Well, he had a private income. I believe he wrote, but I don't think he made much from his writing.'

'Wrote books? What kind?'

DeWitt searched for a word to describe them. 'Academic' would not do, and certainly not 'scholarly.'

'He wrote non-fiction books,' said DeWitt, realizing that the officer had noted his hesitation.

'Ah,' said the police officer. 'Non-fiction books. You mean books that don't tell stories.'

'Well, more or less. I don't know any of their titles. Arthur DeSilva promised to send me a copy of his latest publication, but now he's dead.'

'Yes, now he is dead. That is clear. Well, we have his passport and we know his address in America. We have notified the American consul and he is taking charge. The International Hospital is worried about its bill. It wants to be paid.' The policeman shrugged, world-weary. 'You can tell us nothing more?'

'I really can't,' said Fordham. 'I feel badly because he was stung on a scheduled school trip. But he wasn't a member of our group.'

'Ah. If he were a member, you would have been more watchful. Well, I think that is all. If the American consul has more questions, he will get in touch. Thank you for the coffee.'

'Thank you,' said the younger policeman, in English.

'DeSilva really wasn't our business,' chimed in Monroe Thatcher, roused to renewed volubility by a word in a language he understood. 'He didn't belong to our group. Have you impressed that on the Italian police, DeWitt?'

'Yes, Monnie,' replied Fordham.

'So he wasn't our responsibility,' said Thatcher. Both police officers rose to their feet.

'*Arrivederci*,' said the white-gloved officer, bowing with exquisite courtesy. 'Thank you for the coffee.'

The two policemen nodded pleasantly to the student group

waiting to board their bus, climbed into their Fiat and sped off.

'That younger policeman is a real doll,' Marcia remarked to Paul. 'Wonderful eyes. Did you see them?'

'I didn't notice,' said Paul.

XVIII

THE BUS stopped at the entrance to the archaeological park
that encloses the *Scavi di Baia*, and the students disembarked. Walter Druker was slightly unsteady on his feet,
and Kwame Assante put his hand under his elbow. Monroe and
Millicent Thatcher had remained behind at the Palazzo with
Fordham, Monroe because he felt that he must be there to meet
the American consul if he chose to appear, and Millicent because
Monroe did. Conradin, free of his parents, joined Piers and Yo-
yo Kim. Paul was in good spirits. He had persuaded his room
mate, Percy Bass to leave his guitar behind by warning him that
Camorra regularly filched guitars to feed a growing black market. Whether the Camorra did anything of the sort or not, he
didn't know, but Percy's cautious instincts were aroused and he
put his guitar under his bed.

Sister Stella smiled graciously at him, and Paul smiled back.
His inadvertent pat on her rump on the first day at the Palazzo
had left no trace of ill feeling. Marcia was friendly, almost com-
radely. He would have to perform in bed again, Paul thought
with some pleasure, and probably that meant renting a room
at the *Albergo Felice* for an hour. He could hardly say to Percy,
'Would you go and sing sad songs on the front steps of the
Palazzo and leave our room free for Marcia and me to copu-
late?' Percy would probably understand, but Paul felt that he
could not bear Percy's understanding. And as for Marcia asking Miriam Kuntz to vacate, given Miriam's research interests,

it would be unwise to raise the subject.

The *Parco Archeologico* which encloses the *Scavi di Baia* is a hillside site, sloping down to the Cumana railway which slices along the foot of the slope. Its warm springs must have attracted early visitors even before the Greek colonists reached these shores, for the forces of the underworld made their homes here and demanded sacrifice. But the Romans who came to this area looking for a seaside resort, turned Baiae into a spa. Gregory Donahue chuckled that the Greeks left ruined temples to mark their cities, whereas the Romans built amphitheaters and baths, which decayed without grace or elegance. Still, the baths of ancient Baiae made an impressive ruin.

The Agrippina group passed through the entrance gates and was immediately accosted by a well-groomed Italian male who offered list services as a guide. Dr. Alex declined and produced the appropriate *permesso* which allowed him to lecture on Italian archeological sites. The young man subsided into a chair and polished his fingernails. Sister Stella, who found herself beside Conradin., remarked amiably,

'The Italian male is truly a peacock, isn't he?'

'Yo?'

'Look at that young fellow who wanted to act as our guide,' said Sister Stella. 'All dressed up, very elegant, with a high opinion of his own appearance, I should think.'

'He's not bad looking,' said Conradin.

'And doesn't he know it! You know, I visited St. Peter's when I was in Rome, and it was lovely, but while I was there, a man pinched me.'

'Oh, yes? Why?'

'He pinched me on my –uh—behind.'

'Your rear end, like?'

'There I was,' said Sister Stella, 'kneeling and praying before St. Peter's tomb, and this man came up behind me and pinched me.'

'That must have been fun.'

'But,' said Sister Stella, who felt Conradin had failed to appreciate the enormity of the offense, 'I was kneeling at prayer before the high altar!'

'Well,' said Conradin, 'when you pray in St. Peter's, you got to expect your prayers to be answered quicker than if you were in some Presbyterian church in Hartford, Connecticut.'

'Oh!' said Sister Stella. She shot Conradin an indignant look and moved away from him.

Alex Baker led the group down to the upper terrace built into the hillside and took up lecturing mode.

'Those ruins below us, called temples when people didn't know any better, actually belonged to the Baiae spa that attracted the fast set from Rome. The society that frequented this place was multi-faceted and dynamic. There's the "Temple of Diana" half hidden by the railway station. There's the "Temple of Venus" down there to the east, and notice that great dome protruding from the earth. A dome like the Pantheon in Rome which some of you have seen, only half as large. It's called the "Temple of the Echo" because if you get under it—it's filled to the base of the dome—you get some remarkable echoes. The *Tempio dell'eco.*' Dr. Alex pointed an imperious figure below where a great dome emerged from the ground like a mosque that had subsided into the earth.

'You know,' said Sally Harvey, 'I never put much stock in flying saucers, but that dome down there looks just like a flying saucer that has landed.'

'I heard a story of a woman who was kidnapped by aliens and taken off in a flying saucer,' said Ellen Cross. 'She claimed she was raped, and then put back on earth.'

'What a lot of silliness,' said Mildred Donahue.

'I know a lot of well-educated people who believe in UFOs,' protested Ellen. 'My son, who goes to Yale, you know, said one of his professors actually gave an interesting talk on extra-terrestrial beings.'

Sister Stella nodded with approbation. 'We have to keep an open mind, always,' she said.

On the fringe of the group, Conradin snorted audibly.

'My ex-husband, before he died, used to have an illustrated lecture on UFOs which he gave to Rotary Clubs and the like, and I used to show his slides before he discarded me for a sleek young model,' said Bathsheba Bennett, 'who then discarded him. He was a Dean of Arts and Science.'

Madge Midgely approached with her notebook open, and pen poised.

'Can you give me a quote on the UFO theory, Dr. Alex?' she asked. 'UFOs always make good stories.'

'Nothing I want published.'

'Come on. I need material for an OpEd article in the *Advertiser*. Something catchy, like "Dr. Alex Baker from—where is it? Ancaster University is somewhere up there in Canada up north somewhere?'

'Near Montreal.'

'It's all the same. Ancaster University.' She wrote it down. 'That's all one word, is it? Ancaster?'

Dr. Alex nodded, bemused. Madge Midgely continued,

'I'll write, "From Ancaster University, an expert on Roman archaeology—no, Mediterranean archaeology –that's more attention-grabbing—says UFO theories cannot be discounted. The inspiration for the dome, which we find in St. Sophia in Constantinople and St. Peter's in Rome, may well derive from outer space. Standing on the site of ancient Baiae today, Dr. Baker noted the resemblance of pleasure domes at this ancient Roman answer to Las Vegas to flying saucers..."'

'I was the one who noticed it,' said Sally Harvey.

'My husband thinks.....' began Mildred Donahue.

'But the theory *can* be discounted,' interrupted Dr. Alex. 'Quite safely discounted.'

'Yes, I know, but then the pope discounted Galileo too, didn't he? After all, the Romans had to get the idea of building a dome from somewhere, wouldn't they? They couldn't just think it up themselves. Wasn't Pozzuoli the main port for Rome? This bay would have been a good place for alien ships to land among the merchant vessels from the east and the west that must have anchored here. They wouldn't have been noticed so much in a multicultural region. How about I write that Dr. Baker from Ancaster University near Montreal was noncommittal about the UFO theory?'

'That's a little better,' said Dr. Alex. Madge Midgely had already written in her notebook, 'X-Files in ancient Roman spa.'

'Was this really like Las Vegas?' asked Ellen Cross, as she headed a new page in her notebook with the word, 'Las Vegas', underlined. 'What's a good place to take a picture of that dome from?'

'I need a better hook for this piece,' said Madge, looking about for inspiration and finding none. 'Something to lead into the story. Is there an authority I can quote on the UFO theory? Someone whose opinion will be respected?'

'Well, you can quote *me* as saying it is nonsense,' said Gregory Donahue. Madge glanced at him with malice. A few minutes later, Mildred overheard her saying to Ellen, *sotto voce*, that Donahue was a 'conceited pup.'

'Conceited, yes,' said Ellen, wisely, 'but he's no pup. He's an *old* dog who knows it all.'

'At least,' Mildred told herself resentfully, 'I don't have a dreadful mop of bleached hair like Ellen Cross.' Later in the day she found an opportunity to remark to Sally Harvey that she considered bleached hair and wash-and-wear permanent waves 'absolutely hideous.'

'It's good to see that Conradin has slipped the fetters,' Marcia said to Paul, on the edge of the group. Conradin was talking shyly to Betty Laramie while Piers and Kim climbed down the steep slope for a closer look at the sunken dome of the *Tempio dell'eco* at the bottom.

'How so?'

'He is not under the close surveillance of his mother and father,' said Marcia. 'Thatcher has decided that managing DeSilva's death is more important that keeping track of his son today. Look! He's talking to a girl! Betty Laramie really is a beautiful girl if she would get rid of those glasses.'

'Be good to Conradin,' said Paul. 'That's a difficult father-son relationship. Conradin would like his father to be proud of him, but failing to get into Williamson is a blemish he can't live down.'

'Is he a good student?'

'He works hard most of the time. There may be some minor learning disabilities. But there's no point talking to old Thatcher about it. And his mother is a classic passive aggressive type, as far as I can see.'

'You seem to have them pegged.'

'First impressions only,' said Paul. 'But Conradin has a lot of issues to work out.'

'His sexuality?'

'That too, probably, since you mention it.'

They had descended to the central terrace where there was a crescent-shaped room surrounding a pool, now waterless. Marcia paused.

'I'm going down to the lower terrace to see these so-called temples, Marcia.' said Paul. 'Are you coming?'

Marcia shook her head.

'If I go down there, I'll have to climb up again,' she said. 'I'm not as fit as you. I need a site with escalators.'

'We don't need to save ourselves that much', said Paul and left Marcia to ferret out the meaning of what he said.

He soon found himself alone under the dome of the *Tempio dell'eco.* He shouted. His voice returned once, and then again. He bellowed out his own name, then Marcia's. The words bounced and rebounded off the walls of the dome. Then silence. Paul was suddenly aware of someone standing behind him. He swung round. It was Sister Stella.

'You know, Paul,' she said, 'I know what is going on between Marcia Mellon and you, and I don't mind in the least.'

'Pardon?'

'It doesn't shock me at all,' said Sister Stella, with compassion. 'Some people think that nuns are naïve about that sort of thing because we're supposed to have retired from the world. It's not true. I know a great deal about the world and I quite understand.'

She smiled, turned and left. Paul's last glimpse was of a shapely rump as she stooped to exit the dome. The echo repeated her final words. 'I quite understand.'

XIX

THE NEXT stop of the morning after Baiae was the *Piscina Mirabile*, a great cistern built to store water for the Roman naval base nearby at Misenum. The custodian had been forewarned of the visit by the Agrippina's travel agent, who intimated that a generous tip awaited him if he was close by with the key for the entrance gate when the group arrived. The students descended in single file down the stairway into the cavernous interior. The roof was supported by a forest of square piers so that it looked like a great basilica with five aisles. Like the Odeon of Pericles in Athens, Gregory Donahue commented. Not exactly, said Dr. Alex. Piers, who had reached the floor of the cistern first, gave a great bellow. His cry echoed and re-echoed as if a dozen men were shouting, not quite in unison.

'What a wonderful place this would be for a massed choir,' said Sister Stella. 'The acoustics are splendid!'

'Too sinister,' said Madge Midgely. 'This could be the evil realm of Sauron.'

'Sauron?'

'From the *Lord of the Rings* trilogy, you know. This place could be the domicile of an evil king. His throne would be at the far end and his booming voice would echo and re-echo through the columns. Can't you imagine it?'

'It's a cistern,' said Dr. Alex, firmly. 'A water tank.'

'What a wonderful place it would be for a murder, don't you think, Marcia?' whispered Paul. Sister Stella was within earshot, listening. 'Can't you imagine Aristide Blanchard down here, picking up clues.'

'Aristide has arthritis in his knees,' replied Marcia. 'He'd have a hard time with the stairway leading down here.'

'He could pop an aspirin or two to dull the pain, and climb down, carrying Willoughby on his shoulder. Imagine the body splayed out, bleeding copiously, staining the ancient floor of this great water tank. Aristide looking down at the corpse, his mind working furiously. Willougby saying, over and over, mindlessly, "Who did it?"'

'But who is the victim? What's the motive for killing him? Incidentally, what about your room mate, Percy Bass? He hasn't brought his guitar. I should have thought he would want to sing here. The acoustics are wonderful.'

'He left the guitar under his bed.'

'Has the love affair with the guitar terminated?'

'He's a troubadour. He wants to be recognized as a guitar virtuoso. He claims the guitar is a direct descendant of the ancient Greek kithara.'

'He's also a writer. I've been reading some of his stuff and I've read worse. But why's he teaching school, if he's a troubadour? Does he like working with old Thatcher as a colleague?'

'Good Lord, no. But he's still finding himself. Until he does, he teaches school.'

'He might do as a murder victim.'

Paul snorted. 'Why would anyone kill him?'

'We haven't fathomed Percy's persona yet. Anyway, we'll find a motive once we've got a murder victim. Victim first, then motive. If Percy were the victim, we would scrutinize his record at the Williamson School, and who knows? We might find out something about Thatcher and Conradin....'

'Careful, Marcia. There's an echo in here. Your voice carries,' cautioned Paul.

The vast space amplified Sol Bernstein's voice as he asked,

'Dr. Alex, didn't someone write an article suggesting this was not a water tank but an underground temple?'

'It's not likely,' said Dr. Alex. 'It looks exactly like a cistern.'

'It looks like the great hall of an Egyptian temple,' said Kwame Assante.

Sol Bernstein snorted.

'Well, wasn't the goddess Isis worshipped around here?' persisted Assante.

'Yes, there is an early temple of Isis at Pompeii,' replied Dr. Alex. 'We'll see it when we visit Pompeii.'

'So if there was an Egyptian goddess in this area, there would be Egyptians here.'

'All sorts of people visited this area,' said Dr. Alex, neutrally. 'Pozzuoli used to be the main port of Rome. It was full of dynamic vitality. Very multicultural. And the Roman naval base was nearby. This was a vibrant, dynamic region, and it attracted people from all over the empire.'

From the far corner of the water tank there was a gasp, followed by a howl of agony. Sally Harvey had been trying to line up a photograph with her wide-angle lens, and had backed over a discarded shovel, and tripped. She was sitting on the floor, holding her ankle and grimacing with pain.

'Oh dear, you've twisted it,' said Sister Stella. 'How did you do it?'

'You should watch out,' said Dr. Alex, unhelpfully.

'Well, it's too late to tell me that now,' said Sally. 'How am I going to get out of here? I don't think I can walk.'

'Well,' said Kwame, stepping forward and scooping her up in his arms, 'the first thing to do is to get you back on the bus. Then we'll get some ice on your ankle and hope nothing is broken.'

He mounted the stairs leading out of the *Piscina Mirabilis*, carrying her easily. The rest of the group followed in his wake.

DR. ALEX WAS STILL smiling benignly as he opened the door to his bedroom at the Palazzo Agrippina, but the smile faded the instant the door closed behind him, and he was out of sight. He sank into the wicker chair in front of his desk.

'Screw them,' he muttered.

A few moments before, he had returned with the Agrippina

group from the *Piscina Mirabilis* and with Kwame's help, had taken Sally Harvey to her room and brought her some ice from the kitchen. The ankle seemed to be badly sprained, but not broken.

'We'll see what it's like tomorrow' she said, cheerfully. 'Thanks for your help,' she said to Kwame, patting him on his biceps as he laid her gently on her bed.

Then Thatcher and DeWitt Fordham spied him as he left Sally's room.

'Hey, Alex,' Thatcher barked

Dr. Alex responded obediently.

'We were thinking that someone should say a few words of tribute for poor DeSilva at supper tonight,' said Thatcher. 'He wasn't one of our group, but still he was our guest and it would look good if someone made an acknowledgement of his contribution..'

'We thought you should do it,' said DeWitt.

'Well, I didn't know him,' said Dr. Alex, reluctance breaking like a wave over his face. 'Maybe it would be more appropriate for the director --.'

'No one knew him,' said DeWitt. ' But we need someone with a good unctuous manner to say something to fit the occasion.'

'We agreed you'd be the man,' said Thatcher.

'All you need do is say how much we respected him and what a loss he'll be to the scientific community,' said DeWitt. 'Work in the loss-to-science notion as often as you can. It makes a good impression.'

'DeSilva wasn't one of our Agrippina group,' said Thatcher, 'but we have to acknowledge his death, you know. We want to create a good impression among the group. So keep it light but— you know—properly mournful.'

'Thanks for doing this, Alex,' said DeWitt.

With that, Thatcher and DeWitt walked off down the corridor.

Dr. Alex sat at the desk in his room and nursed resentful thoughts. Hypocrisy, he knew, was not one of the Seven Deadly Sins for, if it were, the ranks of Hell would be overcrowded. What shall I say, he wondered. That DeSilva had revealed new realms of speculation in octopus studies, and its relation to Greek civilization? No. That he was a devoted researcher, an example to us all, whom the scientific community would sorely miss? Then he had an idea of stunning brilliance. He would ask for a minute of silence after the group sat down to supper in the dining room, and the soup was served. He would say a few words, beginning with 'Friends, we must take a moment to remember our dynamic colleague, Dr. DeSilva who became our dear friend though we knew him only briefly' and adding a somber reference to his 'tragic transit to his deserved reward. Here, in this evocative region, replete with its reminiscences of the Underworld and its connotations of Death, fate encountered our friend Arthur DeSilva and summoned him. His evanescent soul has made its final journey to the land of Hades.' Then in a solemn voice, he would ask the group to observe a minute's silence. For a full minute, timed by Dr. Alex's wristwatch, the group would stand and think wordlessly of DeSilva as they watched their soup grow cold. The atmosphere would become suitably gloomy. Monroe Thatcher hated cold soup. Serve the old geezer right.

'Good for me,' thought Dr. Alex. He opened his laptop computer and slipped in a diskette. Out of his briefcase he pulled a letter he had received from Holyrood College just before he left home for Italy, and it required an answer soon.

'Dr. DeWitt Fordham is a candidate for Dean of Arts at Holyrood College, and he has given your name as a reference,' Dr. Alex read. 'We have several well-qualified candidates for the position and we are anxious to make the right choice. So we would appreciate a frank appraisal of Dr. Fordham's strengths and weaknesses, and his potential for this important position. Holyrood College is a top-ranking liberal arts college, and the Dean of Arts must not only have outstanding administrative strengths but also be able to give leadership to a scholarly community of great distinction...'

And so on. The letter was signed by Dr. Edgar Rosenblatt, chair of the Holyrood Search Committee for Dean of Arts.

The Palazzo Agrippina should have its own e-mail server,

thought Dr. Alex. Maybe next year. But he could compose a letter, export it on a floppy disk and take it down to the Internet
Cafe at the *Albergo Felice* where he could get a print-out. He fired
up Word 2002 on his laptop and thought for a moment. Then he
began to compose.

'It is my melancholy duty..' he began. No, that wouldn't do.
'Melancholy duty' was the expression he was using for his eulogy of poor old DeSilva, but it would not do to contaminate
Fordham's reference with DeSilva's eulogy. 'Melancholy' was not
an appropriate adjective. Dr. Alex began again. First line in boldface caps. '**CONFIDENTIAL**'.

'Dr. DeWitt Fordham is a personal acquaintance of mine and
I have enormous respect for him,' he continued. 'Indeed, I count
him as a friend. Yet I feel that you would want me to be honest
in my appraisal. So I shall write frankly but not unkindly, and I
trust that my assessment, which I write *sine ira et studio*, will be
of some value to you .

'DeWitt is first and foremost a man of courage. His struggle
with alcoholism, which he has won with some help from myself,
I am proud to say, is proof of that. Second, I think, his scholarship speaks for itself. His study of violence against women in
Sophocles demonstrates his comprehensive grasp of the latest
trends in literary scholarship. DeWitt has opened interesting
corridors of interpretative dexterity, which will bear fruit in his
book *Time in Sophocles and Shakespeare* which he has been planning for many years to write.'

Dr. Alex stopped, and read what he had written. He began
again.

'I'm sure you will appreciate the need to be candid. I admire
DeWitt tremendously for the courage with which he strug-
gles with his alcoholism and I feel sure that he will achieve
victory.....'

Dr. Alex stopped again and stared out the window. He
fixed his gaze on the tree in the back garden that shaded Sybil
Twickenham's grave, and reflected. Perhaps he should have a
shower before the students exhausted the hot water tank. The
Palazzo Agrippina's hot water supply was limited. What's more,

if DeWitt became dean, he might not have time to be director of the Agrippina program and it would be necessary to find a new director. Dr. Alex himself would be preeminently qualified.

Dr. Alex wondered if he should meditate a little longer before he produced an unbiased assessment of DeWitt Fordham. He put the letter from Edgar Rosenblatt back into his briefcase. He would have a shower before he composed a reply.

MARCIA TOOK A SEDATIVE, crawled into bed and drew the covers over her head. With luck, she would be asleep before Miriam started to snore. But Miriam was wide awake. Something was on her mind.

'Marcia,' she said, 'I don't quite know how to put this.'

'Put what?'

'I know you belong to the sisterhood, and yet there are some requests that it's embarrassing to make,' said Miriam.

Gracious Heaven! Don't tell me she has an unpublished novel, like Percy Bass! How can I tell her I'm far too busy to act as an unpaid literary consultant?'

'It's never too embarrassing,' said Marcia, cautiously. 'Lead on.'

'You know, I have a partner. We've been living together now for six years.'

Marcia didn't know, but she confined her answer to a receptive grunt.

'Another woman, of course.'

'Of course.'

'We've decided we'd like a child.'

'Good for you.'

'It's my partner who would carry it. If I had tenure, I'd carry it myself, but I don't want to do anything that might jeopardize my chances.'

Marcia was wide awake now. 'So what do you want to ask me?'

'We need a sperm donor.'

'Well, there are sperm banks.'

'Yes, but you never know with them.'

'So why are you approaching me?'

'Well, I know you're not a sperm donor yourself,' said Miriam, 'but I can't help but notice that you are on good terms with Paul Kowalski.'

Marcia grunted.

'I wonder if you might broach the question with him.'

'Miriam,' said Marcia, 'that is something you will have to do yourself. I can't act as your agent.'

'I know I'll have to speak with him myself,' said Miriam. 'But I wondered if you could find out first what his reaction might be.'

'You'll have to ask him.'

'I don't know—he might be a prude.'

'He's not.'

'Not with you, maybe, but I think there's a strict Catholic up-bringing in his background.'

'Well, he'll tell you himself. I've no idea what he will say.'

'It's just that he looks like—well, like a likely man to father a beautiful child. My partner would like his sperm, I think.'

'You never can tell. Some unlikely-looking studs father beautiful children.'

'But we'd like to have some idea of the genetic history of our sperm donor.'

'Miriam, go to sleep,' said Marcia. 'Paul won't bite you. Ask him.' She pulled the covers over her head again, this time with finality.

Miriam turned on her side. It was a full hour before she started to snore.

XX

THE ROOM at the *Albergo Felice* was spartanly furnished, but for the price, one could not expect Persian carpets. Marcia and Paul were pleasantly weary. A visit to a couple archaeological sites, lunch, a shower followed by fornication. A dinner with Ischia wine at the Palazzo Agrippina to look forward to. Marcia snuggled up to Paul's bare chest. She felt like a cigarette but she had sworn off. Besides, the hour was nearly up.

'Their operation here is rather mass production, isn't it?' said Paul, as he fondled Marcia's right breast.

'Here at the *Albergo Felice*?'

'They give you an hour. Five minutes over the hour and you're charged for a second hour. There's no time left for romance.'

'But the *Felice's* convenient. The Palazzo isn't set up for civilized copulation.'

'I wonder if any of our fellow students, so to speak, are taking full advantage of the *Felice's* services,' said Paul. 'Should we exit this room together, or separately, in case we are spotted?'

'Does it matter? Do you think Sister Stella is patrolling the hallway? Anyway, do you care?'

'I'm a teacher at an exclusive boys' school, Marcia. No one expects us to be ascetics, like the desert fathers, but we are expected to be discreet. The watchword is zero tolerance.'

'And you all take it seriously?'

'Zero tolerance is the soul mate of multiple hypocrisy at Gilead. But we must keep up appearances.'

'Oh, I see. You really do suspect someone will find you out. All right. I'll leave first. If I see Monnie Thatcher prowling through the hall, I'll pop back and warn you.'

'Comb your hair first. Thatcher is the sort of person who copulates wearing a shirt and tie.'

'Well, if I find him in the hallway, I'll invite him in.'

'Your hair, Marcia! You look as if you've had a roll in the hay.'

'Well, that's not an entirely inaccurate description, is it? All right, all right. Let me straighten my hair and repair my war paint. I aim to please.' Marcia looked at herself in the diminutive mirror over the sink, ran a comb quickly through her hair, and applied some lipstick. 'Did I tell you I had the oddest conversation with my roommate about you?'

'Miriam Kuntz?'

'Yes, Miriam. I'll tell you later. It will give you a laugh.' She headed for the door. 'Ta-ta. I'll see you in the bar. I'm ordering a Campari Soda. Do you want one?'

'I'll take a Cinzano. Be with you in a couple minutes.'

'Don't be long, sweetheart.'

Marcia closed the door softly behind her and headed down the hall towards the stairs. Someone was flushing the toilet in the men's WC. The door of Room 10, just beyond the WC, opened and a youthful face looked out furtively. Conradin. He saw Marcia and closed the door quickly. But not before Marcia caught a glimpse of another face behind him. Tony. A ray of sunlight from the window lit up his face and he looked like a Renaissance youth.

'Well, none of my business,' she thought. 'However, most interesting.'

Luigi was tending the bar by himself, and he was busy. Madge Midgely, Bathsheba Bennett and Ellen Cross were sitting at a table on the patio. Madge had her laptop beside her. The UFO story, Marcia thought. She has no doubt sent a story, titled 'Flying Saucers at Roman Spa' by Hotmail direct from the Internet Café to the Beaumont *Advertiser* editorial room. Ellen was talking with much gesticulation, and Bathsheba seemed perplexed. She looked up as Marcia walked past.

'Have you had any word about your cat?'

'What about Marcia's cat?' asked Madge.

'Marcia's lost her cat,' replied Bathsheba. 'It's called Mikado. I think that's a most interesting name for a cat.'

'No news yet,' said Marcia, who had not thought about the Mikado for more than twelve hours. 'I keep hoping he'll come back.'

'When my son left for Yale,' said Ellen, 'our cat left home for two days. He came back when he was hungry.'

'We'd ask you to join us, but we're just leaving,' said Bathsheba. 'I want to be in time for dinner.'

'Quite all right,' said Marcia, who had been trying to think of some reason not to join them. "I shall suppress my sorrow.' Paul would soon be making his separate way to the bar from their shared bedroom. 'I'll see you all back at the Palazzo in a half hour or so.' She watched them leave with relief.

There was, however, more interesting company at the bar. Perched on bar stools, deep in conversation were Walter Druker and Kwame Assante. Walter appeared slightly drunk and Kwame slightly sober. Neither of them noticed Marcia until she spoke to them.

'Luigi here is acting dumb about our friend Dr. DeSilva,' said Walter.

'How do you know?'

'Well, I asked him. He gave a little shrug. They come and go, I guess.'

Kwame grinned, showing a set of fine white teeth.

'Maybe he didn't understand,' said Marcia.

'He understood. Luigi,' said Walter, turning to face Luigi and raising his voice, 'what was DeSilva up to here? How did he find a scorpion? Do you keep a pack of them here for guests to put in their knapsacks?'

Luigi was very busy washing glasses in the sink. His eyes, when he raised them, were smouldering.

'Let me go and ask him,' said Walter, teetering off his stool and heading in Luigi's direction.

'Take it easy,' said Kwame, checking him with a large hand. Luigi was bouncer as well as bartender, Marcia reflected, and before the summer session was over, Walter might find himself bounced. Kwame, however, was a different matter. Probably a match for Luigi, Marcia reckoned. Walter was lucky in his room mate, she thought.

'I want to order a couple drinks,' said Marcia. 'Paul is joining me.' But Luigi had gone into the kitchen and Tony appeared, radiant in his starched white jacket and looking more than ever like a youth from a Raphael painting. He approached Marcia expectantly.

'A Campari soda for me, and a Cinzano for Paolo, *per favore*, Tony,' said Marcia.

Tony nodded. 'A Cinzano. For Signor Paul,' he said. '*Si.*' With understanding.

Paul came down the stairs from the second floor, heading for the bar. A few steps behind him was Conradin. He saw the little cluster of Marcia, Walter and Kwame at the bar, hesitated, waved a curt greeting and made for the computers in the Internet Café alcove.

'Sorry, I was longer than I thought,' Paul greeted Marcia. 'I met Conradin.'

'Your drinks,' said Tony, setting two glasses on the bar in front of them.

'Don't let us keep you, 'said Walter with a distinct trace of a leer.

'You won't,' said Marcia. 'But won't you join us for a drink? Can we sit outside on the patio?'

'Well,' said Walter. 'sitting outside on the patio should suit us fine, eh, Kwame?' He slid off the bar stool and lumbered out the door after Marcia, with Kwame and Paul following him. 'The hostile vibrations from Luigi were becoming quite palpable in there. Palpable. Nice word.'

But before they went outside, Marcia glanced back at the alcove which housed the *Felice's* two computers. Sitting at one of them were Yo-yo Kim and Piers, and in front of the other monitor was Conradin. Leaning over him, talking earnestly, was Luigi.

I looked for FAFI on the internet. Searched for it with Google and Yahoo and Internet Explorer, and finally turned up a Web Site. FAFI. Fabiola Films. Yeah, sure. It makes sense. I couldn't make out all the Italian. Fabiola Films arranges pictures and tours. Something like that.

Luigi is sort of fun. I don't mind him. But I'm a little frightened of him, too. I don't think he likes to see me with Tony. Bad vibes, I think He wanted to know the name of the good-looking girl with glasses. I don't think he meant Madge Midgely. Even Luigi would find her a lot of woman.

I wish Matthew was with me. I could talk to Matthew. But I can't now he's dead. Kowalski and that woman Marcia Mellon have a big thing going, and he doesn't have any time for me. He said we all have problems. I asked him what his were, and he laughed, but he didn't like my question. But he's not trying to give me the brush-off any more.

Dr. Alex was here at the Internet Café today. Saved a document on the hard drive and then deleted it. But I recovered it. No problem. It was a letter Dr. Alex wrote to recommend Dr. Fordham who, I guess, wants to be a dean at his college, Holyrood which is supposed to be a top-rated school. It was awesome! Like wow! I didn't know that Dr. Alex liked DeWitt Fordham all that much! My dad never told me that Dr. Fordham was all that distinguished! I think I'll tell old Fordham how impressed I am! It will shake him up. But he'll probably be pleased, too.

XXI

'JOSHUA,' MARCIA wrote, 'I hope I am not trying your patience. Please tell me if I am. I shall not heed your objections, but I shall take note of them.' Marcia was writing her literary agent again. 'Where did I leave off? I told you that poor Dr. DeSilva was bitten by a scorpion, didn't I?. Well, he died. Two policemen came to the Palazzo Agrippina next day to interview DeWitt Fordham. That was our morsel of excitement to disturb the even tenor of our life here. The policemen were very elegant and the younger one was quite beautiful. Thatcher had to choose between supervising DeSilva's death, and coming with us to supervise our visit to the *Scavi di Baia*, Roman Baiae, and he gave up the trip. Millicent gave it up too, because Thatcher did. The result was that Conradin had no parents to watch over after him. Piers and Yo-yo took him in tow, and I actually heard him laugh, which he has never done on a school trip before. Piers, Yo-yo, the lovely Betty Laramie in steel-rimmed glasses, and her roommate Shirley Perovic seem to have formed a sub-group and on the Baiae trip, and they included Conradin.

'De Silva was just a visitor here at the Palazzo Agrippina and not our responsibility, as Thatcher has said several times to anyone who cared to listen. The U.S. consul is taking charge. De Silva, it turns out, has a son who is a lawyer in Pittsburgh, and he will take home the body. His Medical Insurance company faxed a letter to the International Hospital here warning them not to undertake anything more than routine medical treatment without notifying them at a one eight-hundred number and I think it may be a little embarrassed when the fax gets into the hands of DeSilva's son. One eight-hundred numbers do not work here between Italy and the United States. I'm told that DeSilva's son is a demon when it comes to torts.

'However, the cause of DeSilva's death turns out to be heart failure. I expect that the scorpion bite had something to do with it, but it will not appear on the death certificate.

'The police also interviewed the manager of the *Albergo Felice*, I gather, but, of course, Luigi and Tony knew nothing. The two policemen seemed on good terms with the *Felice*, for they embraced Luigi and Tony warmly and accepted a free drink. I presume they were detectives. Their uniforms were splendid and they wore white gloves. They picked up DeSilva's luggage and personal effects at the *Felice* and I presume that someone will pay his hotel bill. The management was concerned about that, if nothing much else..

'Something is going on between Conradin Thatcher and Paul. I've established to my own satisfaction that Paul is not gay. At least, not gay enough to matter. He has never forsaken the joys of heterosexuality. Paul takes a personal interest in Conradin, however, which probably goes back to contacts at the Gilead School. Upon reflection, I have decided that Conradin is not a complete pain in the butt. But I haven't decided what makes him tick. We have a repressed memory guru here at the Palazzo, one Madge Midgely, an overweight newshound who writes for the Beaumont *Advertiser* newspaper chain and produces a regular column where she solves personal problems for all comers. In Conradin's case, she diagnoses sexual abuse at an early age, and repressed memory. She says that if she could talk to Conradin heart-to-heart for a couple hours, she could bring his memories to the surface.

'Paul tells me that Conradin's closest friend at Gilead School committed suicide and Conradin went into a blue funk. Monroe Thatcher and Millicent—Millicent in particular—never liked the friend. He was a scholarship boy with not much background.

'I am playing around with an idea for a new novel. It has a

complex plot. A researcher working in the Vatican library on the early church, discovers some new evidence on Pope Pius XII's dealings with the Nazis, which sheds new light on his silence during the Holocaust. He disappears—the researcher, that is—and Aristide Blanchard is hired by his family to discover what his fate was. The story will unfold like a Renaissance drama of murder and intrigue. There will be theft, cover-ups, homicide and undercover activity by the C.I.A, Mossad and MI5. The missing man's corpse will be discovered tucked into a corner of the great *Piscina Mirabile* south of Bacoli, a short drive from here. We visited it the other day and one of our group sprained her ankle there and had to be carried out of the place. You see, my course here at the Palazzo Agrippina will prove useful after all.

'Aristide is baffled as usual, but Willoughby gives him a clue. While Aristide is resting in his favorite arm chair, paging through the latest issue of *History Today* with Willoughby on his shoulder and pondering the case, Willougby climbs down his arm and begins to chew the magazine at page forty-eight. He says, "I'm a clever bird!" Page forty-eight turns out to be the first page of an article which clearly plagiarized the dead man's research. Aristide smells a rat. The author turns out to be a young assistant professor whose application for tenure at his university hinges on this very article. The rest is easy. The young assistant professor is charged with murder and plagiarism, pleads guilty and goes to prison. Life without parole. He is denied tenure. The Promotions and Tenure committee at his university lets him know that, while *History Today* is an excellent magazine, no doubt, it is not sufficiently scholarly for an article published in it to have any weight with a Promotions and Tenure Committee at a first-class university.

'Then would come a surprise ending. In prison, the murderer will write up his story as a television drama and sell it some TV show like *Law and Order*. In the show, the murder is carried out by the Camorra, Naples' own branch of the Mafia.

'The Palazzo Agrippina is a great place. It broadens the mind and the food is very good. I'm becoming comfortable and I think I'm putting on weight.

'Yours faithfully. Marcia.'

Marcia closed her ThinkPad and slid it under her bed. Tomorrow she would send her e-mail from the Internet Café. Before breakfast, if she woke up in time. Miriam was beginning to snore. Marcia crawled between the sheets and closed her eyes, listening complacently to the fugue that rose from the bed against the opposite wall.

She took a sedative and fell asleep.

XXII

'**D**EAR MISS Mellon,
    'I'm very sorry you have been so worried about Mikado, your cat. I think he is living in the sequoia tree in the back yard. I put a dish of *Fancy Feast* outside the back door for him morning and evening, and Mikado comes and eats it. I glimpsed him one morning wolfing it down, but he won't come to me. At least he is alive and looks well. A dead mouse appeared on the doorstep yesterday morning. I think it was a gift from Mikado, payback for the *Fancy Feast*. He doesn't want me to go hungry.

    'I'm glad you are enjoying yourself in Italy. I envy you.

    'All best wishes,

    'Emma Sanchez.' After the name, came Emma's URL for her website. http//www.Sancheznewsandgossip-juicy.com.

    'Hmm. I wonder what's on Emma's web site,' thought Marcia, relieved at the news about Mikado. He was living in the neighbourhood, waiting for her to return. Mikado was a loyal cat; he would not share the house with a house sitter he did not know, but he would keep her supplied with dead mice and he would keep an eye on the house. Marcia sent the e-mail to her agent that she had composed last night, glanced at her watch, signed off the computer at the Internet Café and returned hurriedly along the path to the garden gate of the Palazzo Agrippina. The group was gathering for breakfast when she got back. It would be an easy day: a boat ride to the island of Ischia offshore. The

'Island of Monkeys', the ancient Greeks called it, and it was there that they first started their first settlement, about twenty years before they dared venture to the mainland of Italy and founded the colony of Cumae. Sally Harvey would have a chance to rest her sprained ankle. The next day, the group would go to Pompeii which would be hard on sprained ankles.

Annie Fordham was trying hard to be cheerful at dinner after the group returned from Ischia, and the effort was obvious. Thatcher was taciturn and Gregory Donahue at the far end of the table talked at length about the errors which Dr. Alex had made that afternoon in Ischia where he gave an informal lecture about early Greek colonization in Italy. Yet the mood changed when the Agrippina group left the dinner table at the Palazzo Agrippina for the patio outside where coffee was ready for them. The night was soft as velvet. Lights twinkled on the shoreline of the bay and reflected from the smooth surface of the water. Marcia and Paul disappeared into the darkness of the back garden and out the garden gate. Miriam Kuntz watched them go, expressionless. Piers spotted Betty Laramie standing in a corner talking with her roommate, Shirley Perovich. He approached them hesitantly.

'Would you like to go for a walk on the beach with me and Yo-yo? We might see some action.'

Betty looked uncertain. 'Would it be safe?' she asked.

'Me and Yo-yo will fight off the attackers,' said Piers, manfully.

'Wouldn't it be wonderful to go for a walk on the beach,' said Bathsheba, who was standing within ear shot.

'Could we come with you?' asked Sister Stella.

'You probably don't want old people like us,' said Bathsheba. 'You want to be by yourselves.'

'No, no,' protested Betty. 'We'll all go. We'd love to have you along.'

'Sure,' said Piers, with no great enthusiasm.

'Certainly,' agreed Yo-yo.

'We'll take the air, like ladies in Jane Austin novels,' Bathsheba said.

'Like what?' asked Piers.

'Ladies in Jane Austin novels.'

'Don't know them,' said Piers.

'I used to want to be a lady in a Jane Austin novel,' said Bathsheba. 'Instead I'm a middle-aged assistant professor. Well, it could be worse.'

'It could be a lot worse,' said Sister Stella.

'I thought assistant profs were young,' said Piers. 'I'm mean— don't get me wrong. I don't mean you're not young, Professor Bennett–'

'I'm not,' said Bathsheba. 'I'm deep in middle age, and no one ever listens to what I have to say. Except Shlomo, sometimes.'

'I mean,' Piers blundered on, 'the assistant profs I've met aren't all really young—some are almost forty, I think, --, but they're not about to retire, either.'

'So why haven't I been promoted to a full professor? That's what you want to know, Piers, isn't it? I'm not a full professor because I was never promoted,' Bathsheba said with some heat. 'I preferred to be a good teacher rather than write a lot of papers no one ever reads. I wouldn't play the publications game. I wouldn't lower myself to do it. That's why.'

'But you can do research and be a good teacher, too,' protested Betty Laramie.

'If so, I haven't met anyone who is,' said Bathsheba. 'The sort of stuff my colleagues turn out to be promoted—I wouldn't stoop to write that sort of stuff.'

'But my work on the three-barred sigma is ----'

'Three-barred sigma!' snorted Bathsheba.

'I could change a date in the history of classical Athens by as much as two or three years with my research,' protested Betty.

'The three-barred sigma sounds interesting,' broke in Piers. 'My frat is Sigma Delta Chi.'

'But how did you ever get tenure at your college if you didn't publish?' interposed Shirley Perovich. 'I thought it was all publish or perish.'

'I was a special case,' said Bathsheba. 'Anyway, back then there weren't a dozen applicants for every job.'

'Didn't you tell me your husband used to be the Dean of Arts and Science?' asked Shirley, sharply.

'Awesome,' said Piers.

'No!' Bathsheba looked thunderous. 'I know what you suspect. I got tenure because I was an excellent teacher! And you can't be a good teacher and do a lot of research too. So I got tenure but I wasn't promoted. And anyway, the Dean is not my husband any longer. The jerk.'

'What happened?'

'He dumped me for another woman. His secretary. He used to tell me how flexible she was. She could do any job he wanted her to do. I took it all at face value.'

Well,' said Piers, 'I'm the product of my mom's starter marriage. She's on number three now. Did your husband and his secretary live happily ever after?'

'She put up with him for a year or two, and then she discarded him. That shattered the male ego, and a good thing, too! He's dead, now.'

'What the fuck!' commented Piers.

'My best teacher also did some excellent research,' said Betty.

'Humpf! That's the rare exception, then,' scoffed Bathsheba, looking cross. 'I wouldn't play the publishing game. The stuff that gets printed in these so-called scholarly journals,—why. I wouldn't lower myself to write it!'

'It's nice to have two strong young men to escort us,' tittered Sister Stella. 'We wouldn't have dared walk along the beach without an escort.'

'Why's that?' asked Piers.

'Well, we might be attacked,' replied Sister Stella.

'Who'd want to attack you?'

'Well, you never know who's out there,' said Sister Stella. 'Did I tell you what happened to me in St. Peter's basilica in the Vatican? In broad daylight?'

'Isn't the water calm tonight?' remarked Shirley. 'Almost as if there was oil on its surface. You can almost hear singing in the distance. Listen!'

'I was kneeling to pray at the high altar, before St. Peter's tomb,' went on Sister Stella, disregarding the interruption.

'Well, across the water, I mean, across the bay, was where the Sirens lived,' broke in Bathsheba. 'At Sorrento, I mean. Half woman and half bird, and they sang beautifully. Maybe that's the music we hear.'

'Lured men to their deaths,' remarked Yo-yo, who had been listening silently to the conversation.

'Let that be a lesson to you, Piers,' said Bathsheba. 'An attractive woman is a dangerous woman.'

'Yeah,' said Piers. 'That's what my dad says. He should know, too. His alimony keeps him poor. He's had to sell his boat.'

'I was kneeling at the altar and a man pinched my behind! Can you believe it!' Sister Stella edged into the conversation.

'It happens all the time, Sister,' said Bathsheba. 'Men are interested in only one thing. Nothing else. But I got my own back, I can tell you. With my ex-husband, I mean.'

The beach nearest to the Palazzo Agrippina was almost empty. The sunbathers who filled it by day had all gone home. The surface of the water mirrored back the lights along the Pozzuoli waterfront, and a radio on a boat offshore was blaring a tune. Further along the beach, a crowd had gathered, and policemen in a zodiac seemed to be probing the sea bed. An ambulance broke away from the crowd and headed off, its siren wailing. Piers spotted Percy Bass on the edge of the crowd. He was wearing a sweat suit and sneakers; evidently he had been jogging when the crowd attracted his attention.

'What's up, Percy?' asked Piers.

Percy responded with a start, and he peered warily through the darkness at the little group that had come up behind them.

'Oh, it's you,' he said, recognizing them.

'What's happening here?'

'There's a body that's been washed up on the beach.'

'A body?' asked Piers.

'Yes.'

'What sort of body?' Piers queried.

'You mean a dead body?' broke in Bathsheba.

'Quite so.' Percy's tone was dry. 'Anyway, he smelled of death. The ambulance took him away. If he's not dead yet, the hospital will finish him off.'

'What a fu ---' Piers caught himself. 'That's not a cool way to die!'

'What are those men out there in that rubber boat looking for?' demanded Bathsheba.

'The policemen in the zodiac? I think they're looking for another body.'

'Poor man' said Sister Stella. 'I wonder if he was fisherman from Pozzuoli.'

'Another dead man,' said Shirley. 'First DeSilva and now a someone washed up on the beach, within sight of Pozzuoli.'

'He was a black man,' Percy volunteered. 'An African.'

A stocky camera-man in front of them was having a loud altercation with a policeman. He was carrying a video-recorder on his shoulder, and on its side was stenciled in white paint, FABIOLA FILMS.

'Quite possibly an illegal immigrant from Africa who was trying to cross from Libya,' Percy went on. 'There were a couple of bodies reported the other day. Maybe he tried to swim ashore.' Percy shrugged. 'Maybe he had a contact in Arco Felice who took his money and then dumped him.'

'How terrible!' said Sister Stella.

'Will we ever find out?' asked Bathsheba. 'Who he is and what happened, I mean.'

'Who knows?' said Percy. 'The newspapers might report it if there's no other news that's more important.'

Sister Stella shivered.

'Maybe it's time we got back to the Palazzo,' she said. 'We're off to Pompeii early tomorrow.'

'Will you come back with us, Percy?' asked Bathsheba.

'I was just starting my run,' Percy replied. 'I'd like to jog a little more before bedtime.'

'We'll see you safely back to the Palazzo, ladies,' said Piers, with a burst of gallantry. 'Yo-yo and me.'

'Wasn't that fellow with the video-recorder the man who tried to pick you up, Betty?' Shirley asked Betty Laramie, quietly, so that no one else could hear..

'The Fabiola Films man?' asked Betty. 'Same height, same build, but I didn't get a good look at him.'

XXIII

THE DAY at Pompeii was hot and tiring. It was the heat and the crowds of tourists which Marcia remembered most about the visit after it was over. The bus left the Palazzo early, fought its way through the Naples traffic and past the heaps of garbage and the smells of the grimy Naples outskirts. It paused for a fifteen-minute stop at Donadio's shop along the road, where some of the group bought cameo brooches and those in need visited the WC. It still reached the entrance gate of the Pompeii excavations a few minutes before the great deluge of tour buses that visit the site every day in the tourist season. DeWitt Fordham took his *permesso* to the ticket seller and got entrance tickets for everyone, ignoring a complaint from Monroe Thatcher from the rear that entry permits should all have been arranged in advance.

Miriam Kuntz approached Paul and cast a furtive glance about her before she spoke.

'Paul,' she said, 'the guides here approach tourists and offer to sell postcards of wall paintings from the Pompeii whorehouse, but they sell them only to men, not to women. So I wonder if, that is, if you get a chance, could you could pick up a set of postcards for me?'

'Dirty postcards?'

'They're only for research,' Miriam assured him. 'I need illustrations of phallic tyranny and female exploitation for my book.'

'I'm told the wall paintings from the brothel simply show coitus in various positions,' said Paul.

'Well yes, that will do very nicely. It's evidence of phallic tyranny any way you look at it. And you've no idea how hard it is for researchers to get the illustrations we need.'

Paul told himself that he would avoid any guides with postcards like the plague, but a few minutes later he heard a 'Psst!' at his elbow. *'Signor! Signor!'*

The hand plucking his sleeve belonged to a wrinkled old man in an elderly seersucker suit and a Panama hat, and only a few stained teeth remaining in his mouth.

'Dirty pictures?' he whispered audibly, with an expression that was half appeal, half a leer.

Paul was on the point of a righteous negative when he spotted Miriam's gaze full upon him.

'Quanto?' he asked.

He paid. He wondered how Miriam would enter this item on her research grant account. But Miriam who had been watching the transaction, collected her pictures immediately, and she was very grateful.

'You know,' she said, confidentially, 'there's a glass ceiling for women at my college, and the only way a woman can break through is to be better than the men. This book I am writing must attract attention.'

'Yes, I'm sure it will.'

'I'll include a thank you to you in the introduction,' said Miriam. 'I'm really indebted to you. I know you don't usually buy pornography like this.'

How does she know? Let this not get back to the Gilead School, please God!

Aloud Paul said, 'Think nothing of it. You needn't thank me in your introduction, though.'

'I won't say what you did to deserve the thanks, Paul. I'm very discreet.'

'Are you buying dirty pictures, Mr. Kowalski?' asked Conradin, who appeared at Paul's elbow. He clapped Paul on the shoulder. 'You're awesome, Mr. Kowalski.'

'No—I mean yes,' said Paul. 'But they're for research only.'

'They always are,' said Conradin, withdrawing his arm and striding off.

'You know,' said Miriam, 'that boy may never grow up to be a man. Someone will murder him first.'

'Oh, Conradin's all right.'

'He's a mouthy brat,' said Miriam. 'With braces still on his teeth.'

The group made its way into the forum of Pompeii. In the middle of it was a group of young Japanese tourists being herded along by a voluble guide. DeWitt cleared his throat significantly.

'Here we have a perfect example of a forum in a Roman provincial city. It was the centre of commercial and civic life. Over here on the west side,' DeWitt made a sweeping gesture with one arm, 'is a temple to Apollo. There was an earthquake here twelve years before Vesuvius erupted and when the temple was repaired, the columns of its portico were changed from Ionic to the more up-to-date Corinthian style by adding some fancy stucco work. Over there on the east side is a market building like the so-called Temple of Sarapis you saw in Pozzuoli, which was an open market with stalls and latrines.' DeWitt coughed. 'Over there at the north end is a temple to Jupiter, standing on a high platform with Mt. Vesuvius rising up behind it. Dramatic, isn't it? The earthquake did it a lot of damage, too. Let's just walk down to the south end, here, away from the Japanese tourists.' He coughed again, fumbled in his pocket, found a lozenge and popped it in his mouth.

'Everyone of those Japanese tourists has an expensive camera,' observed Ellen, as she adjusted her hat over her mop of blonde hair.

'I wish they'd get out of my way so I could get a picture of the temple with the mountain behind it,' said Miriam.

'Over there on my left is a large structure built by a priestess called Eumachia for fullers of wool and linen, and probably they sold their goods there too' announced DeWitt.. 'And on my right is a basilica....'

'What's a fuller?' asked Ellen.

'You can answer that one, Alex,' said DeWitt.

'Didn't they use piss for fulling cloth?' asked Sol. 'They went around and gathered it from private houses, didn't they?'

'How awful!' said Ellen. 'But what's fulling?'.

'Felting,' said Dr. Alex..

'Oh,' said Ellen, still puzzled.

'Here at the south end of the forum,' said DeWitt, 'you can see three large halls, and the big one in the centre is where the town council met. Elections here were lively affairs and there were posters painted on the walls of the houses facing the street which boosted various candidates. One of these smaller halls on either side of the council chamber was the office of the two may- ors of the city. Roman municipalities had two mayors, not one. They called them *duumviri* which means two men.'

'They had two mayors so that they could watch each other?' interjected Thatcher, with a guffaw. 'No hanky-panky, huh?'

'Remember, the Roman republic didn't come to an end when Rome got an emperor. In fact, the first emperor, Augustus claimed to have restored the Roman republic. And over there,' Fordham pointed across the forum, 'where the Japanese group is entering, is the basilica we just passed. Basilicas were Roman law buildings, where judges heard cases and lawyers met their clients.'

'But lawyers didn't charge fees, I hear,' said Sol Bernstein.'

'Well, they got rich just the same,' said DeWitt.

'We try to,' said Sol,, 'We don't always succeed.'.

The group advanced down the street, past the Temple of Jupiter to the *Vicolo di Mercurio*, then turned right and paused in front of the monumental entrance of the *Casa del Fauno*. DeWitt stopped to speak. This, he explained, was the House of the Dancing Faun, so-called because of the bronze statue of a danc- ing satyr found in the middle of the atrium. A fine male nude with a diminutive tail at the lower end of his backbone. The house was already old when Pompeii was overwhelmed. The stucco imitation of marble panelling on the walls was old-fash- ioned. At the front door was a black-and-white mosaic with the letters 'HAVE' which in the Oscan tongue meant 'Welcome'. The wealthy family that built this house probably spoke Oscan, the language of the Samnites, not Latin, the language of the Romans who conquered the Samnites.

The house was excavated in the 1820s, DeWitt pointed out, and had stood open to the elements for going on two centuries, to say nothing of the multitudinous feet of tourists. In the Second World War, a bomb had damaged it. Time had been unkind.

'This was the largest house found in Pompeii,' said DeWitt, 'and it's richly decorated. The mosaics found here on the floors have been lifted and they're safe in the Naples Museum, which is just as well. There's a magnificent mosaic from this house which shows Alexander the Great meeting king Darius of Persia in battle. He defeated Darius in two pitched battles, and we don't know which one the mosaic shows, nor does it matter much. Ellen, if you want to take a picture of the dancing faun, you should take the lens cover off your camera lens first.'

'I just want to get a picture with the group standing behind that faun, to show the folks back home,' said Ellen.

'It is clear that an important person lived here,' continued DeWitt. There's a good deal of speculation about who he was. A Roman colony was settled here in the first century B.C. about one hundred and sixty years before the eruption of Vesuvius, and maybe the house was taken over by the Romans at that time.'

'This place could stand some fixing up,' remarked Conradin to no one in particular.

'There are two peristyles at the back,' DeWitt went on. 'The gardens here must have been splendid.'

'Dr. Fordham,' asked Conradin, 'what's a peristyle?'.

'Well, Conradin, it's a colonnade enclosing an open space.'

'A garden, like?'

'That could be.'

'And the temple of Isis?' asked Kwame Assante. 'Where's it?'

'We'll come to it,' said DeWitt. 'Unfortunately there's not a lot to see.'

At the reconstructed House of the Vettii, a guard saw Piers and Yo-yo Kim by themselves and gestured them over to the corner of the atrium. He pulled out a key with a wink and opened a closet door. Inside was an ithyphallic statue with an impressively erect penis. Piers and Yo-yo looked impressed and a little startled.

'What's this?' said Miriam, coming up behind. The guard closed the door quickly.

'What am I missing here?' demanded Miriam. Piers pulled a couple euros out of his pocket. The guard took them, and re-opened the door.

'Oh, very nice,' said Miriam, aiming her camera. The guard closed the door again, his sense of propriety offended.

'But I got one picture,' said Miriam, triumphantly. 'Good for you, Piers. That's what it means to be a man. If you're a woman academic, you get doors closed in your face.'

'Free time,' croaked DeWitt, his voice almost gone. 'Unless you want to say something more, Alex?'

Dr. Alex didn't.

Percy Bass headed off in the direction of the amphitheatre, with his copy of *The Last Days of Pompeii* tucked under his arm, and climbed to the top row of seats. He sat and read for a few minutes, and then closed his book and meditated. This amphitheater was where the young gladiator Lydon was killed in his first fight. Like a poppy that is touched by the plough as it cuts a furrow across the field. As part of the same entertainment, the Athenian Glaucus was to be thrown to the lions for a murder he did not commit, just moments before Vesuvius spewed a mushroom cloud into the sky. Percy looked up at the cone of the volcano looming over Pompeii.

Suddenly, one day in August in 79 A.D., life had stopped at Pompeii. Storekeepers made the last sale they would ever make. Gladiators fought their last battle. The worshippers of Isis made no more sacrifices. Careers for the young and ambitious Pompeians—there must have been some --had ended abruptly. Percy thought for a moment about careers. His own career had nearly shipwrecked only a few months ago. He was playing a gig at the *Magenta Swan*, a club near the Williamson School which was out of bounds to Williamson boys, and a couple of them were caught there smoking marijuana. Someone had squealed to the principal that Percy was in the club at the same time as the delinquent students. He could have lost his job at Williamson and his reputation as well, except that he recalled that he had spotted the principal's daughter several times at the *Magenta Swan*. After due deliberation, the principal decided to overlook Percy's behaviour. Monroe Thatcher had given Percy a fishy-eyed stare for a week or so, and then overnight he became all affability. Percy had faced his first contest and survived. He had done better, he thought, than Bulwer Lytton's young gladiator, Lydon. Poor Lydon had faced his first enemy in the Pompeii amphitheatre on the last day of the city's life, and lost, only a few moments before death would enfold all the bloodthirsty audience watching the show on their stone benches.

But it was a disappointing amphitheatre. Here, to this provincial town, the impresarios who ran the gladiatorial schools would send their third-rate fighters. Frightened men, past their prime, dreading an encounter with a young gladiator with swift reflexes like Lydon. The spectators waited impatiently for violence and blood. Like a hockey game, thought Percy. But there were no amenities in this amphitheatre. No dressing rooms. The stairs leading to the upper tiers of the seats were narrow and precipitous. Stone benches to bruise Pompeian buttocks. However the spectators would have been on their feet half the time, cheering, hurling insults, brandishing their fists, stretching their legs.

All that's left of it is this bare structure, thought Percy. He stood on top of one of the exterior staircases, and looked across at the Great Palaestra where Pompeii's young men exercised and sculpted their bodies. Some of them had fled to the Palaestra's latrine for shelter when Vesuvius exploded, for their skeletons were found there when archaeologists unearthed the building. Percy sat down on a stone bench in the arena, and thought of death and the vanity of human life.

But first, before death overtook him, Percy had some scores to settle.

Down below, in the arena, he spotted a familiar figure. Betty Laramie. And beside her, Madge Midgely was struggling along gamely. They were in earnest conversation. Percy's first instinct was to slink away, unnoticed. But then, on second thought, he climbed down to join them.

'YOU KNOW, SALLY,' SAID Miriam, 'internalized oppression always haunts the female. The whole system is rigged against women.'

Sally Harvey nodded, and thought bitterly of her own divorce. The scars still hurt. Shirley Perovich had paused to take a picture. The three of them had exited Pompeii by the Herculaneum Gate and were trudging along the Street of the Tombs outside the walls, on their way to the *Villa dei Misteri*.

'We are enslaved by the culture of romance,' Miriam went on. 'It's compulsory heterosexuality that's at the root of it. Our culture has institutionalized practices which presume that all women are sexually orientated towards men.'

'Well, you're right down in the trenches when you teach high school,' said Sally. 'The girls in your class are nubile young women at fourteen and the boys are either long and gangly, or they haven't reached their growth spurt. They aren't very satisfying sexual objects.'

'They grow up,' said Miriam, 'and they don't improve.'

Sally's ex-husband had been eleven years younger than she. He had matured to discover that he did not like Sally. Three years had passed, but Sally still brooded on it. She had come home early from school to find him in bed in the arms of the gardener, who was an illegal immigrant from Mexico. Sally still remembered how she had entered the bedroom, and the gardener looked up at her , surprised, with the large, melting eyes of a startled deer.

'I'm sorry, Mrs. Harvey,' he had said. Her ex-husband looked guilty and said nothing.

'Sometimes,' she remarked, aloud, 'men are nicer before they have quite grown up.'

Miriam gave her a chilly glance. 'If you take young Conradin as an example, they have some rough edges to lose. Mark my words, someone will strangle that young man before the summer is out.'

'Piers and Kim are a different sort, though,' said Sally, charitably. 'Piers should clean up his language—not every second word has to be "fuck"—but the Korean boy is a nice, well-mannered fellow. I told him I thought I had an affinity with Korea, for we used to drive a little Kia. It was a nice little car. My ex-husband took it when our marriage broke up.'

'And left you to get around on a bicycle, no doubt,' said Miriam.

'Oh, no. I kept the Jaguar. I wasn't going to let him have an expensive car like a Jag.'

Shirley rejoined them, her digital camera dangling from her wrist.

'I got a picture of the tomb of Aulus Veius,' she said with satisfaction. "I think it's the right one. The *Blue Guide* said it looked like a semicircular seat.'

'I'd like to be remembered by a seat for the bums of the common folk,' said Sally. 'It would make me feel useful.' Sally's sprained ankle was still hurting.

'This is amazing, these tomb monuments,' said Shirley. 'The Romans built their tombs along the road leading into the city, so they wouldn't be forgotten. You know, in Roman funerals, when someone died, they actually hired actors to walk in the funeral procession wearing death masks of the man's ancestors? A man was buried in the presence of his ancestors. Symbolically, I mean.'

'It's the patriarchal society again,' said Miriam.

'It was a male culture, for sure,' agreed Shirley, amiably. 'Roman women never thought outside the box. They wouldn't push the envelope.'

'That's the way the patriarchy maintains control,' insisted Miriam.

'I've always been fascinated by the cult of death,' said Sally. 'These Pompeians were desperate to be remembered. Look at these monuments!'

'Who does?' said Miriam. 'You'll notice the preponderance of tombs for men. It's the male ancestors that mattered. Not the women. They can be consigned to oblivion.'

'Well, there is the tomb of Caecilia Metella on the Appian Way,' said Sally. 'It's impressive enough. I don't think Caecilia wanted to be forgotten.'

'Tomb of who?' said Miriam. 'Whom, I mean?'

'Caecilia Metella. She was immensely wealthy. She wanted to be remembered.'

'Well,' conceded Miriam, 'it could happen. But I get mad when I see women going along with the male-dominated society as if life were a Harlequin Romance. Marcia Mellon is carrying on with Kowalski, you know. She came in late again last night. If this keeps going on, I'm going to demand another room-mate.'

'It's her business,' said Sally. 'Kowalski is the kind of man my fourteen-year old girls would go crazy about.'

'Well,' said Miriam, 'I don't hang out with Kowalski to all hours at the *Albergo Felice,* and I don't see why I should have to put up with Marcia doing it.'

'I wonder how he gets on at his school for boys,' said Sally. 'The Gilead Academy. That's the name, isn't it? Young Conradin goes there.'

'Here we are,' Shirley broke in. 'The Villa of the Mysteries. Let's see what our indispensable guidebook has to say about it.' She opened her *Blue Guide.* 'The villa was being remodeled when the eruption buried it, it says. There was an olive press found here in a courtyard.'

'I wish Baker or Fordham would guide us around more of Pompeii than they did,' grumbled Miriam. 'It's their job to answer questions, not to sit in the coffee shop. This college Baker is from, Ancaster University, does anyone know anything about it?'

'I know someone who taught there, once,' said Sally. 'He liked the place, but he had three children and they were growing up without being taught American values. He felt he had to move them back to the States even though he took a slight drop in salary. The children were not getting the right upbringing in Canada, he thought.'

'Values are so important,' said Shirley.

'Yes,' said Miriam. 'Now tell me, what was this villa for?'

'Well,' said Shirley, as they paused in the entrance, an apse which gave on a hall leading to the atrium. She paged through her guide book, and a card fell from it to the floor. 'It's a big farmhouse, I guess. Quite a house, though I don't like these black walls.'

Miriam spotted the card and picked it up. 'Fabiola Films,' she read. 'Is this yours, Shirley?'

'Oh, that? I didn't know I'd kept it. Throw it away.'

'What is this Fabiola Films?'

'Well, Betty Laramie and I were having a Cinzano two or three days ago on the patio of the *Albergo Felice* and this young Italian—he would have made a great statistic for you, Miriam—well-dressed, well-groomed—almost as handsome as he thought he was—he tried to make a move on Betty. She's a very pretty woman, you know, behind the glasses. I think Piers worships her from afar, but the least whiff of scholarship scares him off.'

'The poor girl,' said Shirley. 'You know, her university pays her a pittance to teach two courses as a teaching assistant, and then takes most of her salary back in tuition? She has to live on student loans!'

'So what's this about Fabiola Films?' asked Miriam.

'Oh, his line was that he made films and would very much like to take pictures of Betty,' said.

'Porn films, no doubt,' said Miriam. 'They peddle them on the Internet.'

'He wanted her to take her glasses off.'

'He wanted her to take off more than that, I'll bet,' said Miriam, disposing of the card in a flower pot.

'Take a look at this,' said Sally. They had entered a room with a great frieze on three of the walls. Figures against a vermilion background seemed to tell a story of religious ritual. First there was a child reading from a book, while a young bride and a seated older woman listened. Then there was a scene of sacrifice and next to it, a painting of spirits of the woodland making music. A woman peered into a cup held by a satyr while behind her, another figure raised up a hideous mask. In the far corner, a woman naked to the waist knelt before a veiled object, and across the corner of the wall, a winged demon raised a bullwhip to strike her.

'What is it?' asked Sally, awed at the sight. 'What is under that veil?'

'The *Guide* says it is a phallus,' said Shirley.

'A penis? Wearing a veil?' said Miriam. 'What is that poor woman doing to it?'

'Unveiling it, or protecting it with her body. The *Guide* thinks its one or the other.'

'And she's being flogged?' said Miriam. 'It makes you want to vomit, doesn't it?'

'Next we get the woman performing a wild dance with tambourines, and then we get her being dressed as a bride. It's an initiation into the cult of Dionysus.'

'Then the initiate becomes the bride of Dionysus?' asked Sally.

'I'm going to have to learn more about this,' said Miriam. 'Here we have the whole ritual of male domination. It's rape as a religious cult!'

'This is fantastic,' said Shirley. 'No wonder they call this the Villa of the Mysteries. This isn't what you'd expect to find in your ordinary farmhouse.'

'Not your ordinary farmhouse,' said Sally, who had pulled her copy of Baker's *Monuments* out of her satchel. 'It had sixty rooms. I wonder what sort of worshipers gathered here?'

'They came for the rituals of male dominance, whoever they were' said Miriam. 'The poor woman is flogged, kneels before an erect phallus, if that's what it is under that veil, and then it's the marriage bed. After that, probably death in childbirth. If not, another pregnancy. Another childbirth. By the way, where is Betty?'

'Betty went off with Madge Midgely,' said Shirley. 'She feels she needs advice, poor girl, and Madge is a good person to talk to. Besides, she moves slowly, so they can talk without Betty getting out of puff.'.

'Advice? Why does Betty need advice?'

'Well, here she is, with thirty thousand dollars in student

loans, and a dissertation that's not going well. After all her research, she thinks she will have nothing new to say about whatever it is she is writing about.'

'I know how it feels,' said Miriam. 'I sometimes reflect that no
one cares about Roman hegemony and the phallus, the subject
of my book. But then I think that *I* care, and that's enough say to
myself, Still, a topic like the three-barred sigma!'

'It makes you wonder,' said Shirley.

'THAT GREAT VOLCANO BROODS over us', said Sol Bernstein,
looking up at the cone of Vesuvius rising above Pompeii.

'Before it blew, they thought it was extinct,' said Piers who had
joined him, along with Yo-yo and Conradin. 'The explosion must
have been a fucking surprise.'

'This is where the gladiators practiced,' said Yo-yo Kim. They
were in the great colonnaded courtyard behind Pompeii's large
open-air theatre.

'Is that what Dr. Fordham said?' asked Sol.

'That's in Dr. Baker's *Notes*,' said Kim. 'There was armour for
gladiators found here, and skeletons. A woman's skeleton, too,
with expensive jewelry.'

Piers laughed. 'Guess what she was up to? She must have got
a fucking surprise.'

'Imagine fighting for your life like a gladiator,' said Kim.
'Dying if you lose.'

'It was a fucking great life,' said Piers. 'The crowd cheers, you
win your fight, you kill the other guy. Then the next fight, maybe
you die. Someday your fucking luck will always run out. It always does, eventually.'

'Brief glory,' said Sol. 'There's always someone younger, faster
and stronger waiting to do you in if you don't know when to retire. Have you ever read A. E. Housman's poem to an athlete dying young? We all read Housman when I was in school.'

Only Kim knew it. He had read it in his English as a second
language class.

'But,' said Piers. 'the gladiators knew that if they didn't retire in time, someone would kill them. The fucking reflexes always slow down with age.'

'A lot of them were slaves,' said Sol, 'and they retired when their owner let them retire. A lot of them even fought with their chests bare, if you look at their armour.'

'I remember that,' said Kim. 'Remember the gladiators' armour we saw in the museum?'

'That was stupid. Why didn't they protect their fucking chests?' asked Piers.

'They laughed at death. Remember the mosaic of a skeleton we saw at the museum?' said Kim. 'It came from Pompeii. People tramped on the skeleton..'

'But death's always there, no matter how fucking often you tramp on it,' said Piers.

'Maybe it's the good way to go,' broke in Conradin. 'Like, you have your great moment in the amphitheatre. The crowd cheers. You look Death in the face, like. You shoot the dice, and sometime you lose, and you die. It's awesome.'

'You're too young for talk like that,' said Sol.

'No, I mean it,' said Conradin. 'My best friend at Gilead died. I think about him a lot.'

'When?'

'Six months ago.'

'How did he die?'

'He just died. He didn't mean to die. He looked Death in the face—like, and he died. We never thought the pistol was loaded.'

'Nobody means to die. You young fellows can talk about looking Death in the face because you think it's far way', said Sol. 'Once Death comes closer, it's less fun to look at.'

Piers suddenly thought he understood Conradin's meaning.

'Suicide sucks,' he commented, with finality.

'It wasn't suicide,' Conradin protested. 'Matthew didn't mean to shoot himself. He didn't want to, no more than these gladiators wanted to die.'

'What do you plan to be when you grow up, Conradin?' Sol asked, after a moment's silence.

'I don't know. I want to do something to help people. Maybe in Africa, or somewhere like that.'

'Ah. You want to be a teacher. Like your father.'

'No, not like my father. Definitely not like my father.'

'And you, Piers?'

'Me? I want to be a lawyer, like my stepfather. I want to make money.'

'Well, you're looking at a lawyer,' said Sol. 'My money goes to alimony and supporting three kids, and of course, there's my high-priced shrink, to say nothing of my rabbi, whom I've got to keep happy. But I like to think I achieve something.'

'What do we look at next?' asked Piers, breaking a moment of uncomfortable silence. 'Where's the amphitheatre?'

XXIV

'I STILL feel a little choked,' Miriam Kuntz said to Dr. Alex as the group waited in the shade at the exit from the site of Pompeii for the stragglers to join then. 'The guard in the House of the Vettii showed that ithyphallic statue to Ellsworth and Kim, but he virtually slammed the closet door in my face. I was a woman and I wasn't supposed to see it!'

'That's a wonderful house, isn't it,' said Dr. Alex, refusing to be drawn. 'Did you know that the excavators identified the plants that grew in the peristyle before the eruption by examining the traces their roots left in the soil, and then they replanted the garden with the original plants?'

'If it weren't that I was keeping an eye on what Piers and the guard were up to, I would never have seen it,' said Miriam, who would not be diverted from her chosen subject.

'Have you seen Sir Kenneth Dover's remarks on the Priapic statuettes with erect phalluses which have been found in considerable numbers in Roman orchards and olive groves?' asked Dr. Alex, taking refuge in the sanctuary of arcane scholarship.

'What's that?' said Miriam.

'Priapus, you know, was an agricultural god who saved the crops from fungus diseases like rust, or from locusts or hail. A pagan scarecrow.'

'And they've found these in Roman olive groves? Wouldn't the Christian church have destroyed them?'

'These were little votive offerings of terracotta Priapus figures, buried in the orchards.'

'So what does Sir Kenneth say?' asked Miriam.

'Well, he suggests that these ithyphallic votive figurines were probably intended to guard the boundaries of a farmer's orchard. He finds parallels in the behaviour of primates.'

'You mean they were guardians of a peasant's property?'

'Well, that's the general idea.'

'Isn't that like men!' said Madge Midgely. 'They could have built a fence with a gate to keep intruders out, but instead, rather than just lock a gate, they bury an idol made of crockery, of a man with an erection.'

'I don't know how that theory would fit into my book,' said Miriam, troubled.

'You could lock the gate,' Dr. Alex said to Madge Midgely, 'but that wouldn't keep out fungus infections, or foot-and-mouth disease.'

'I'm not sure those terracotta Priapus figures fit into feminist theory very well, if, as you say, they were guardians of the fields,' said Miriam. 'I think that overlooks their significance for Gender Studies. There's only one reason why males have erections. What did you say the reference was?'

'Check out Kenneth Dover's *Greek Homosexuality*,' replied Dr. Alex. 'Somewhere around page 100.'

'You know, you've got to go with the flow when you're writing a book like mine,' said Miriam. 'I can't believe that men get erections to scare off intruders, when it's obvious that what they are doing is trying to lock women into inferior status.'

'Well, then you'll break new ground.' The stragglers had arrived and Dr. Alex was trying to herd the group in the direction of the bus.

'I'm not sure about that. You know, if your book gets a bad review in the *Journal of Feminist Theory* or the *Liberated Women's Monthly*, you might as well not have written it. Or worse, if it's never reviewed at all.'

'Send me a review copy, 'said Madge Midgely, generously. 'I'll give it a good write-up in the Beaumont *Advertiser*. The sisterhood must support one another.'

'Thanks,' said Miriam, thinking to herself that an effusive review in the Beaumont *Advertiser* would make, at best, an uncertain impression upon her Promotions and Tenure Committee.

XXV

THE GROUP was tired when it returned from Pompeii, but there was hot water in the showers, and a change of clothes and supper revived them. Sol Bernstein, Bathsheba Bennett and Sally Harvey went out to the patio overlooking the back garden, where Mario served after-dinner coffee, Sally hobbling along with the help of a cane. Her sprained ankle had been over-exercised at Pompeii, and was throbbing painfully. The night was cool and sensuous, the sort of night when one could imagine the spirits of the dead returning to the world of the living to taste a few short hours of pleasure. Bougainvillea in full bloom covered the Palazzo wall, and the oleander bushes were blossoming at the foot of the garden. Bathsheba found a wicker basket the gardener had abandoned, turned it upside down and fitted it under Sally's sore ankle as a footstool. Sol produced a deck of cards and shuffled them. Millicent and Conradin joined them.

'What a wonderful evening,' said Millicent. 'I love the smell of the good earth of Italy.'

'Except for the whiff of perfume from septic tank, mom,' added Conradin. 'Infusing the night air with a scent that is not Heaven-sent.'

'We were just talking about poor Dr. DeSilva,' said Bathsheba. 'It's odd, the way he died. Tragic, too.'

'We did what we could,' said Millicent. 'We got him to a hospital where he got medical attention.'

188

'I guess the doctors in that place knew what they were do-ing.' Bathsheba's voice conveyed enormous doubt about doctors in Naples.

'Well, they goofed this time,' observed Sally. 'I don't think DeSilva needed to die.'

'He didn't belong to our group,' said Millicent. 'We can't take responsibility for every Tom, Dick and Harry who turns up at the Palazzo. Not that we wouldn't give what help we could. We're always helpful.'

'The question that bothers me,' said Sol, 'is how that scorpion got into his knapsack in the first place. Are scorpions really all that common at Paestum?'

'It bothers me, too,' said Bathsheba. "The best guess is that he took the knapsack with him to the beach and left it open, lying in a place where a scorpion could find it.'

'But, Sheba, did he ever take his knapsack off the bus?' asked Sol. 'I wasn't paying much attention, but I didn't see him do it.'

'It stands to reason he did,' said Millicent. 'He would have carried his bathing suit in it.'

'This is getting ghoulish,' said Conradin, getting to his feet. 'I'm leaving.'

'Where are you going, Conradin?' asked Millicent, sharply.

'Just for a walk, mother.'

'Well, don't be long,,' said Millicent.. 'We start early tomorrow.'

'I won't, mom.'

'We've got just the right number for a game of bridge,' said Sol, shuffling his cards. 'Millicent, do you play?'

'Yes,' said Millicent, abstractedly, as she watched her son leave the garden by the back gate. 'Yes, I'd like a game. But we can't be late.'

'We won't be,' said Sally.

In the lounge Walter Druker was holding forth.

'So,' he said to Betty Laramie, 'you're a hopeful graduate stu-dent. Young, pretty and eager. Ah, I remember my graduate student days.' He rubbed his expansive belly contemplatively. 'I read everything and argued about everything, and it all seemed so terribly important. None of it does now. What are you working on?'

'It's not anything to do with philosophy,' said Betty, a little defensively.

'So much the better. You might have a concluding chapter that really comes to conclusions if you stay away from philosophy. You're not working on pots, are you?'

'Pots?'

'I mean you're not doing a dissertation on Greek or Roman pots, are you? Vases, urns, whatever you call them now. Broken chunks of earthenware pots, you know. Pot shards. You're not working on them, are you?'

'Pot shards can be very important for chronology,' Gregory Donahue stated, with a wise nod of his head.

'Chronology. Dates, you mean,' said Walter, with scorn. 'Betty, honey, if the study of Greek pots ever gets you a secure date that no one will contradict, I'll do cart wheels in the back garden of the Palazzo Agrippina, and you can imagine how ridiculous that would look.'

'Indeed we can,' interjected Kwame Assante.

'Never fear. But what is your dissertation all about?'

'Well,' said Betty, 'my advisor is an epigrapher who works on Greek inscriptions and he suggested a topic in that field.'

'Oh?' said Gregory Donahue, who began to find the conversation interesting. 'That's my field, too. I'm an epigraphy expert myself. What's the topic?'

'It's on the date when the three-barred sigma first appears in Greek inscriptions.'

'The *what*?' said Walter.

'Sigma is a letter in the Greek alphabet,' interjected Mildred Donahue.

'So I believe. But isn't that an old potato? Does anyone care any more whether the sigma has three bars or four? Sorry, Betty. Obviously you care. But what's the point?'

'It's an extremely important question,' interposed Gregory

Donahue. 'The sigma is tool for dating inscriptions, and without a date, inscriptions lose half their value. There's a lot of literature on the three-barred sigma.'

'I know it, Heaven is my witness!' Druker put a hand over his heart. 'But does anyone read this bountiful literature? And anyway, who wants more dates in history? I'd like to banish them from my classroom.'

'But see here,' protested Gregory. 'You can't do that. Let's say you're trying to discover the cause of an event we'll call "x", and you think the cause was a happening we'll call "y". But if I prove to you that "y" happened after "x", then "y" can't be the cause of "x". Right?'

'Wrong, because we always figure out the causes of an event in history after it has happened. If the event doesn't ever happen, it won't need a cause. There are all sorts of causes in this world which are still looking for something to cause.'

Donahue's body language expressed distaste. He changed the subject.

'Tell me, Betty,' said he with solicitude, 'have you seen the article by Wilhelm von Krauthammer in the latest *ZPE*? The *Zeitschrift*, you know. You know it, don't you? He says everything that can be said about the three-barred sigma, in my opinion.'

'No, I haven't,' said Betty, looking worried.

'You should. It's not a long article. In German, of course.'

'Greg can read German,' interjected Mildred.

'I haven't seen the last *ZPE*, said Betty.

'Well, it would be good to know the latest work on the subject,' said Gregory, magisterially. 'Von Krauthammer is a very thorough scholar. You wouldn't want to repeat what he's already done and have your dissertation out of date before you start.'

Betty looked a little tearful. 'I've been working almost two years on this subject,' she said. 'I don't know what I'd do if I had to change it now. I have an enormous student loan. It will keep me in debt for years. I could come here this summer only because the Palazzo Agrippina gave me a scholarship.'

'Hum,' said Gregory, feeling in his jacket pocket for his pipe.

'Good Lord, but I'm in desperate need of a drink, Kwame,' interrupted Walter Druker.

'Here, have some Perrier water,' said Kwame.

'I hate the stuff, but for you, Kwame, I'll drink it. Now, Betty, I don't think you'll have to abandon your topic. You'll be able to find an angle that old Krauthammer's overlooked. Something that grabs attention. Something that's in style and up-to-date. Has Krauthammer said anything about the three-barred sigma and gender relations? I'll bet he hasn't even thought of it.'

Gregory Donahue snorted.

'You see?' Druker went on. 'There are all sorts of unexplored angles. What about the three-barred sigma and the changeover from oral to written culture? Is the three-barred sigma a hot medium or a cool medium? You must show that the way a stonecutter forms a letter on the marble he is carving expresses his inner being. It is his reaction to the *Zeitgeist*. Maybe you can work in a reference to Affirmative Action. What evidence do we have for visible minority stonecutters carving inscriptions with three-barred sigmas? You see, I'm writing your dissertation for you.' Druker took another swig of Perrier water. 'But if you do have to give up on the three-barred sigma,' he went on, 'find another topic that grabs some real interest in the modern world. A topic you can tie up in eight months or so. A doctoral dissertation shouldn't be a life's work.'

'But my advisor is an epigrapher,' said Betty.

'Ditch him. Give up inscriptions. What about tackling a topic from Black History? Martin Bernal's *Black Athena* has blown that field wide open. Deal with it judiciously, *sine ira et studio*, as old Tacitus said, as he set forth the history of Rome with rage and prejudice. Now what about Queen Cleopatra of Egypt? Kwame here tells me she was a black woman....'

'I said we shouldn't dismiss the notion,' corrected Kwame. "I say she can usefully be considered black.'

'And I say,' went on Walter, 'that we must examine the question. It needs a dissertation. In your first chapter you'll show that she was born and brought up in Africa, and so she was an African. Then...'

'You're making it all too simple,' interrupted Donahue, with a grimace.

'Well, you can't deny she was an African. Egypt is in Africa, you know. Anyway, how black do you have to be to be black? Personally I don't think it matters much, but if Kwame thinks Cleopatra can be usefully black, let her be useful. It's poets and movies and school teachers who make history, not the poor devils who fight battles and do things like that. We need useful history, with good guys and bad guys.'

'Now hold on,' said Shirley Perovich. 'History is about truth. We all have to confront our pasts and learn to live with them.'

'Nonsense,' said Walter. 'We all create histories that minister to our self-esteem. Then every so often along comes an historian with a heart of flint, armed with a lot of dates and footnotes, and starts looking for truth. He chops down our private historical edifice. Historians are really a merciless lot. They talk about confronting our past, as if history were some damned battle-line we have to face. Who wants it?'

'But,' said Shirley, 'as educationalists we are shaping young minds. We have to train them to ask questions. We're not propagandists.'

'Well, Gregory thinks....' began Mildred, but Walter ploughed ahead.

'No, we're all propagandists. The difference is some admit it, most don't. We want history that makes us feel good. We want to hear how upright and valiant our ancestors were, and how they survived oppression and all that sort of thing. We want to know they were victims, never oppressors. History does not live by footnotes alone, and, anyway, bad history, no matter how bad, is far better than bad wine. Bad wine's a crime; bad history is pure fun.'

'You're asking us to change our ideas about accuracy,' said Madge Midgely, who had been listening carefully. 'A good reporter reports facts. If someone on the editorial staff of the *Advertiser* took your line, he wouldn't last long.'

'Oh yes, he would, so long as what he reported didn't offend a powerful interest group. A successful newspaper story has to reproduce patterns that most people accept. The trouble is, we don't admit to ourselves what we are doing. Now Marcia, you write murder mysteries. I suppose you think that the important thing is to catch the murderer.'

'Well, that's the general idea,' said Marcia. 'Justice should be done.'

'Justice should be seen to be done,' said Walter.

'That, too.'

'It's not the same thing,' said Walter. 'For justice to be seen to be done, you've got to find the right sort of person for the murderer. A person who fits our idea of what a murderer should be. Whether or not he actually committed the murder is not nearly as important. In law courts, husbands beat wives. Wives never beat husbands. In real life, maybe, but never in the courts of law. If justice is seen to be done, it has to provide suitable verdicts that maintain the proper conventions. It doesn't matter if it's right or wrong.'

'Oh, come now! Why do you think we have trials before juries, if not to prove a man who is accused is really guilty?'

'Because trials are dramas. You have a lawyer who tries to prove the accused person is guilty. You've got a lawyer who tries to prove he is innocent. You've got a judge to see to it that it's all done according to the popular prejudices of our historical period. The jury serves as the audience. The drama's all done according to the rules Aristotle set down in his *Poetics*. He said a tragedy is ridiculous if the right sort of person doesn't suffer. Kwame, this Perrier water is destroying my spiritual being. Is there nothing I can add to it?'

Kwame extended a long arm and nabbed a bottle of Stock brandy.

'Take a drop of this. Not too much. You're getting too heavy for me to roll into bed.'

'You're a saint, Kwame. A true saint. What was I saying?'

'You were saying that a courtroom drama is an Aristotelian tragedy,' said Sister Stella. 'And is the final aim *katharsis*?'

'*Katharsis*? Yes, of course it is. Nowadays we call it "closure" and we pay grief counsellors good money to lead us to it. *Katharsis*. Nice word, but it's never been translated properly. We translate it "purgation" as if Aristotle thought of tragedy as a detergent. But the translation is quite wrong. *Katharsis* means "fart." A simple old-fashioned fart. Aristotle thought of the Greek audience gathered in the theatre, watching the climax of the play, and then, when emotion is at its peak, when the grief is unbearable and the audience is in tears, there is a great communal fart. It fills the theatre. There is a huge sigh of relief. Then everyone goes home feeling much better.'

'What a fragrant place the theatre must have been,' said Madge Midgely.

' Not at all,' said Walter. 'Farts stink only when people eat a lot of meat. Stick to bread and olive oil and they're not half so miasmal. Anyway, Greeks had open-air theatres.'

'But,' said Marcia, 'the primary aim of a trial is not closure for the victims, but rather to find out who the perpetrator of the crime really was, and punish him so that he won't commit the crime again.'

'Ah, Marcia, you write murder mysteries. Now tell me, if your aim is to punish the perpetrator so he won't commit the crime again, then you must believe in the death penalty, No dead criminal ever commits a crime again.

'But it so happens that I don't believe in the death penalty.'

'Marcia, you're a liberal. In Spearfish State U., that is a misdemeanour. But look here: for centuries governments got rid of their criminals by killing them. It was cheap and effective, and provided public entertainment. Squeamishness about hanging is a modern notion, and all of us here are by definition old-fashioned, I should think.'

'I still can't accept the death penalty. Governments shouldn't be in the business of taking human life.'

'Then you must believe that punishment is an educational experience. Courts punish convicted crooks to make them mend their ways. Do you really believe that?'

'Well, there's also the need to make the punishment fit the crime.'

'But no punishment ever fits the crime. The murder victim won't come to life no matter how long the murderer stays in jail

at the taxpayers' expense. The Romans here in Pozzuoli had a
better idea. They would thrust a convict into the arena in that
splendid amphitheatre they built here, and let him fight it out
with a couple hungry lions. He got to fight a desperate life-and-
death battle with wild beasts just as his primitive ancestors did
hundreds of times during their short lives. The crowd loved it.
That's *katharsis* for you, Marcia.'

'It's horrible,' interjected Madge Midgely.

'What a cynical old sod you are,' said Marcia. 'So why do you
think we have trials before juries?'

'Well,' said Walter, after a moment's thought, 'I'm not against
them. We must not let an unnecessary death go unremarked.
A murder trial is our homage to a life cut short. That's why
DeSilva's death seems so sad to me. It went unremarked. It was
an unnecessary death and no one noticed, except for a couple
questurini wearing white gloves.'

'But that wasn't murder,' said Sister Stella.

'I guess not. Depends on how you define murder.'

'How did we get on this topic?' spoke up Mildred Donahue.
'We were talking about inscriptions, I thought.'

'So we were,' said Walter. 'Does anyone have anything more
to say about inscriptions before we abandon the topic?'

'Just one thing, Betty,' said Gregory Donahue. 'Read Wilhelm
von Krauthammer's article on the three-barred sigma before you
give up on it. It's not a long article. Just four pages.'

'Gregory just had some good news,' interjected Mildred.

'Now, Mildred,' said Gregory.

'Oh,' said Walter. 'Let's hear some good news for a change.'

'It was just before we heard of poor Dr. DeSilva's death that
we got it. Greg has been working on a committee to choose the
next president for CPC—the College of the Pacific Coast, that is—
for the past six months, and we just learned that the man Greg
backed got the job.'

'Good for him,' said Walter.

'You must be glad,' said Sister Stella. 'Your university will
have got good president, and that's an achievement.'

'Well,' said Gregory, 'Brent Fenwick, the man we chose, is not the sharpest tool in the toolbox, I'd be the first to admit.'

'He's a psychologist, you know,' interjected Mildred. "He did his PhD at Mississippi University.'

'But as president he won't change much,' Gregory went on. 'He's grounded. He'll fit in.'

'He used to be the assistant vice-president academic and he's a very sound man,' Mildred went on. 'Our children went to the same school as his. He told Greg that if he became president, he would back Greg for the next Dean of Arts.'

'There you go,' said Walter. 'There is justice in the world, after all.'

Mildred beamed. Gregory Donahue looked faintly embarrassed.

'The dean we have now should go,' said Mildred. 'He was a pal of the last president. He owed his appointment to him. But he's just a dollars and cents man. No vision'

'Well,' Walter went on, 'I hope your school—what's its name?—is better than the seat of higher education where I teach. Spearfish State is the place where the academic brain goes to die.'

'Oh, CPC is a good school,' said Mildred. 'Greg wouldn't be there if it wasn't.'

The door opened and Thatcher thrust in his head. He cleared his throat at the decibel level of a six-inch cannon.

'Have any of you seen Conradin lately?' he demanded, fixing Betty with a suspicious stare.

'He's not here,' said Walter.

'I haven't seen him all evening,' said Betty.

'It's time for him to go to bed,' said Thatcher.'

'So it is for us all,' said Walter, 'but alas! This is an educational institution and our room partners are assigned to us, with no consideration for our sexual needs.'

Thatcher withdrew, closing the door firmly behind him.

Ellen Cross, who had been listening carefully, said the last word.

'I think it's wonderful to be here where we can all improve our minds,' she said. 'You know, Betty,' she added, turning to

Betty Laramie, 'I was thinking about your three-barred sigma. That would be a wonderful name for a cocktail lounge, don't you think? The *Three-Barred Sigma*! Three separate bars. One wild west, the second art deco, and the third very modern, My husband's in the hotel business. Wait till I tell him.'

'Good for you, Ellen,' said Walter Druker. 'Who says that our research lacks a practical dimension?'

THATCHER STUCK HIS HEAD out the back door of the Palazzo, and saw the game of bridge in progress on the patio.

'Have you seen Conradin?' he asked.

'He went for a walk, Monnie,' said Millicent.

'I asked Percy Bass to look out for him,' said Thatcher, 'but I don't know where Percy is.'

'He should be back by now,' said Millicent.

'Well, Conradin's a big boy. He'll find his way home,' said Sol Bernstein.

Thatcher looked doubtful, but he withdrew.

'Conradin can be such a worry sometimes,' complained Millicent.

'Annie Fordham seems very low,' said Sally Harvey, after a pause for more comment on Conradin.

Bathsheba nodded. 'She should be at home,' she said. 'She can't cope any more.'

'Does anyone know what's the trouble?' Sol wanted to know. 'She and DeWitt, they both soak up a lot of wine at supper, I notice.'

'Yes, I noticed too,' said Sally. 'Madge Midgely diagnoses repressed memories of sexual abuse as a child. That's her pet theory. She's quite stuck on it.'

'That's a load of crap,' said Sol.

'Well, Madge would dispute that,' said Sally. 'She's had a lot of experience with women writing to her for advice. You know she writes an advice column called "Ask Madge" or something like that, and several newspapers reprint it. She says one-third of American women have suffered incest before the age of eighteen, and they don't remember it because they repress the memory.'

'They don't remember it because it didn't happen, you mean,' snorted Sol.

'Well, Madge would say that's being in denial. I don't buy everything she says,' Sally went on, 'but she's my room mate, and I've learned not to argue with her.'

'I think Annie's just depressed,' said Millicent.

'Madge's been telling me about a number of cases that were reported to her,' Sally continued. 'One woman wrote that she suffered from depression off and on until a therapist revealed that her father had changed her diapers when she was a baby. Her father admitted it, but he wouldn't admit any guilt! She sued him.'

'Poor devil,' said Sol. 'He probably lost, too'

'Well,' interjected Bathsheba, 'I'm sorry for poor Annie, but this is not the place for someone who's suffering from depression. It's not a restful life here for the wife of a director. But I guess it's her choice. I think it's time for my bed.'

'I'll follow you, Sheba,' said Sol. 'It was a busy day. I'm tired.'

'Breakfast at six-thirty tomorrow,' said Bathsheba. 'My biological clock doesn't really fit this program schedule. My stomach isn't ready for the digestion business until eight in the morning!'

XXVI

THE AMALFI Drive with lunch at Ravello, washed down with good Ravello wine. It was to have been a great day, with lunch served on a terrace far above the blue Mediterranean, looking down over a great swath of southern Italy spread out like a landscape painting. The Agrippina group would visit Amalfi, stop in the Piazza del Duomo and visit the cathedral, which claims to have the bones of St. Andrew, the professions of Scotland notwithstanding. Then the bus would climb up the side of the Dragone gorge through many twists and turns to Ravello. It should have been a great day.

The group gathered for breakfast early in the dining hall. They looked sleepy, except for Percy Bass who had returned from a morning jog, followed by a quick shower. The day would be long, but the scenery would be spectacular. Annie Fordham planned to join the Agrippina group for the trip.

'Ravello is too beautiful to miss,' she said. 'If I take a Gravol before we start the climb up to Ravello, I'm OK. Otherwise those switchbacks get to me.'

Dr. Alex, who was sitting at the end of the long table at DeWitt's left elbow, next to Percy Bass, leaned down to pick up his briefcase from the floor. 'I'd better see if I've got my notes here,' he said. 'I don't want to lose my Ravello lecture.' He pulled out a notepad, set it on the table, and as he did, a letter, stamped and ready to be mailed, fell accidentally on top of it. Dr. Alex picked up the pad and in the process knocked the letter almost under DeWitt's nose. DeWitt read the address: 'Dr. Edgar Rosenblatt, Chairman, Search Committee, Holyrood College'.

'A letter to Rosenblatt, eh?'

'Yes,' said Dr. Alex, genially. 'He asked me for a reference for you.'

'I hope you weren't too accurate?'

'If my letter were any more flattering, it would sprout wings and fly stateside itself,' said Dr. Alex. 'Don't worry.'

'Well, thanks,' said DeWitt, still slightly ruffled. Percy Bass, at Dr. Alex's elbow, giggled nervously for no particular reason, and seemed about to say something..

'I didn't know you were being considered for Dean of Arts,' Dr. Alex went on. 'You kept it to yourself.'

'Well,' replied DeWitt, modestly, 'some of my friends urged me to throw my hat into the ring. I wasn't so sure, myself. But you know how it is. If I ever want to get into administration, it's now or never.'

'So what do you think your chances are?'

'Well,' replied DeWitt, 'I have a good friend on the selection committee who tells me I'm at the top of the list along with one other candidate. Maybe your letter will put me over the top.'

'Well, it should.'

'But I've made it clear,' DeWitt went on, 'that I'll need six weeks off in the summer months so that I can fulfill my commitments here at the Palazzo Agrippina. I'll never let the old Agrippina down.'

'Absolutely,' said Dr. Alex, his tone earnest. 'We'd miss your dynamic –'

'I said I was needed here, and the search committee said no problem,' said DeWitt.

'Good,' said Dr. Alex, without complete enthusiasm. 'I was worried about that.'

DeWitt looked down the long table where the Agrippina group, some of them still half asleep, were eating breakfast. The Palazzo always served a good breakfast. Continental breakfasts were banned in its dining hall. Tour groups that had only *caffè latte* and a hard roll for breakfast flagged by half-past ten, and that did not do..

'Something is bothering Millicent,' DeWitt said. 'Where's Conradin? What time did he come in last night?'

'He'd better not hold us up this morning,' said Dr. Alex. 'We've a long day ahead.'

Sitting at mid-point along the table, opposite her husband, Millicent Thatcher was toying with her boiled egg and toast.

'I wonder where Conradin is,' she said. 'He should be up by now.'

'Someone bang on his door,' said Monnie. No one moved. 'I'll go up myself.' A minute later he was back. 'He's not in his room.'

Millicent looked worried.

'He's probably stepped outside,' said Annie. "DeWitt, ask Mario to look.'

Fordham said a few words to Mario in Italian, and Mario headed out the back door. He returned a moment later, pale, with shock written over his face. He burst into a flow of excited Italian to DeWitt, who got up and followed him.

'What is it?' asked Thatcher.

'Did you understand what he said?' Marcia murmured to Paul.

'Something is wrong with Conradin.'.

Millicent overheard, even though Paul had spoken in little more than a whisper. "Conradin?' she said, sharply. 'What has happened to Conradin?'

Fordham returned and spoke urgently to Thatcher, who rose and followed him out, for once with nothing to say.

'What is going on?' asked Millicent. Her hand holding her *caffè latte* shook so badly that the coffee slopped into the saucer. 'What is it?' She got up and followed her husband outside. In a moment, her high-pitched cry, like the howl of a wounded beast floated back to the group at the breakfast table. By now they were all on their feet and making for the back door, Sol Bernstein leading with Marcia only a step behind.

Conradin was hanging by his neck from a lower limb of the tree that shaded Sibyl Twickenham's grave. One end of a leather belt had been passed through the buckle and then fitted around his neck, and the other end was looped over the limb, and fastened by shoving a bent nail through two holes in the belt. At Conradin's feet lay an old armchair upholstered in threadbare brocade on which he had climbed to attach the belt to the limb, and then kicked aside. Marcia recognized it. She had last seen it inside the back door of the Palazzo that led to the garden.

'Is he dead?' It was Ellen Cross who asked.

'Quite dead, I fear,' said Marcia. The silver buckle of the belt had pressed deeply into Conradin's neck. He was wearing a new pair of sneakers on his feet, and Marcia spotted his footprints in the soft earth under the tree. Prints Conradin must have made with his new shoes. There was another set of footprints as well, sneakers about the same size as Conradin's, but with worn treads. Both sets of footprints were rapidly disappearing under Thatcher's feet, for he had thrown his arms around his dead son's waist and was swaying back and forth with grief.

'Conradin! My son, Conradin! Oh, Conradin!' It was a feral cry, the voice of an animal in anguish.

DeWitt, his face ashen, moved forward, and took Thatcher by the shoulders. Kwame and Walter Druker followed him. Druker took a Swiss army knife from the pocket of his ample Dockers and started to cut the belt. The belt buckle had broken the skin on the left side of Conradin's throat but there was no bleeding.

'Is he dead?' asked DeWitt, his voice flat.

'I think so,' said Kwame.

'Best leave him, then, until the police come.'

'Can't do that, DeWitt,' said Druker, and continued to saw the belt while Kwame wrapped his arms around Conradin's inert torso and lifted until the belt hung loose. It revealed a scarlet ring around Conradin's throat where the belt had chafed, and marks made by the edges of the buckle.

Millicent's face crumpled as if the realization that Conradin was dead had just struck her like the blow of a fist in the gut. She collapsed into a canvas chair and Ellen Cross knelt beside her and put her arms around her shoulders.

'Poor dear Millicent. There, there.' Later, Ellen was to say, with tears in her eyes, 'I couldn't find the right words. All I could do was to put my arms around her. I wanted to give her a shoulder to cry on.'

But Millicent did not weep. She sat very still, looking at her husband, and her eyes were full of bitterness.

'He killed him,' she said, as if she were unaware of Ellen's presence. 'It's Monroe's doing. It's even his belt.'

XXVII

THE TWO elegant policemen with white gloves reappeared. For the moment they had questions only for Fordham and Thatcher, and Thatcher, pulling himself together, announced that the group should not cancel the trip to Amalfi and Ravello. Dr. Alex could act as leader. The lunch for the group at Ravello had ordered and paid for. It was pointless to miss it. The policemen could question the students when they returned, if they thought it necessary.

Annie Fordham retired to her room, looking as if she had been pole-axed, and Thatcher became suddenly anxious about his own wife, who sat, dry-eyed, looking into space. Marcia managed to take a careful look at Conradin's body after it was cut down. She felt a trifle ghoulish: a detective-story writer drawn to a corpse like a bee to honey. Rigor mortis had not yet set in. Conradin had not been dead for long. There was a angry red mark on the left side of his throat where the silver buckle of the belt had cut into the flesh and on the right side, a smaller wound with a trickle of blood oozing from it, as if Conradin first had tried on the belt and adjusted it once before he climbed on the chair to attach one end to the tree. A cursory search was done of his room. There was no suicide note, but there were several videotapes and a floppy disk labeled 'Doc. 1, Notes for Creative Writing next term. Doc. 2, Poem for Matthew.' The policemen took them with them, promising to return them later.

The group left the Palazzo later than the hour of departure

announced on the day's schedule, and Giuseppe had to steer the bus through a gauntlet of traffic as he drove across Naples. A seething mass of Fiats, Peugeots, Rovers and Volkswagens driven by Neapolitan drivers bent on self-destruction charged the bus on every side. By the time the group reached Sorrento, some sanity had returned to the road, and a measure of oxygen to the air, but the driver was still trying vainly to make up for lost time. Mildred Donahue was looking ill and Madge Midgely was distinctly green.

'Paul,' Marcia said, 'I think you have something to tell me.'

'If you saw my lips moving,' said Paul, 'it was because I was praying to St. Christopher. I hope the bus driver realizes that one death is enough for the day.'

'I think you are holding back something,' said Marcia. 'Let me be your mother confessor. Absolute confidentiality guaranteed.'

'Why do you think I'm holding something back?' Paul's voice was cautious.

'You knew Conradin well.' It was a statement, not a question. Paul was silent for a moment before he replied.

'Yes, he was my student, and teenage boys who want to talk things over will turn to male teachers who don't have grey hair yet. It often happens. That's what Conradin did. He couldn't talk to his father. The age gap was too great.'

'And he was a disappointment to his father.'

'He thought he was. Yes, that was a barrier too.'

'What did he talk about?'

'You're sticking your probes in deep.'

'I'm a writer,' said Marcia. 'I'm a ruthless old bat when I smell something that's not quite straight.'

'If you're insinuating something more than a teacher-student relationship, you're wrong,' said Paul with a flicker of anger. 'Conradin wanted a father figure.'

'But he already had one,' said Marcia.

'Point taken.'

'Who was this friend called Matthew, that I hear about?'

'Yu do have a nose for scandal, Marcia. Matthew was Conradin's best friend at the Gilead Academy. He shot himself accidentally. Conradin saw him die. It must have been terrible for him.'

'Was Conradin gay?'

'I thought you might ask that. I think Conradin didn't know the answer to that, himself. Marcia, I don't feel right being here. Here we are going along to Amalfi drive and up to Ravello for lunch, one of the most beautiful places in a beautiful country wherever man hasn't spoiled it. And Conradin is lying dead.' There were tears in his eyes. 'I loved the boy, Marcia. If I ever have a son, I hope he can be like Conradin.'

'I'm sorry, Paul. I didn't mean to probe an open wound. But I'm an old bat who has seen a lot, and if you want to talk, I'll listen.'

Paul looked out the window of the bus, expressionless, as the magnificent scenery bordering the *Via Nocera* flashed by..

'Do you know that Mary Shelley used this mountainous country south of Sorrento for a Gothic novel of hers which was published after she was dead, long after she wrote *Frankenstein*?'

'Yes, I've heard of it,' said Marcia. '*The Heir of Mondolfo*.'

'The young prince of Mondolfo hated his father for maltreating his mother.'

'Are you saying –'

'No,' said Paul, 'I'm not claiming there is any parallel. Thatcher does not maltreat his wife. But she is a possession of his, like his car and his old dog that follows him on his early morning walks, always one step behind. Millicent had a good brain once, but Thatcher never noticed it, and I don't know if she has one anymore. Brains cannot be left unused.'

'I think that might be true of Mildred Donahue, but Millicent? Surely not.'

'No, no. Mildred is her husband's manager and spin doctor, efficient and not too obtrusive. Millicent Thatcher is just an outlying province in the Thatcher empire. Conradin was another. Heaven knows it's no great empire: an endowed chair at the Williamson school and alumni who've made a mint on Wall Street who greet him on Commencement Days. So there you have it. Conradin wanted his father to approve of him and love him. His father didn't notice. At the same time, he hated his father because he saw how the supreme ego left his mother no room to breathe. Then came the teenage hormone rush. In the Gilead common rooms, conversations can start on any number of subjects, some even intellectual, but they always turn rapidly to sex.'

'I thought they sometimes talked about sport.'

'That, too. It still ends up with sex.'

'And Conradin was mixed up?'

'You could put it that way.'

'Well,' said Marcia, moving forward cautiously, ' what about Conradin's relationship with Luigi and Tony at the *Albergo Felice?*'

Paul stared at her. 'You are an old bloodhound, aren't you? Well, the *Felice* is respectable on the surface but as we both know, it rents rooms by the hour to couples who want exactly sixty minutes of mad passion. Or one hundred and twenty minutes if the mad passion lasts that long. It's equal opportunity, too. The cost is the same for heterosexual or homosexual couples. And yes, Luigi and Tony are available. Are you surprised?'

'Paul, you remember the first time we used the *Felice's* facilities? We exited our room separately, remember? And as I sneaked down the hall, I saw Conradin stick his head out of a room. Behind him was Tony.'

'Tony?' said Paul. 'I misjudged Conradin.'

'What do you mean?'

'I suspected Luigi. That explains something I wondered about.'

'I think I'm out of the loop. Is something going on between Tony and Luigi?'

'Well,' said Paul, with an exasperating smile, 'that depends on what the meaning of "is" is.'

'Don't play with me, Paul. There are two levels of reality at the *Albergo Felice::* what you see on the surface and think is real, and what is really happening, well beneath the surface.'

'That's true enough. The *Albergo Felice* seems respectable enough, but don't ask where the financial backing comes from.

Luigi and Tony are very close. They are related, you know. Cousins, I think, though there's no family resemblance that I can see. Don't try to come between them. From what you tell me, maybe Conradin did. I never thought Luigi really liked Conradin very much.'

'I knew the relationship between the Palazzo and the *Felice* was a little tangled, but this isn't what the Agrippina's brochures led me to suspect.'

'Oh, the Palazzo Agrippina is good business for the *Felice*,' said Paul, with a dismissive gesture. 'We're a tight-assed lot, but just the same, business at the bar shoots up whenever the Palazzo's in session. DeWitt and Alex are well-known there. Walter and Kwame are regulars. Walter soaks up cognac like a sump pump, and Kwame sees him back safely to their room. It's good it's not the other way around. If Kwame were ever drunk and disorderly, even beefy Luigi would have a hard time handling him.'

Luigi. Marcia wondered if she should tell Paul that she had seen Luigi and Conradin in the back garden at the Palazzo. No, she decided. Instead she said,

'I suppose you think it was Luigi who put the scorpion into Arthur DeSilva's knapsack.'

'I don't know. Could be Tony. He looks like an angel but that doesn't mean he is one.'

'But why should either of them do it?'

'They had a motive. Old-fashioned retribution. DeSilva was not an ideal guest at the *Albergo Felice*. He complained a lot, and even gave them the Evil Eye. They didn't like it. They told me so. But if they did it, they needn't have expected DeSilva to die, would they? DeSilva died of heart failure. The scorpion bite was just a trick that went wrong.'

'You've not got proof, have you?' said Marcia.

'That's the problem,' said Paul. 'I have a suspicion that's grown into a notion that's grown into a conviction. But no proof. No good evidence.'

XXVIII

THE ROAD from Amalfi to Ravello rises on a series of switchbacks and at each turn there is a breathtaking view of the Dragone valley below. The beauty of Ravello itself was heartbreaking. The Palazzo Agrippina bus parked, and the group disembarked, glad that the succession of switchbacks was finished. They went to the edge of the terrace overlooking the road that they had ascended, and gazed at the vista spreading out below. Ellen Cross fished her camera out of her handbag and took a picture.

'I want my husband to see this,' she said.

Kwame Assante watched her, soberly. He looked like a troubled man. Walter Druker, standing beside him, took in the panorama, his face impassive.

Gregory Donahue stopped at a kiosk to buy a postcard.

'The group is heading off for the cathedral, Greg,' said Mildred, coming up behind him.

'I just want to buy a card of this view to send to Brent Fenwick,' said Gregory.

'Oh, yes,' said Mildred. 'Poor Conradin's suicide put it out of my head.'

Donahue scrawled on the card: 'Greetings from Ravello, Brent, and congratulations on your appointment as CPC's next president! We've got a good man! Yours. Greg Donahue.'

'That should do,' he said, and fished a postage stamp out of his wallet. 'I don't want him to forget me, now he's president-elect.'

Inside the cathedral, Alex Baker noted that Paul knelt in the chapel of San Pantaleone briefly, and his lips moved soundlessly. Alex moved over to where a knot of students was examining a mosaic of Jonah and the whale that decorated one of the pulpits.

'Yes,' he said, in answer to a question, 'this is called an ambo. It's actually Norman. Remember that the Normans moved into southern Italy and Sicily about the same time as they took over England. They were a dynamic tribe.' Out of the corner of his eye, Alex noted that Paul had joined Marcia and they moved towards the high altar. 'The Norman interlude in Sicily was a brilliant period in Sicilian history. The Normans drove out the Arabs, but they continued to use Arab workmen and artists and Norman culture was a curious amalgam of Byzantine and Arab. This wonderful mosaic here is just a sample of what you can see at Monreale on the hills above Palermo in Sicily.' Baker looked around and discovered that he had an audience of only one. Sister Stella.

'It's very interesting, Dr. Baker,' she said.

'Yes,' said Alex.

'It's heartbreaking. Here we are in the midst of such beauty, and back at the Palazzo, that poor boy is lying, dead. It's as if evil has insinuated itself into a Garden of Eden. Perhaps I shouldn't say that. But the contrast seems so stark to me.'

'Conradin was a troubled boy,' ventured Dr. Alex.

'He must have been troubled. But to think that his troubles drove him to commit a mortal sin! Was there no one he could talk to, to unburden himself?'

Dr. Alex cleared his throat. 'I don't think we have the answer.'

Sister Stella looked up the nave towards the chancel where Paul and Marcia were standing.

"I wonder what Paul and Marcia are thinking,' she said. 'You know, Paul was Conradin's teacher.'

'It would be nice to know.' Baker's expression grew speculative. 'Yes, I gather that Conradin was in Paul's class at school.'

Sister Stella moved off, genuflected in front of the altar, and continued across the nave.

At lunch, Alex Baker resolved to do a little probing. Marcia and Paul had been talking earnestly on the bus, and he had strained to overhear what they were saying, but the roar of the engine prevented eavesdropping. Marcia was a well-seasoned old hen, he thought, but Paul was more naïve. He knew more than he was saying, and a well-directed conversation with him, aided by fine Ravello wine, might lead him to blurt out some background to this suicide. A suicide? Dr. Alex played with the question for a moment before he suppressed it. Of course Conradin's death was a suicide. It had to be. A suicide was bad enough, but anything else would be a grave embarrassment for the Palazzo Agrippina. A murder would be the end of the summer programme.

Lunch at Ravello was a little hurried, and the group was subdued. Piers Ellsworth and Kim Young Sam sat together, but they barely spoke. Percy Bass, enveloped in gloom, picked at his food. The soufflé for dessert was a culinary triumph, but it failed to lift spirits. Betty Laramie remarked that Conradin had been looking forward to the Ravello trip. He knew that the restaurant was famous for its soufflé. Percy remarked that, if so, Conradin should have postponed his death for an extra day, and then hastened to beg pardon when he saw the look of pain that passed over Betty's face. There were a few moments over a last glass of Ravello wine before the Agrippina group had to push on, and Dr. Alex took them to advantage.

'I'm truly sad and heartsick at what happened this morning,' he said as if some suppressed emotion forced him to speak. 'It puts a pall on our visit here.'

Marcia agreed and Sol Bernstein said, 'I was a little surprised we went ahead with the trip today.'

'Oh,' said Dr. Alex, 'lunch here was ordered and paid for. It was better for us to come.'

'I am so sorry about his death,' said Miriam Kuntz. 'I liked Conradin.'

'He was such a nice boy,' said Sister Stella.

'Poor Conradin,' Miriam continued. 'He had a lot to offer. And now his life has been snuffed out. I was very fond of him, you know.'

'We all were,' said Sally Harvey. 'He was a good young man.'

'We don't expect the young to die,' said Bathsheba Bennett, twisting her wine glass with a hand sprinkled with freckles. 'We accept death for old people, but not for teenagers. Conradin was sort of—sort of a special case, I guess.'

'Our educational system fails these adolescents,' opined Shirley Perovich. 'They have the bodies and hormones of adults, but inside their minds they are still children. You know, there's been a study that shows that a teenager's brain is actually larger than an adult's.'

'Teenage suicides are so sad,' said Madge Midgely. 'There was a story about one in the Beaumont *Advertiser* only a few months ago. His parents were both professionals. The boy seemed completely normal. And then, without warning, he took his father's revolver from the bedside table drawer and shot himself. If only he'd got help from a therapist in time, it needn't have happened. But how was one to know?'

'Well, if this tragedy had to happen,' said Sol, 'this view from Ravello is balm for the soul.'

'It surely is,' chimed in Bathesheba.

'I consider myself something of an expert on Suppressed Memory Syndrome, since there's so much of it around,' Madge went on. 'Poor Conradin roused my suspicions. But of course, I couldn't collar his father and demand to know the whole story.'

Sol Bernstein transfixed her with a gaze usually reserved for the willfully ignorant.

'Monnie Thatcher held up well, didn't he, in spite of the shock?' said Dr. Alex.

'He's a tough old bird,' said Madge. 'He knows a lot more than he's saying. But I felt sorry for him,' she added quickly. She shot a sharp glance at Percy Bass.

'I guess that after the incident at the Gilead Academy, we should have been more ready for this,' said Dr. Alex, glancing significantly towards Paul. 'Of course, hindsight is a lot clearer than foresight.'

Paul was listening intently now, but said nothing.

'What incident?' asked Madge, her reporter's antennae quivering.

'Something about a suicide attempt, I think. I never got a clear story.' Dr. Alex shot a significant look in Paul's direction, but got no response.

'What suicide attempt?' Madge demanded. "What's this about?'

'Well, it was only a rumour,' said Dr. Alex. 'I didn't believe it, myself. Best let bygones be bygones.'

'You teach at the Gilead Academy, don't you?' Madge said directly to Paul. 'What do you know about this suicide?'

'It's news to me,' said Paul. 'There was an accident with a revolver about six months ago. Conradin's best friend, Matthew Bell, killed himself.'

'Did Conradin witness it?'

'No, Madge. Conradin and Matthew were in adjoining rooms. Conradin heard the shot and got there in time to see Matthew die.'

Betty Laramie spoke up. 'That must have been a horrible experience for Conradin.'

'I wonder if it was a case of repressed memories of sexual abuse,' said Madge. 'They're so common.'

'It's love affairs that are usually behind these teenage suicides, I think,' broke in Sister Stella. 'Did Conradin fall in love with some girl, Paul?'

'All boys his age fall in love,' said Paul. 'Conradin was no different from any other student.'

'Well, it's all in the past now,' chimed in Ellen Cross. 'Poor boy. I'm so sorry for his mother—and his father, too.'

'Repressed memories of abuse are at the heart of so much of the *angst* that young people have,' said Madge. 'My column "Ask Madge" in the *Advertiser* gets dozens of letters from people who are victims. They were in denial until the memories of the abuse were unlocked from their bodies by therapy.'

Sol Bernstein gave a derisive snort and a red flush of anger started to rise up Madge Midgely's neck.

'What do we really know about Conradin's past?' interjected Bathsheba. She glanced at Percy Bass as if she expected him to speak, but Percy's gaze was fixed on the view spread out below the terrace.

'What do *you* know about this story of attempted suicide at Conradin's school, Alex?' Sol Bernstein asked with a sharp look at Dr. Alex. 'You obviously think you know something that Paul here doesn't.'

The good doctor looked enigmatic.

'It's best to say nothing about it,' he said. 'It's over and gone, now.'

'I think you're fishing for information,' said Sol. 'You don't know anything about it.'

Dr. Alex's eyes glinted with indignation behind his glasses and both chins quivered in unison.

'It's best not to spread rumours,' he said, judiciously. 'Let them die, I say.' He rose heavily to his feet. 'Regrettably we must get on the bus now and leave this beautiful place. We must become our dynamic selves again. So let's take a last look around!'

'Yes,' said Sol, rising to his feet, too. 'We must act like dynamic students.'

Dr. Alex's ears grew red, but his tone remained magisterial.

'This awful tragedy has been a crushing blow for our beloved president,' he said, 'and poor, dear Millicent! I feel for her. I feel for them both. Now I'll just go and round up the bus driver, to come and pick us up at the bus stop.' He moved off at a dignified pace towards the bus parking lot.

'Yes, poor Millicent,' murmured Bathsheba, rising stiffly to her feet.

'You know,' said Madge, *sotto voce* to Bathsheba, 'I'd like to get to the bottom of this. I'd like to get to the bottom of Paul Kowalski, too.'

'Well, as interrogations go, that was a dud,' thought Marcia, as she gathered up her camera and notebook. 'I wonder what actually did happen at Gilead.'

WALTER DRUKER FELT BETTY Laramie standing behind him before he saw her. Years of experience with students had taught him to apprehend when they wanted to tell him something before they spoke.

'Here we are, ready for the bus at the bus stop,' he said, 'and no bus yet.'

'It will be here in a minute,' said Betty. 'Dr Druker, I was thinking about what we were saying last night.'

'About your dissertation? Don't pay any attention to what I said, Betty. I'm just a cynical old college hack who drinks too much.'

'I was thinking that as we were talking, maybe Conradin was making up his mind to ...'

'To kill himself? There's no connection.'

'I was thinking that, really, life is rather short. It was too short for Conradin. I have a brother his age. You know, I was brought up on a farm. My father and mother worked hard, and they were very happy when I got a chance to go to college. I was the first in my family to go, but now I think my brother will follow in my footsteps.'

'You worked hard and went to church and were a conscientious student,' said Walter, wondering if no one had ever told her how beautiful she was.

'Yes, and I got a scholarship to a small college where I played the organ in chapel for a little extra money. I had a wonderful teacher of Greek and Latin there. She made classical studies live for me. It's because of her that I went on to graduate school at the state university.'

'Do you regret it?'

'No. The big state university frightened me at first, but I got used to it. I made some friends. My graduate advisor told me I should work on the three-barred sigma and so that's what I did. I just took his suggestion. But I've been thinking. If I write a dissertation on the three-barred sigma and manage to finish it, how many people will read it? Fifteen, maybe, at the outside?'

'Two,' said Walter. 'Your advisor and your outside examiner, and they'll just look for misprints and grammatical errors.'

'Just two. That's all. And I've gone into debt up to my ears just to write it.'

'It's a mad world,' said Walter. 'No one values true worth. Our bus is coming now. I wonder what held it up.'

'So I'm going to change,' said Betty. 'I don't want to end up like Conradin.'

'Good Lord, no,' said Walter. 'Don't even think of it. Change your dissertation subject. Get a new topic. Something you can put your teeth into.'

'I'm going to do more than that,' said Betty. 'I'm going to drop out. I want a new career.'

'Don't be too hasty. This is not a good time to make decisions like that. We're all under stress.'

"I have thought about it a lot. I want a new start.'

'What sort of career are you thinking of?'

'I don't know yet. What do you think I would need to get a job on television? As an announcer, I mean. Someone who does interviews. What would I need?'

Walter turned to look at her directly.

'Contact lenses,' he said. 'A good hairdresser. You'll knock them dead.'

'You don't think I'm too stupid?'

'No, and anyway, if you were, whoever would notice?' Walter replied.

They boarded the bus, and as Betty made her way down the aisle, she took off her glasses and smiled sweetly at Piers Ellsworth, who looked stunned, as if he had encountered an unexpected vision of beauty. He uttered his ultimate compliment, in a voice too low for anyone to hear. 'What the fuck!'

XXIX

ONE COMPUTER station was free at the Internet Café and Marcia took it. Tony arrived with a drink, and she balanced it on the desk while she typed in the e-mail address of her agent. Her fingers flew. Paul would meet her here in fifteen minutes.

'Yes, Joshua,' Marcia e-mailed, 'go ahead with the contract with Harper Collins. Sounds good. A lot has happened here since I last wrote. Yesterday morning we found Conradin Thatcher hanging by the neck from a branch of a tree growing in the back garden of the Palazzo, not far from the final resting place of the founder of the Palazzo Agrippina program. Mario was the one who found him first. He was hanging by his father's leather belt. Monnie Thatcher's waistline is of generous proportions and so his belt was a suitable length. The consensus here is that he committed suicide, though Millicent, it seems, muttered something about Monnie killing him. But by now she seems to have resumed her supportive wife role. Monnie himself looks like death warmed over, but he is presenting a brave face. The party line seems to be that Conradin was a very troubled lad, and that maybe there was some problem at school, and so on. Over lunch at Ravello, Alex Baker tried fishing for information and dropped some of his best lures in front of Paul, but Paul didn't bite. Paul is shocked by it all, and doesn't want to talk, but trust me to extract whatever wisdom he has to offer on the case.

'Another member of our group who I thought would have

something to say is Percy Bass, who is a junior teacher at the Williamson Academy where old Decimus Monroe Thatcher is the classics master. But during lunch at Ravello, Percy was morose and silent. The Thatchers will want to blame someone for the suicide and Percy must be wondering if they will choose him.

However, those of us who are uninformed are full of theories and hypotheses, and those who knew the Thatchers in the past have nothing to say.

'The same two policemen who visited us after DeSilva's death paid us another visit after Conradin's suicide was reported. The older one still wears white gloves and they are still spotless. The younger one is as handsome as ever, and he knows it. I think they harbor a few suspicions under their bland exteriors. They took Conradin's videotapes but they've now returned them. Nothing but pictures of archaeological sites with the Agrippina group crawling over them in ungainly fashion. But whatever suspicions the police have, they seem happy enough with the suicide verdict. It saves them a lot of trouble, whether it is true or not.

There will be no autopsy. Monroe and Millicent will cut their Italian holiday short and fly back home with Conradin's body, suitably embalmed. The Palazzo's travel agent is working on the details. The Palazzo's travel agent, who is a Neapolitan bred in the bone, spends much of his time playing cards with his cronies in the back room of his office, but in spite of (or possibly because of) that, things get done. He knows all the strings to pull and how to deal with all the right people. In a crisis like this he is invaluable. He had a long conversation with the senior white-gloved policeman in Neapolitan dialect which no one here could follow, and I suspect that they decided between them what the official report should say about both DeSilva's and Conradin's deaths.

'It is all very interesting. Sad, too. I am not immune to tragic *angst*. Paul lapses into long silences. I have tried my lean-on-my-shoulder-and-tell-all trick on him, and have elicited a morsel or two of information. He was Conradin's mentor at the Gilead Academy. He knew Conradin was a mixed-up boy, and I can imagine there were long heart-to-hearts, but nothing sexual, he says. I'm a suspicious old bag as you know, but I believe him. In the right hands, Paul is a very enthusiastic heterosexual.

'So the session so far as been interesting. I know a little more about human nature and a great deal more about Roman archaeology. Perhaps next year, the bulletin board at the Palazzo will have a post card from me pinned on it, saying how much I loved the session I attended. Or perhaps not. Keep in touch. Marcia."

SOL BERNSTEIN SAW MONROE Thatcher sitting alone in the back garden, staring at the spot where he had found his son's body hanging by the neck. Sol approached cautiously.

'I'm terribly sorry,' said Sol. 'I wish I could be some help.'

'Thank you, Mr. Bernstein,' said Thatcher, formal and very stiff upper lip. 'I'm grateful for your sympathy.'

Sol patted him on the shoulder with gentle compassion, and Thatcher looked up at him, his eyes suddenly filling with unwanted tears.

'Thank you,' he said. 'Thank you. You know, I wanted to have a son who would be a credit to us and a credit to the family. Was that wrong?'

'No,' said Sol.

'I tried to be a good father,' said Thatcher. 'God knows I tried.'

'Of course you did,' said Sol.

'I spent a fortune to have an orthodontist straighten his teeth. That's all money wasted now.'

'It shows you cared,' said Sol.

'But I went wrong somewhere. Millicent thinks I killed him.'

'You didn't,' said Sol. 'She doesn't mean it.'

'It was my belt. I mislaid it and Conradin must have found it. He used it to kill himself. What does that mean? A son kills himself with his father's belt.'

'It was handy,' said Sol, practically. 'He didn't have any rope. So he used the belt.'

'No, it wasn't that,' said Thatcher. 'I thrashed him once with that belt because...' The words trailed off. Sol waited, but the stiff-upper-lip Thatcher was beginning to re-emerge. The repressed guilt retreated into the recesses of his mind.

'Thank you, Mr. Bernstein,' he said. 'I would just like to be alone for a while. We'll be leaving with Conradin's body early tomorrow. It will—uh—deteriorate quickly in this climate.'

He got slowly to his feet, moving like an old man. At the back door of the Palazzo, an acanthus grew luxuriantly, encouraged by various libations of dishwater from the cook. Thatcher paused to look at it, as if he had never seen it before.

'You know, Mr. Bernstein, I'd like to plant something like that acanthus in remembrance of Conradin. A plant that puts out new growth each spring. A plant that doesn't die.'

'Go for it,' said Sol.

XXX

'Paul, it was not suicide. It was murder,' said Marcia as the two of them walked from the Palazzo Agrippina to the *Albergo Felice* on the second last day of the session. The Thatchers had left for home. Giovanni had taken them to the Naples airport in the Volkswagen bus. The Fordham's and Dr. Alex bid them a subdued farewell. Annie was red-eyed and tearful, and trying bravely to appear sober; after the Thatchers were gone, she retired to her bedroom and was rarely seen. Thatcher paused as he was about to enter the Volkswagen bus and looked critically at the suitcases which Mario was loading.

'You know, there's no need to take all of Conradin's things. They'll be excess luggage on the plane. We could give his clothes to some of the Italians around here.'

Millicent looked with some distaste at the man she had lived with for twenty-three years.

'It would create a good impression,' Thatcher went on.

'I've packed Conradin's clothes,' said Millicent, with deadly calm. 'We shall take them with us.'

Mario loaded the last of the suitcases, and a moment later, the Volkswagen disappeared down the driveway in a cloud of dust.

Dr. Alex led the remaining excursions to the archaeological sites. and DeWitt Fordham stayed behind at the Palazzo with Annie. However, he appeared regularly for happy hour with a benign smile on his face and the summer school session limped on to its close.

'It wasn't suicide,' said Marcia again, since Paul had received her verdict with no more than a grunt.

'Your imagination is running amok,' said Paul. 'What happened is that Conradin stole his father's belt. You must have seen that strange notice which old Thatcher put on the bulletin board? He said he had mislaid his belt. It was a hand-tooled leather belt with a silver buckle. Quite unusual. Conradin took it and hanged himself. Teenagers sometimes do.'

'Do what?'

'Commit suicide.'

'I see. So Conradin was a suicidal teenager.'

Paul hesitated a moment. 'Well, I shouldn't have said so. But you saw what happened.'

'Well, let me pick holes in your theory. You're walking too fast. More slowly, please. The *Albergo Felice* is not going to run away. First, if Conradin took his father's belt to hang himself, then the suicide was not merely premeditated. He actually planned it several days or more in advance. Is that typical of teenage suicide?'

'No,' Paul admitted, 'though it's not impossible. But maybe he took the belt for some other reason?'

'Second, the belt itself. Not the best instrument for suicide. Did Conradin take it and give it to someone else? Or did Monnie really mislay it, and someone else found it and gave it to the murderer? Did Monnie give it to the murderer himself? Maybe Conradin had nothing to do with the loss of his father's belt. Have you thought of that?'

'Yes,' said Paul. 'But how?'

'The staff at the Palazzo come and go. Only Giovanni is an old retainer. The cook is hired for the summer season. Giovanni's daughter is one of the maids, but the other was hired new this season. If a maid found a hand-tooled leather belt, she wouldn't know who it belonged to. More likely she'd say "Finder's keepers." As for Mario, this is his second season at the Palazzo, I think, and he and Conradin seemed to strike up a friendship. Did you see his face when he came in to tell Fordham he had found Conradin hanging from the tree? He was starting to cry.'

'So how does that add up to a murder case?'

'All right, then, the real evidence. There were two punctures in Conradin's throat where the buckle of the belt bit into the flesh. I was not the only one who saw them. Conradin got the one puncture from the belt buckle which pressed against his throat as he hanged himself, and it didn't bleed. What of the other one, where there was a trickle of blood?'

'Conradin tested the belt once before he kicked the chair aside and let himself swing.'

'Not bloody likely. Remember the one puncture bled. Conradin was still alive when it was made. I can't swear it was made by the belt buckle. But the second puncture which the belt buckle made as he was swinging from the tree didn't bleed. That's because he was already dead when it was made. What is likely is that someone garroted Conradin with the belt first, and then hung him by the neck after he was dead.'

'It would take two men to do that,' said Paul, 'Remember Conradin would have to be lifted into position and he would be a dead weight.'

'A strong man might do it by himself.'

Paul looked doubtful.

'Then I come to the second piece of evidence,' Marcia went on. The footprints at the scene of the crime were quickly obliterated, I'm afraid, but I got a good look at them first. There were two sets. One was made by a pair of new sneakers. Conradin's, I think. I managed to take a look at the soles of his shoes. The tread was almost like new. The other, more numerous set of prints was made by similar sneakers, about the same size, but the tread was well worn. Two persons were there. Two at least. Conradin was one, and another man.'

'And what's the motive?'

'That's a problem. I'd like to know what was on Conradin's floppy disk, which the police found in his room.'

'I can tell you that. The *agenti* interviewed me when they learned I was Conradin's teacher and I knew Italian. It was notes for an assignment in the Creative Writing course that Conradin wanted to take next term at Gilead. Evidently a story of a black man who tried to make it from Libya to Italy and the snakehead who collected a thousand euros from him for the trip dumped him overboard. The last thing he heard before he died was the sirens singing.'

'Singing on the shore of the Gulf of Naples.' Marcia looked thoughtful. 'Luring men to their deaths.'

'If you're thinking that Conradin discovered a connection between a Camorra mob and the *Albergo Felice*,' said Paul, 'think again. We all suspected a mob connection with the *Felice*. None of us was killed.'

'But throw in a personal motive and we may have the answer.'

'A personal motive?'

'Conradin came between Luigi and Tony. Have you thought of that?'

'Humpf! I know what you're thinking and I can't believe it. What's more you've got a loose end. The chair.'

'The chair? You mean the chair he stood on to fasten the belt to the bough of the tree?'

'Yes. It came from inside the Palazzo. Did you notice that?'

'Of course,' replied Marcia. 'Someone brought it out into the garden.'

'And that someone was likely Conradin. Conradin must have cooperated in his own death. Sounds like suicide to me.'

'The chair's a loose end. I agree. But there are possible explanations. The back door was usually left unlocked so that our bar flies could straggle in from the *Albergo Felice* at all hours. The murderer may have entered the Palazzo and taken the chair. Fingerprints won't help us. Half the Agrippina group left fingerprints on that chair.'

'Well, if your murder theory is right, someone, who may have had help, wanted Conradin dead, and I don't know why,' said Paul. 'Anyway, everyone, you know, wants Conradin's death to be suicide. DeWitt does. It saves trouble. Conradin's father and mother accept it. The staff at Williamson will feel sorry for them, whereas if Conradin were murdered in Italy, there would always be questions. The Italian police are happy to accept it. They can close their books. So the murderer will escape.'

'I'd love to give the murderer a few uneasy moments just the same,' said Marcia.

XXXI

WALTER DRUKER and Kwame Assante were sitting at a table in the bar of the *Albergo Felice* when Marcia and Paul came down from the room they had rented for an hour. Their coupling had been brief but tender. Perhaps they would keep in touch, as they promised they would, but these meetings in the magic nights of Pozzuoli would never be duplicated. They joined Walter and Kwame who greeted them gravely, though there was a familiar knowing grin on Walter's lips.

'We were talking about Capri and the emperor Tiberius' villa on a cliff overlooking the sea which we visited a couple days ago,' said Kwame.

'Brutal climb up to the villa,' interjected Walter.

'The climb wasn't too bad. The view was worth it. But imagine old Tiberius hiding there on his lonely cliff, too scared to return to Rome, even when his throne was in danger. He tried once, but couldn't do it. He didn't have the guts.'

'He was a classic recluse,' said Paul. 'Afraid of the world.'

'I started a biography of Tiberius once,' said Walter. 'While we were on Capri I floated a new idea about him before the Midgely woman, that Tiberius suffered from childhood trauma. Sexual molestation. She nearly bit my head off. I thought it was a good idea.'

'Oh, Tiberius couldn't stomach life in Rome,' said Paul. 'Probably it reminded him too much of his wife. He was his own prisoner.'

'We are all our own prisoners,' said Walter, drunk enough to be philosophical. 'I am; you are, Kwame. As much as Tiberius.'

'No, Walter,' said Kwame. 'We don't all of us make our own beds. Some people get breaks. Your big success story who tells you he is a self-made man, you look at his career and you'll always see he got some breaks along the way. If you don't get any breaks, you don't go anywhere.'

'I never had any breaks,' said Walter. 'I got an Oxford M.A. and then I went to Stanford for a PhD. Paid my way with bit parts in movies. I wrote a first-class dissertation. The outside reader said it was one of the best dissertations on Velleius Paterculus he had ever read. But alas! who knows anything about Velleius Paterculus?'

'Never heard of him,' Marcia began. 'But didn't Dr. Alex mention his name when we were at the emperor Tiberius' villa on Capri? What's left of it, anyway.'

'Good for you. You remembered,' said Walter. 'Most people wouldn't. He was an old soldier of Tiberius. Took to writing history in his retirement. He liked the old geezer. Tiberius, I mean. But my dissertation didn't get me a job. I got a one-year appointment at one place, and then a year appointment at another, and then another, hopping from place to place, never getting any research done. If you don't publish a single-authored book in your first ten years, you can kiss tenure goodbye. At last I landed at Spearfish State. There I've stayed. I came for a one-year appointment there, too, but they noticed about the time my year was up that one old sod on the faculty was brain dead too obviously to teach, and I was asked to stay on. So I did. That was my one big break, Kwame. I lecture to two sections of world history from the primeval slime to the Vietnam war, and two on the great thinkers of western philosophy from Socrates to Wittgenstein. Each thinker gets ten minutes if no one asks questions to slow me down.'

'I've heard of Spearfish State in some connection,' said Marcia. 'I can't think what.'

'Neither can I,' said Walter, 'unless it's for the production of graduates most proficient at mangling the English language.

The Spearfish campus consists of a monumental entrance gate, a large modern football stadium, a big air-conditioned administration building, an edifice the size of an outhouse called the Whitcombe Memorial Library, and a sprawling ramshackle firetrap which is the Arts and Science Building.'

'Walter's really better than he makes out,' said Kwame. 'Do you know that Miriam Kuntz has asked for his sperm? She has a partner who wants to get pregnant.'

'She has?' exclaimed Marcia, startled. 'My roommate has asked for Walter's sperm?'

'Yes, your roommate. She and her partner want a child and you can't get pregnant without a stud.'

'Good for you, Walter,' said Paul. 'No one would ask me for my sperm.'

'Nor mine,' said Kwame.

'What did you say, Walter?' asked Marcia, a little breathless, remembering that she had intended to pass on Miriam's request for Paul's sperm to him, and never did. 'Did you say yes?'

'Well, I'll think about it. My first reaction was no. But the idea of someone carrying my genes, standing over my grave twenty-five years from now, saying, "Alas, poor Druker, I wish I'd known him well", it intrigues me. I like it. I told Miriam to keep in touch. I expect she'll find someone else, and I won't hear from her. But I sort of hope I do. You know, I'm not all that bad. I rowed for Oxford when I was a student. I have an Oxford M.A. That should qualify me as a good stud. I like the idea.'

'How will the son you sire with your borrowed sperm find out who his father is? Marcia demanded.

'My son,' said Walter, 'will find out who his father is. My son will be the sort of man who'll find the answers to things.'

'You know, you should thank Miriam,' said Kwame. 'You'll have an unknown son who carries your legacy. Not all of you will die. The Druker genes will live on.'

'You're a good man, Kwame,' said Walter. 'You haven't given up on the rat race yet and you can listen to an old fart philosophize on and on with patience from outer space. You know, I liked this Agrippina summer course. It reminded me that I once found excitement in the world of scholarship, and now that I'm going to be a stud, I'm going to start work again on my book on the emperor Tiberius. I want my child to be proud of me, even if he never finds out who I am. I'm tired of being the poor man's Socrates, as Kwame calls me. I want to publish, and be promoted to full professor at good old Spearfish State. I like being asked for my sperm. I'll bet no one ever asked Socrates for his. Luigi, another drink, *per favore*.' Luigi, watchful, poured another brandy. 'Poor old Conradin,' Walter went on. 'Giving up so soon. He should have had a better run at life than that.'

'I was surprised he killed himself,' said Kwame. 'I talked to him. We had several conversations. He was a nice guy, trying to find himself. Not depressed at all.'

'I didn't expect it, either,' said Paul.

'It doesn't add up,' said Marcia.

'Well, it bothers me,' admitted Walter. 'Conradin was down here several times. I don't think his father knew. He would join us for a Campari Soda, but he never got drunk. He was a bright young lad but not the sort who does well at examinations. I meet a lot like that. A real computer nerd. Like Tony, here at the *Felice*. They struck up a real friendship. With Luigi I don't know.'

'The chemistry with Luigi was different,' said Kwame.

Luigi brought Walter's drink to the table. He seemed wary, Marcia noted. He must have heard Kwame and Walter mention his name and was trying to follow their conversation, but Walter's speech was slurred and hard to understand. Luigi lingered a bit, as if expecting a tip. His white jacket was unbuttoned, and the fake rubies decorating his belt glinted in the sunlight.

'His classmates at the Gilead are going to be shocked,' said Paul. 'He was a leading member of what we called our Computer Nerd circle at school. He'll be missed.'

'Luigi has a new belt,' said Walter. 'Even more vulgar than the one he had before.'

Suddenly, in Marcia's mind, a missing link snapped into place.

'What was the belt he was wearing a couple days ago?' she asked.

'A couple days ago, I don't know I didn't see what he was wearing. I don't notice these things unless they are under my nose,' said Walter. 'But last week he was sporting a belt with a big silver buckle.'

'DeSilva mentioned it,' said Kwame. 'Luigi and his tooled leather belt, which was long enough to circle his gut twice.'

Slowly in Walter's befuddled mind, and more swiftly in Kwame's unclouded brain, a suspicion began to form. Marcia and Paul exchanged glances.

'Hey there, Luigi.' Walter raised his voice drunkenly. 'That's a fine new belt. What happened to the old one?'

Luigi ignored Walter's bellow. Tony, who was making a cappuccino coffee, stiffened visibly.

'I'm talking to you, Luigi,' roared Walter, rising unsteadily to his feet, upsetting the table and spilling the drinks on to the floor tiles. 'What about your belt? You need a new one studded with rubies to hold in your expanding gut, do you?'

Luigi's glance was uncomprehending but venomous.

'Take this, eh?' said Walter, making the sign of the evil eye with two fingers. 'You don't like that, do you?' Luigi was at his side in a moment, grabbing his elbow purposefully.

'You go, now,' he said with menace.

'The hell with that,' said Walter. Luigi's muscles bulged under his jacket and Walter found himself being propelled, willy-nilly, towards the door. But before he had gone three feet, Luigi felt a powerful arm around his neck and he was hurled back.

'Take your paws off him, you damn thug,' roared Kwame.

Luigi recovered and launched his two hundred and twenty pounds of bone and muscle at Kwame. But before his charge reached its target, Kwame caught him with a blow to the jaw that would have felled an ox. Luigi sprawled on the floor, and before he could recover, Kwame leaped on him as he lay spread-eagled, caught him by the throat and rapped his skull sharply on the floor tiles.

'That's for Conradin,' he said. He rapped Luigi's skull again, hard. 'And that's another for him.'

Paul was on his feet, ready for battle if necessary. Walter

swayed unsteadily, his expression a mixture of belligerence and surprise. Luigi lay on the floor, dazed, and Tony stared, astonished to see the *Albergo Felice* Hercules in so atypical a position, flat on his back with no fight left in him. Marcia who had armed herself with an empty bottle of Stock brandy, took a good look at his feet. He was wearing a soiled pair of sneakers with soles worn smooth. The last piece of the puzzle fitted into place.

'Let's go,' said Kwame. 'This is no place for us.'

'I wish I had met you twenty years ago,' said Marcia to Paul. He was carrying the heavier of her two suitcases down to the Volkswagen bus, which was about to leave for the airport. Marcia's flight left five hours before Paul's, and the Volkswagen was shuttling back and forth between the Naples airport and the Palazzo Agrippina.

'No,' said Paul. 'Twenty years ago the love of my life was my dog. But if I had met you ten years ago, you might have saved me from some self-doubt.'

'Well, it's nice to know this old bag is still of some use,' said Marcia.'

'Don't be bitter. Let's keep in touch. I can't believe we'll not meet again.'

'Well, you have my address and I have yours. I could arrive at the Gilead Academy and titillate your students. Now, don't turn pale,' Marcia admonished, as Paul's expression changed. 'I'll be the soul of discretion.'

'Marcia,' said Paul, 'I don't feel right about Conradin's murder.'

'Why?'

'You know why. Murderers should be punished. Justice demands it'

'Of course it does, but you have to prove, first, that it was murder, and then, who did the deed. I know --*we know*—who did the murder. Walter and Kwame both have guessed the truth. But we couldn't prove it in any court beyond reasonable doubt, and we certainly couldn't prove it here. Moreover the Palazzo Agrippina wants it to be suicide. Suicide is bad enough but it is less embarrassing than murder, for all concerned.'

'Even to Conradin's parents?'

'Even his parents.'

Paul sighed. 'Well, that's the cynical view.'

'The incident can usefully be considered a suicide by a troubled adolescent,' said Marcia.

'The verdict meets the standard of competitive plausibility,' said Paul. 'I think that your Aristide Blanchard would have done better job with this case, but maybe you're right.'

'I *am* right. We're looking for closure, not strict justice. You'll understand if you think about it. Good-bye, Paul. It was a great summer course, all in all, wasn't it?'

'Good-bye, Marcia. You are a great commercial for heterosexuality, you know. I'll miss you.'

'Then how about a farewell kiss?'

Paul took her in his arms and their lips met, while Giovanni and Mario looked on with approval, and Walter Druker and Kwame Assante, who were coming out of the front door, broke into applause.

'Bravo! Bravissimo!' bellowed Druker.

'Encore!' shouted Kwame.

'Good-bye, Marcia,' said Paul, looking a little deflated.

'Good-bye, Marcia,' intoned Dr. Alex, appearing in the doorway behind Walter and Kwame. 'Be sure to come back! Include us all in your next murder mystery!'

'Don't worry! I will! You're too good to leave out. And I shall be back,' replied Marcia. 'I haven't finished improving my mind.' Then, turning to Paul, 'Shall we do a reprise for our audience?'

Paul took her in his arms and kissed her again, with passion.

'Oh, Marcia,' he said, almost in a whisper. 'You're quite a dame.'

The Volkswagen disappeared down the driveway and Paul returned to the room he shared with Percy Bass to finish his own packing. Percy had spread his clothes out on his bed, and was stuffing dirty laundry into a suitcase.

'You said a fond, sad farewell?' asked Percy.

'Sad enough,' Paul replied. 'But it will be good to get home.'

'We've survived the brief summer course, spiced with one accidental death and one suicide,' Percy went on. 'Tony at the *Felice* has become gloomy Tony after Conradin died, and Luigi has become grumpy. His jaw must stay wired together until it heals. Kwame packed quite a wallop.'

'Luigi will survive a broken jaw.'

'Well, anyway, I did learn something this summer,' said Percy. 'I'm glad I took the Agrippina course. I learned something about human nature, and I gave my new digital camera a good workout, too.'

'Well, that's O.K., then.'

'I've made up my mind to find a new job and leave Williamson Academy as soon as I can. I'm stuck there by my contract for another year, but that's my limit. I want to get away. I'm not made out to be a teacher.'

'You're really a troubadour.'

'And a long distance runner.' Percy threw his track shoes on top of his suitcase. They were large shoes, and Andrew noted that the soles were worn smooth. For a moment a suspicion crossed his mind. Percy Bass? Percy and Conradin? They seemed barely to know to each other, and seldom spoke. But Percy was Monroe Thatcher's colleague at Williamson and there was no love lost between them.

No: it was impossible. Paul dismissed the thought.

'I won't forget poor Conradin,' said Percy, soberly. 'I pitied the poor guy. Now if it were his father who died instead of him, it would show there is such a thing as justice in the universe.'

XXXII

TONY SAT in front of the computer monitor. It had been a fairly busy day, but now the *Albergo Felice* bar was empty, and Luigi had left on his motorcycle. He didn't say where he was going. He had sworn vengeance on the big black man who had broken his jaw, but now the black man was gone. A new session of students had arrived for the Palazzo Agrippina and it would take them a day or two to discover the *Albergo Felice*. Mario would recommend the Internet Café to them, as usual, though Mario was taking Conradin's death hard. Luigi was in a black mood. Tony hoped he would be careful. A motorcyclist had been shot in Naples a day or two ago. A gang member. Tony recognized his name.

Tony entered Luigi's password. Luigi kept it secret, but Luigi was no Einstein. Tony figured that all he had to do was to take the letters in Luigi's name—Luigi Fini—and rearrange them according to a simple pattern which would not strain Luigi's brain cells to remember. 'iLguiiFni'. Unscrambled, it was Luigi's name. Luigi's in-box filled up with messages.

He was receiving some interesting e-mails, Tony thought. There was his girl in Napoli. Her mother wouldn't let Luigi within a kilometre of her. She was sure he was a thug, mixed up in something he shouldn't be. An e-mail from Giacomo at Fabiola Films. He was coming to Pozzuoli to see his mother and pick up his laundry. Paolo had a boat, Giacomo reported. Everything was ready. The blacks could be dumped south of Salerno. That will be risky, Tony thought. The police were suspicious and they can't be bought off forever. Rome was cracking down on the Camorra in Napoli. .

Another e-mail in Luigi's in-box. 'Conradin is too curious. What's he know? Get him out of our business.'

Conradin was always asking questions, Tony reflected. He liked to make up cloak-and-dagger theories. But he didn't know anything. He was just a big kid.

A e-mail from Paolo. 'Idiot! Why were you bothered by the DeSilva guy? We don't want the police to start sniffing around the *Albergo.*'

Luigi's reply. 'The scorpion can't be traced here. Anyway, scorpions don't kill. We didn't kill him.'

No, thought Tony, but DeSilva deserved the scorpion. He was a ugly guy. He gave us the Evil Eye.

Luigi's girl friend again. 'Luigi, I'll always love you, no matter what.'

Poor dumb broad.

Giacomo Fini again. 'We can't have the Thatcher kid screwing things up.'

Luigi had hit the reply button. 'No problem.'

No problem, Tony thought. Not for a big, powerful guy like Luigi.

I cut through the corner of the Palazzo Agrippina garden that day, on my way to work early in the morning. The light at daybreak is so beautiful and the bougainvillea was a mass of red flowers. I felt good. Then I saw a parcel swinging from the tree. No, not a parcel. Not a parcel at all. It was a body. But I keep out of trouble. It was best to just keep going. Then I heard someone coming. Through the gate walks the tall guy with the guitar, coming home late. He sees Conradin hanging, goes up close, looks at it, and then hurries into the Palazzo, fast, like he had a red hot poker up his ass. He must be going for help, I thought, and I waited a while, but nothing happened. He didn't come back. Conradin just hung there, twisting a little in the breeze. The morning light played on his face and the bougainvillea dripped petals down on him. I waited. Then at last Mario found him, and the Palazzo emptied as everyone rushed out to see Conradin hanging there. I slipped away. Luigi was working at the bar when I got to the Albergo. *He looked up when I came in, and said, 'You're late.' He knew. But we are both honourable men.*

Poor Conradin. He was so sure he knew the difference between right and wrong. Everything was black or white. If he found something he thought was wrong, he would tell everyone. He never learned that nothing was simple, that you shouldn't ever get too involved, and that silence was always the best policy. Now he would never learn.

Tony turned off the computer and went to the door of the *Albergo* where he could look out into the night. The velvet darkness, pierced by pinpricks of light, stretched across the bay, shrouding numberless ghosts of the indignant dead, whimpering for justice. For two thousand years they had lamented. Somewhere out there, among them, was the ghost of Agrippina, the mother of Nero. Still lamenting the impiety of her ungrateful son.

Tony felt sad and suddenly very lonely..